Firing erupted from the embassy grounds

"Hit the brakes!" Encizo shouted as he reached inside his jacket for the Walther P-88 holstered under his arm.

McCarter had already jumped out before the bus came to a halt. A Browning autoloader clenched in one fist, he hit the ground on his feet, knees bent and body angled forward. He tumbled across the pavement as a gunman tracked him with an Ingram SMG.

Katz opened fire from the door of the bus. Bracing an Uzi machine pistol across his mechanical arm, he drilled a trio of 9 mm parabellums into the terrorist who had lined up McCarter in his sights.

A figure appeared from behind the wreck of the automobile at the curb. The terrorist's uniform was torn and bloodied, and his features were twisted by pain and anger as he raised a bottle in his fist.

The cloth jammed into the mouth of the bottle was already ablaze, and the man was poised to lob the Molotov cocktail at the bus.

Mack Bolan's

PHOENIX FORCE.

PHOENIX FORCE®

GAR WILSON

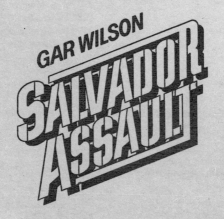

SALVADOR ASSAULT

A GOLD EAGLE BOOK FROM
WORLDWIDE®

TORONTO • NEW YORK • LONDON • PARIS
AMSTERDAM • STOCKHOLM • HAMBURG
ATHENS • MILAN • TOKYO • SYDNEY

First edition September 1990

ISBN 0-373-61349-0

Special thanks and acknowledgment to
William Fieldhouse for his contribution to this work.

1

San Salvador seemed peaceful and almost quaint. The capital city of El Salvador reminded Lawrence McKeller of a large sleepy village as he strolled along Alvarado Avenue, but he knew that the impression was an illusion. San Salvador was usually crowded, noisy and anything but quaint. Furthermore, peace never had much of a chance to play a major role in the history of El Salvador.

The Embassy security personnel, whose names he didn't remember, were a constant reminder of the dangerous and unpredictable environment. The bodyguards had been assigned to him that morning. Young, quiet men with stern faces and short, clipped hair, they were polite when they spoke and they dressed in neat gray suits that barely revealed the bulge of the pistols carried in shoulder holsters under their jackets.

McKeller wasn't accustomed to being escorted by bodyguards in broad daylight, and he felt awkward accompanied by the pair. He was basically a public relations man for the U.S. State Department. Armed guards hardly seemed necessary, because McKeller had met with the assistant curator at the Tazumal Museum to discuss an exchange of archaeological displays. Several museums in the United States were eager to arrange a deal to loan artifacts from their collections if the Tazumal Museum would agree to let the American institutions borrow exhibits of sixteenth-century Spanish conquistador relics and Nahuatl Indian tools and pottery that likely dated from much earlier.

Carbon-14 radiation tests had not been done on many of the Tazumal pieces, and both American and Salvadoran scientists wanted to establish the age of these relics by employing the radioactive isotope tracer evaluation. The curator was interested in the exchange, but the matter would have to be decided by the board of directors and cleared by the government.

McKeller's visit had been a start. He had a better than average layman's knowledge of archaeology and he spoke Spanish fluently, which helped him discuss the project with the curator. Cultural exchange was one of the key methods of improving relations between nations. The United States and El Salvador had a long and frequently strained association. American support of El Salvador was not very popular with the public in the U.S., and a great many Salvadorans resented American involvement and blamed many of their country's problems on Washington's policies in Central America.

El Salvador certainly had its share of problems. Terrorism, civil war and military juntas had plagued the republic since it was formally proclaimed in 1859. McKeller hoped an exchange of art and culture at least might improve relations between the two countries. But improving the turbulent political atmosphere of El Salvador was a task no one seemed to have any idea how to manage. How El Salvador would fare under the leadership of Alfredo Cristiani remained uncertain, but there was no doubt that the unofficial civil war in the small Central American country was far from over.

Nonetheless, Cristiani had claimed that he would try to heal his nation and establish a truce with the leftist factions. Washington had grave doubts about Cristiani's ARENA Party, which was regarded as being more right of center than the Christian Democrats formerly in power. Considering the record of Duarte and Magaña, it was hard for McKeller to imagine that the new regime would be less successful unless Cristiani deliberately worked to make matters worse.

Maybe the ARENA leader was doing something right, McKeller thought as he walked along the avenue with the bodyguards. He had been in El Salvador for one month, and things had been fairly quiet. There had been hit-and-run strikes by FMLN—Farabundo Martí National Liberation Front—rebels in the western region, near the Guatemala border, and the military had responded with the usual heavy-handed tactics. Yet, compared to past actions, both sides were acting with restraint.

That Sunday afternoon seemed pleasant enough to McKeller. Church bells pealed in the distance. Families, dressed in their best Sunday clothes, strolled the sidewalks on their way to or from church services. It seemed to be a fine autumn day for a walk, and most Salvadorans were used to it, since there weren't that many private vehicles. Although the rain is heaviest in summer and autumn months, McKeller didn't see a dark cloud in the bright blue sky as he headed back to the U.S. Embassy.

"I still think we should have taken a car, sir," one of the bodyguards stated as he glanced about the tranquil streets suspiciously, though only a few cars made their way through the streets, aside from the ever-present army patrol vehicles.

"The museum isn't that far from the Embassy," McKeller replied. "And I could use the exercise. You fellows are young and active. I'm on the wrong side of forty and spend most of my time sitting behind a desk. Besides, this has turned out to be a nice quiet day."

The sudden snarl of an engine abruptly challenged McKeller's opinion as a dark blue sedan raced through the street and swung toward the curb. The bodyguards responded automatically to the threat. One man quickly shoved McKeller to the pavement and covered him with his own body. The other dropped to one knee and drew a Beretta 92-F from shoulder leather. He grasped the 9 mm pistol in both hands and aimed it at the sedan.

The car simply skidded to a halt. A rear tire bounced onto the curb, and the frame banged against the metal post of a street lamp. The driver seemed to wobble unsteadily behind the steering wheel. His head bobbed limply as he hugged the wheel like a sick child seeking comfort.

"What the hell," the bodyguard growled with a frown. "Is this guy drunk?"

"Stay down, sir," the other protector told McKeller as he remained sprawled across the State Department PR man.

McKeller felt foolish and none too comfortable with the bodyguard draped over his prone body. The guy shifted his weight to one side, and McKeller groaned as pressure on his kidneys increased. The bodyguard had to change position in order to reach inside his jacket to draw his pistol.

Both watchdogs eyed the car suspiciously. The driver appeared to be the only occupant in the sedan, and he didn't seem to present a threat. A Salvadoran army patrol witnessed the incident and headed for the scene in a jeep. The soldier in the back seat unslung his M-16 assault rifle as the vehicle approached. An NCO in a seat next to the driver had the handset to a field radio in his fist and had already reported the incident.

From his awkward observation post, McKeller almost felt sorry for the reckless driver of the sedan. The soldiers would certainly come down on him hard for such a stunt. Still, the man from the State Department was relieved that the driver of the car was just a bum behind a steering wheel and not a terrorist. The bodyguards weren't convinced the driver was harmless and they kept their weapons trained on the sedan.

Neither man noticed the two figures that emerged from an alley and stepped onto the sidewalk behind them. Young men dressed in field pants, fatigue jackets and green berets, they carried compact, boxlike weapons with stubby barrels. The gunmen opened fire before the bodyguards even realized the new threat had arrived. High-velocity projectiles smashed into McKeller's bodyguards. They toppled to the sidewalk, propelled by the force of the multiple bullets.

Blood squirted across McKeller's face and eyes. Half-blind from the red mist, he still saw the bodyguards fall. Their bodies twitched violently as crimson spilled from their bullet-torn flesh. He heard their dying moans and the metallic rattle of the gunmen's automatic weapons. More rounds thudded into the fallen bodyguards and split open their skulls to spread gray matter and bone splinters across the pavement.

The army jeep bolted forward to come to the rescue of the Americans. The driver grimly clutched the steering wheel and stomped the accelerator while the soldier with the M-16 tried to bring his weapon to bear as the military vehicle closed in. The NCO in the passenger's seat had taken a .45 Colt autoloader from his holster and was ready to jump from the jeep as soon as it came to a halt.

The back door of the sedan burst open, and another young killer emerged. Dressed in the same manner as his comrades, the man held a bottle in one fist and a cigarette lighter in the other. He held the flame to a rag stuffed into the mouth of the bottle and hurled the Molotov cocktail at the jeep.

The bottle struck the windshield and shattered, spewing flaming gasoline across the open-top jeep. Hideous screams erupted from the vehicle as the NCO and driver were drenched in burning fuel. The other soldier cried out and leaped from the moving vehicle, flames dancing along his shirtsleeve and trouser leg. The jeep swung out of control as the driver released the steering wheel to claw at his fire-eaten face with both hands. It hopped the curb and plunged through the plate glass window of a small café. The blaze continued to consume the jeep and spread within the building. Black smoke billowed from the shattered window. The screams ceased, but the sickly sweet stench of charred human flesh filled the air.

McKeller blinked to try to clear the blood from his vision. He glanced up and saw the muzzle of a machine pistol pointed at his face. The PR man was stunned by the attack and numb with horror at the carnage that surrounded him. McKeller knew he was about to die, and he was surprised not to be as frightened as he would have supposed he would be when facing his own death. He had never considered himself a particularly brave man, but when he actually found himself staring into the black tunnel of the enemy's gun barrel, he felt an odd sense of acceptance.

"If you're going to do it," McKeller said without even realizing the words had formed in his mouth, "get it over with."

The machine pistol snarled. McKeller glimpsed the flash from the muzzle, but he didn't hear the report of the weapon. The high-velocity slugs traveled faster than sound and punched through McKeller's skull and knifed into his brain. He was dead before he could hear the shots.

"*¡Eso basta!*" the leader of the terrorist hit-team snapped when he saw the other gunmen were about to fire on the lifeless trio of Americans once more. "That's enough! They're dead. Let's get out of here. *¡Dése prisa!*"

The gunmen hurriedly climbed into the sedan while the driver shifted gears and nervously waited for all three triggermen to get in the vehicle. The car doors slammed shut, and the sedan shot into the street. It raced from the scene of the murders as blood trickled from the curb to the gutter.

2

Rafael Encizo breathed deeply as he grasped the handles of the Roman chair and wrapped his feet around a twenty-five pound dumbbell. He held the bar between the insteps and pressed his ankles together. Encizo braced his back and buttocks on the chair and raised the weight. He inhaled as the strain on his abdominal muscles forced him to clench his teeth.

Exhaling slowly, he lowered the weight and repeated the process again and again. Working out didn't get easier with age. Encizo was no longer the hot-blooded youth who'd participated in the Bay of Pigs invasion in 1961. He was nearly three decades older, and his passion was balanced by the self-control and wisdom acquired through experience.

Many of those experiences had been harsh, but the lessons were never forgotten. Encizo was more careful, more observant and inclined to use his head instead of his emotions. He was also less idealistic and more cynical. That was also part of what he learned over the years. Bitter lessons were often the most valuable.

In most ways, Encizo believed he had improved with age, though his body didn't always agree. The older he got, the more time he had to spend with physical training to keep his muscles toned and his waist trim. His thighs and abdomen were taut and hard as he carried out fifteen repetitions in the Roman chair. The dumbbell seemed to get heavier each time he raised it from the mat. His sweat suit was damp, and his face felt flushed and red.

The Roman chair workout was just part of more than two hours of vigorous exercise. The Cuban had pumped iron, performed a series of stretching exercises, worked on both the light punching bag and heavy bag and practiced judo with a second *dan* black belt instructor. The *sensei* had been embarrassed during the match because Encizo successfully countered every move he made and each time sent him to the mat. The Cuban had applied armlocks and choke holds that forced the judo teacher to say *matte* in surrender.

The *sensei* would have felt relieved rather than embarrassed if he knew that Encizo had restrained himself from actually breaking bones or throttling his opponent. The Cuban was accustomed to kill-or-be-killed combat situations. His fighting skills had been developed to an extraordinary level. Rafael Encizo had long ago lost count of the number of men he had bested.

His first battlefields had been in his homeland after Castro's revolution. Eventually, most of his family having been wiped out, Encizo and other survivors had fled Cuba. They wound up in the United States, where the CIA recruited them for operations against Havana. Unfortunately the Bay of Pigs was a fiasco. Many of the invaders were killed, and others, including Encizo, were taken prisoner and sent to the infamous El Principe political prison. Encizo was subjected to various forms of mistreatment, starvation, torture and efforts at brainwashing. Eventually he managed to escape and return to the United States.

Encizo had been employed in many capacities since the Bay of Pigs, among them as scuba diving instructor and professional bodyguard. Occasionally Encizo had been recruited by the FBI and DEA to assist in criminal investigations and drug busts in Hispanic communities and along the border.

He had done other covert jobs in various Central American and Caribbean countries. Sometimes for government agencies, sometimes for private outfits. A few of these had not been entirely legal, but Encizo had believed the motivations had been legitimate. Eventually he moved into a more respectable and almost conventional profession as an insurance investigator in Miami. Encizo was a naturalized U.S. citizen with a job that was interesting and fairly stable. He hadn't planned to charge after any more windmills. At the age of forty, it had seemed time to settle down and avoid putting his neck on the figurative chopping block.

That was before he was contacted by Hal Brognola and brought to the top-secret headquarters of Stony Man operations. They wanted him to be part of a special five-man unit comprised of the best antiterrorists, commandos and experts in covert operations in the free world. If he accepted, Encizo realized his life would change forever and he would never be able to go back to the way things were before. He could continue with a relatively safe and sane career as an insurance investigator or he could dedicate his life to an elite fighting unit, assigned to the highest risk, most dangerous missions imaginable with the probability of survival somewhere between slim and none.

Rafael Encizo had chosen the latter. He had agreed to become a member of Phoenix Force. And, he reflected as he left the Roman chair and headed for the locker room, he'd never looked back.

He took a long, hot shower to work out any stiffness in his muscles and got his clothes from a locker. Other men were either about to leave the gym or start their workouts. Encizo didn't know any of them. He'd spent little time in Miami since he joined Phoenix Force and he rarely used his membership at the fitness center. A couple of months had passed since the latest mission, and the members of the unique team had returned to their homes for a little R&R.

He slipped his wallet into a pocket and slid into his boots. Encizo reached for a small, battery-operated message beeper. The message light was blinking. Encizo frowned. He should have kept the beeper with him during the workout, but people in Miami had a tendency to think anyone with such a contraption was either a doctor, a policeman or a drug dealer. He didn't care to be mistaken for any of the above.

Encizo clipped the beeper on his belt and slipped on his Levi's jacket. He stuffed his workout clothes into a blue gym bag and left the fitness center. The sky was bright, and the weather was pleasantly warm without being too humid or hot. Encizo liked warm climates, and he was perfectly comfortable with the Little Havana district—at least in the daytime. The gangs and drug dealers came out in droves after sundown.

Eighth Street was fairly quiet that day. A couple of prostitutes stood at a corner, trying to attract passing motorists. Two long-haired youths hung around the bench at a bus stop with a twin-speaker radio turned up loud enough to annoy people two blocks away. A shop owner examined some gang graffiti on the wall of his establishment and debated whether it was safe to wipe it off. The gangs thought they had a right to use public and private buildings and walls to leave messages as on a community bulletin board. Anyone who thoughtlessly destroyed their notes could suffer the consequences.

Encizo shook his head as he walked to the parking lot and located a public phone booth. Gangs were becoming a major problem all over America and nobody seemed to know how to deal with them. The kids were making millions in the drug trade. They could buy cars, apartments, fine clothes and automatic weapons. They were well armed, well organized and dangerous. Because they were minors, they couldn't be charged as adults even when they committed the worst kinds of felonies. The gangs could literally get away with murder and they knew it.

The kids involved in the gangs seemed to get younger and younger. Fifteen-year-old enforcers and ten-year-old "mules" were not uncommon. Even younger children were sometimes used as lookouts for teenage drug pushers. The gangs were an odd and extremely dangerous combination of technical sophistication and emotional immaturity.

But Encizo was mainly concerned with other matters. Phoenix Force was not set up to deal with the growing problem of youth gangs in America. That would have to be somebody else's headache. Phoenix had enough of its own, and Encizo needed to get to Stony Man to see what the newest crisis was about.

He moved to the phone booth and entered the glass-and-metal box. Encizo was relieved to discover the phone hadn't been vandalized. He inserted some coins into the phone and dialed a Watts-line number. An odd musical beeping, not unlike a Pacman machine, sang from the receiver before he was cut off. It sounded like a malfunction on the line, but it was actually proof his phone call had been recorded and confirmed by Stony Man headquarters. Brognola knew he was in Miami. The call would be traced to learn its origin, and Stony Man would know who called to confirm he was on his way to HQ.

Encizo slid open the folding glass door and discovered the two long-haired youths from the bus stop had wandered to the call box. The pair approached the booth as Encizo emerged. They were tough-looking kids. One was more than six feet tall, clad in imitation leather jacket and pants, with a scruffy black beard and shoulder-length hair that was held in place by an Indian headband. His companion was short and wiry, his beard little more than dark fuzz around his jaw and cheeks. Both had cruel smiles, and their faces were aglow with the frenzied excitement cherished by lovers of violence. They eyed the dark-haired, handsome man with open contempt.

"Hey, man," the larger kid began as he placed a hand on a sheath knife on his belt. "I don't think you asked for permission to come into our neighborhood."

"Yeah," the other one added. His hand emerged from a pocket with a plastic-and-metal object in his fist. The thumb pressed a button, and four inches of sharp steel sprang into view. "Guess you'll have to pay a fine, asshole."

He pointed the switchblade at Encizo's face. "Hand over the wallet, or we'll carve you up like a Thanksgiving turkey."

"Yeah, like a turkey," the other hood echoed with a snicker.

Encizo glanced at the switchblade and looked at the owner with an expression that seemed weary and almost bored. The Cuban sighed as he swung the gym bag by his side.

"Are either of you familiar with the term 'edification'?" he inquired.

They seemed baffled by the question and the Cuban's calm reaction to the threat of armed robbery. The larger hood started to draw his knife as the punk with the switchblade lunged. Encizo's gym bag rose adroitly to block the knife attack. The point of the switchblade stabbed the bag and caught on cardboard under canvas. Encizo's free hand balled into a fist and punched the kid in the mouth to knock him five feet away.

Growling an obscenity, the big thug charged with his Bowie knife. Encizo swung about and lashed the gym bag into the second blade to parry the attack. He grabbed the kid's jacket sleeve at the elbow and pulled hard, increasing the attacker's own forward momentum. The punk crashed into the side panel of the phone booth. Glass shattered, and he cried out as his hand and face were cut by sharp fragments of the shattered pane.

Encizo whipped a backfist to the temple and landed a hard blow. The youth fell to the pavement. His scrawny partner spat blood from a split lip and prepared to launch another attack with his switchblade. Encizo suddenly hurled the gym bag into the junior hoodlum's face, startling and distracting him without causing any real injury. However, the maneuver allowed Encizo a split second to aim his boot at the knife-wielding wrist.

He kicked the switchblade from the kid's hand and suddenly slashed a karate chop to his upper lip. The blow broke two front teeth and sent the youth reeling backward. Encizo quickly grabbed his wrist with one hand and yanked him forward. The Cuban ducked low and thrust his other arm between the dazed punk's legs, then slung him across his shoulders and whirled him around in a variation of a fireman's carry.

The larger punk was starting to get to his feet, but Encizo heaved his burden and sent him flying like a projectile to crash into his partner. Both would-be muggers hit the sidewalk. Encizo followed the pair and stomped on the wrist of the larger jerk with one boot and kicked the Bowie knife from his fingers with the other.

"'Edification' means to enlighten and educate one in improved moral or spiritual conduct," Encizo told the battered, semiconscious young criminals. "I hope you'll learn from this demonstration and become better individuals and citizens."

He retrieved his gym bag and glanced over a shoulder at the pair. Neither was able to get to his feet, and they were shaking their heads dazedly, trying to clear the cobwebs from their throbbing skulls.

"If you don't learn from this," the Cuban added in a voice as cold as frozen steel, "next time I'll kill both of you."

Satisfied that he had done his part to assist in the rehabilitation of misguided youth, Encizo headed for his car in the lot. The amateur muggers had wasted enough of his time, and he had an important appointment to keep.

3

"I had a meeting this morning with the President of the United States at a secret conference room at the basement level of the White House," Hal Brognola began while he chewed a cigar butt as if trying to be certain it was dead. "He's very concerned about recent events in El Salvador."

The Fed sat at the head of the conference table at the Stony Man War Room. He was a weary-looking, rumpled figure in a wrinkled white shirt and a narrow tie pulled down to allow his top button to be open at the throat. Brognola needed a shave, and coffee stains marred his sleeve, but he didn't notice and wouldn't have cared if he had. Other things were more important than his appearance at the moment.

David McCarter had entered the room as Brognola spoke. The tall, fox-faced Briton had been the last member of Phoenix Force to arrive. He had the most distance to travel to attend the meeting. McCarter had caught a flight from London as soon as he could manage it and arrived at Stony Man with the greatest haste possible. The British ace lived for the excitement and action provided by Phoenix Force and he was always eager to get on with the next mission regardless of the danger involved. In fact, the greater the danger, the greater the appeal to McCarter.

"Did I miss anything, gents?" the Briton inquired as he headed for the table, a can of Coke Classic in one hand and a pack of Player's cigarettes in the other.

"You mean besides an ironing board," Gary Manning asked as he glanced at McCarter's typically wrinkled slacks and sports jacket. "What the hell, David. Do you sleep in your clothes all the time?"

"Not when I'm with a bird," McCarter replied with a mild shrug. "But I've been sleeping solo lately."

Manning grunted. A big Canadian with a powerful physique and rugged features that reflected his limitless reserves of strength and determination, Gary Manning was the unit demolitions expert and the best rifle marksman of the group. He tended to approach the missions with businesslike precision. His serious manner caused a certain degree of bickering between the Canadian and the adrenaline-addicted Briton.

"You haven't missed anything, David," Yakov Katzenelenbogen assured the British commando. "Take a seat. The briefing has just begun."

Katzenelenbogen was the commander of Phoenix Force. Middle-aged, slightly overweight, with short-clipped gray hair and with a prosthetic device attached to the stump of his right limb, Katz did not look like a super commando ready to charge into combat. His deceptively harmless appearance had caused more than one opponent to underestimate Katz in the past. That was a mistake that generally cost a man his life.

"Okay," Brognola continued. "I'm sure you guys have followed what's been going on in El Salvador for quite a while now. The conflict between right-wing and left-wing factions in El Salvador has been a major concern for the United States for almost a decade."

"A lot longer than that," Rafael Encizo stated as he leaned back in his chair and drummed his fingertips along the edge of the table. "The U.S. has always been worried about El Salvador. It's had a long history of warring against other Central American countries. The more recent leaders like Romero and Duarte have been too similar to Somoza or Batista. Washington has long been worried that the Communists could take over in El Salvador just as they did in Cuba and Nicaragua.''

"That's why Washington has been backing a lot of the right-wing dictatorships in Central America,'' Calvin James commented. "Though I don't know if that's been such a brilliant idea, because those tinhorn tyrants tend to get people pissed off and eager to throw out whoever is in power and replace 'em with some other form of government, *any* form of government. I can't say I blame them. Pretty hard to convince people communism is so awful when they're living under a system that already denies them human rights and forces them to exist in poverty and fear.''

A tall, lanky black man from the South side of Chicago, James was the only native-born American member of Phoenix Force. He was an ex-Navy SEAL and former policeman with the San Francisco SWAT team. In addition to his skills with weapons and tactics, James was also a chemist and the unit medic of Phoenix Force.

"I must admit I haven't followed some of the things all that carefully lately,'' McCarter commented as he lighted a Player's. "But didn't El Salvador have an election last year and they booted the bloke who was in office out the door and put in a new chap?''

"That's right,'' Brognola confirmed. "Alfredo Cristiani of the ARENA Party is the president in El Salvador now. The President...that is, the President of the United States...isn't so sure that's a good thing. Washington has a lot of reservations about the ARENA Party. One thing is nobody seems to be sure who the hell actually runs it.''

"Who the hell runs the Republicans and Democrats here?'' James remarked with a cynical snort. "Seems to me they ought a be doing a better job, whoever they are.''

"Yeah,'' Encizo said with a nod, "but there's a definite difference here. One thing that is known about ARENA is it was founded by Roberto D'Aubuisson, who's been accused of running death squads in El Salvador back in the late seventies. Also, he's never been a great fan of the United

States. Of course, he blamed America for sticking El Salvador with Duarte for a leader. There's a certain amount of truth to that accusation, too.''

"Well, I don't think anyone really thought that the shit wouldn't hit the fan in El Salvador again," Brognola remarked as he consulted a computer printout sheet. "And, sure enough, it has. An official of the U.S. State Department named McKeller was attached to the U.S. Embassy in San Salvador to negotiate some cultural exchanges with our government and El Salvador. Yesterday he was murdered in broad daylight. Terrorists blew him away right on the street. They also killed two American Embassy security personnel who were McKeller's bodyguards, and they hit a Salvadoran military patrol jeep that was in the area. Two soldiers were burned to death by a Molotov cocktail, and another wound up in a hospital. His condition was listed as fair, but it looks like he'll be okay. That is, if you consider living with the results of third-degree burns over more than one-fourth of his body for the rest of his life as doing okay.''

"That sounds like a rather bold hit," Katz remarked. "I assume we're supposed to find out who did it.''

"You got it," the Fed said with a nod. "The Salvadoran government is already convinced the hit was carried out by the FMLN. The President isn't so sure. Like Rafael said, ARENA has its share of anti-American zealots. For that matter, three American nuns and a female volunteer worker were killed in an ambush outside San Salvador in 1980. They never proved who did it, but a lot of people figured it was done by the right-wing death squads or even Christian Democrats. At this point, nobody can be ruled out as possible suspects.''

"Bloody hell," McCarter complained as he sipped some cola. "We're not criminal investigators. Why do we keep getting these damn missions where we have to go to a foreign country and dig up the villains of some goddamn conspiracy? I thought Phoenix Force was meant to find a target and hit the bastards.''

"That's right," Brognola said with a slight smile. "You guys go to El Salvador and find your target. Then you get to hit it. Just finding it might be the hardest part of the mission."

"What's the CIA doing?" Encizo inquired. "The Company had people in El Salvador in 1961 and probably before that. They ought to have personnel who know the country and the people. I'd think they'd be better choices than we are."

"First thing is the President wants you guys to handle this," Brognola began. "He's been pretty impressed by you fellas in the past, and he thinks this is a mission that can best be handled by a small team of extremely good men operating with a very low profile and complete White House authority. He also suspects the CIA personnel in El Salvador haven't been able to maintain such great security. Too many people know who some of them are."

"That's wonderful," Manning said with a sigh. "I take it we'll be working with the Company, and they've already blown their own cover down there?"

"You'll be working with a case officer named Sommers, who has a pretty good reputation for handling matters in Central America," Brognola explained. "He's also tight with the Salvadoran authorities. You're gonna need their cooperation down there. There's a real good chance you won't like working with these guys, but you'll need their help."

"That thought sure gives me a glow all over," James muttered. "I don't know about this, Hal. Sounds like we could go down to El Salvador and be sandbagged by the Company and the Salvadoran government because both will be trying to cover up their own dirty laundry and only willing to pursue their pet theories about who the terrorists were who killed McKeller."

"McKeller getting killed is serious," Brognola began. "But there's more at stake than the lives of three Americans killed in the line of duty with a U.S. Embassy. If this turns out to be a new wave of activity by the FMLN, we need to know whether they're getting backing from Cuba or Nicaragua. This could be the beginning of a concentrated effort by the Reds to take over all of Central America."

"So much for the death of communism under *glasnost*," McCarter remarked dryly as he stuck the butt of his cigarette into the now-empty soft-drink can.

"*Glasnost* concerns the Soviet Union and the Iron Curtain countries of Eastern Europe," Katz reminded the Briton. "Castro still maintains that his government in Cuba is part of the 'people's revolution,' and the push for democratic reforms aren't likely to happen there as long as Fidel is running the show. It's even possible he sees the division between Moscow and Havana as a signal to push for Marxist revolution throughout Central America and possibly the Caribbean, as well."

"True," Brognola confirmed, "but it's also possible the FMLN isn't responsible for the incident in El Salvador. It could be a splinter group that isn't really connected to the guerrillas. There are five factions that comprise the FMLN, and even if one is responsible, it doesn't mean the others are. For that matter, fanatics from the Christian Democrats or another right-wing outfit might be the guilty party, and the Salvadoran government could be barking up the wrong tree."

"Or it could be a new death squad working for the ARENA government now in power," James said grimly. "If that's the case, we might wind up working with the bastards responsible."

"That's sure a cheerful thought," Manning commented.

Brognola swept his glance around the table. "We have to find whoever is responsible. Washington has split opinions about Cristiani. Probably the only fair attitude is to wait and see what kind of leader he'll turn out to be. However, considering El Salvador's track record, this incident will almost certainly lead to new repressions and restrictions on the rights of citizens. By cracking down on the 'other side,' the government can create an atmosphere ripe for revolution. Somoza did it in Nicaragua, the Shah did it in Iran and a whole bunch of other countries have done it and continue to do so today."

"And the FMLN has gotten a lot of support from the peasant classes," Encizo explained. "It's also said they get support from refugee camps in Honduras. The possibility of revolution or an escalation of violence in El Salvador is very likely."

"More than seventy thousand people have been killed already in the ten-year civil war in El Salvador," the Fed declared. "Uncle Sam has been shoveling hundreds of millions of dollars into Salvadoran governments in the past. Of course, we did that in Nicaragua, too, and you know what the outcome was. All that money was spent to keep El Salvador afloat and fend off growing Communist influence in Central America. It's been a hell of an investment, and so far there hasn't been much evidence it was money well spent."

Brognola checked his information on the computer sheets as he continued. "McKeller isn't the first American to be killed in El Salvador, either," the Fed stated. "The Reagan Administration sent military advisers to El Salvador in 1981 to help train the Salvadoran military and observe the situation there. Officially, at least, they were under orders not to engage the enemy. Still, Lieutenant Commander Albert Schaufelberger was killed by terrorists in 1983. Staff Sergeant Gregory Fronius was slain during a rebel attack on a Salvadoran army base in 1987. There have been several others killed in El Salvador who aren't as well known. The point is, if there's an escalation of the civil war in El Salvador, Washington will probably respond by increasing financial aid and military assistance."

"Yeah," James said grimly. "That's how we got involved in Vietnam, too."

"Unfortunately that's true," Brognola admitted. "Central America is one of the biggest political powder kegs in the world today. From Washington's point of view, it might even be hotter than the Middle East. There's already been quite a stink about American support of the Contras in Nicaragua and sending troops to Panama. Our policies in El Salvador have already gotten widespread criticism from the public.''

''I'd say there's some justification for that,'' Encizo said with a shrug. ''The U.S. supports dictators in charge of repressive and often brutal regimes simply because they're anti-Communist. Hitler was anti-Communist, too. Then Washington can't figure out why people in many of those countries don't like Americans. When someone has a boot on your throat, you're not terribly concerned with politics or whether communism is as bad or worse than fascism. You just want that boot off your throat.''

''You guys aren't expected to help the Salvadoran government or even like them,'' Brognola stated. ''Our concern is to find out what the hell is going on in El Salvador. The President would rather send Phoenix Force to nip things in the bud—if possible—before the situation mushrooms into something that could end with U.S. troops flooding into Central America. In other words, this could turn into another Vietnam.''

''There may be nothing we can do to stop that,'' Katz remarked with a sigh. ''It is probably up to the politicians and the rebels to determine the ultimate destiny of Central America.''

''God,'' Manning muttered. ''I don't think they've got a prayer.''

''Phoenix Force can only do what it can,'' Brognola said. ''You guys know more about what you're capable of and what your limits are than anybody else does, including me. If you take the mission, you'll handle it your way, like always.''

''Then I think we should get ready to leave,'' Katz replied.

4

Colonel Martillo calmly puffed on a short black cheroot as he watched the figure writhing in agony. The man was strapped to a wooden chair. His naked body was drenched with sweat and stained with his own blood. Alligator clips wired to an electrical generator were clamped to his nipples. Captain Ortiz stood beside the generator, one hand covered by a thick rubber glove.

"Hacer el payaso," Martillo remarked with a sigh. "To play the fool for those who are willing to let you suffer so. I do not understand you, Rodriguez. You feel you owe them your life?"

"No soy comunista," Rodriguez moaned, his voice little more than a harsh croak.

Ortiz swatted the back of his hand across Rodriguez's mouth. The victim's head recoiled from the blow, and more blood oozed from his cut lip. Martillo looked at Ortiz and shook his head. He didn't want the captain to knock Rodriguez senseless. An unconscious man couldn't answer questions.

Martillo was conducting the interrogation in a musky cellar in a remote farmhouse near Santa Ana. He had converted it into a torture chamber. A single light bulb hung from the ceiling, powered by another small generator. Martillo had to duck his head to avoid the light bulb as he approached Rodriguez. The colonel was a tall man, athletic and physically strong. He was barely forty years old, quite young to be a lieutenant colonel in El Salvador. His strong jaw and piercing dark eyes seemed to dominate his face, and one barely noticed the pock-marked cheeks or the irregularities of his features.

The steel head of a claw hammer jutted from a ring on his belt. Martillo meant "hammer" in English. Allegedly his ancestors had been Spaniards who were supposedly carpenters before they accompanied Cortés to the New World. Martillo took great pride in his heritage. The hammer on his belt was a fetish and a favorite close-quarters weapon. He was pleased that others spoke of Colonel Hammer in whispers, like old women afraid to say the names of evil spirits out loud.

"There is nothing to be gained by denying you are a Communist, Rodriguez," Martillo told the prisoner. "We already know that much about you. What we don't know is where the terrorists are hiding."

"If you want to find terrorists," Rodriguez replied as he stared back at the colonel, "you need only look in a mirror."

Colonel Martillo tapped the ash from the end of his cheroot. It fell on Rodriguez's naked groin. The prisoner trembled in terror as he felt the warm cigar ash on his private parts. He glanced up at the glowing tip of Martillo's cheroot. Rodriguez imagined what agony the Hammer could inflict with the hot point of the cigar.

"Insulting me under these conditions is rather stupid," Martillo told Rodriguez as he lowered the cheroot to the captive's face. The burning end hovered centimeters from Rodriguez's right eye. "One might even call it blind stupidity."

"*¡Madre de Dios!*" Rodriguez rasped as he turned his head away and tried to avoid looking at Martillo and the threatening cigar.

Captain Ortiz stared down at him. Martillo's aide was as sinister as his boss. A thin, waspy man with flat, emotionless features, Ortiz seemed almost reptilian. His dark cold eyes reminded Rodriguez of a viper, and he seemed frozen in place while he waited for Martillo to utter the next order, like a great lizard sunning itself on a rock.

"I thought you Communists do not believe in God," Martillo remarked as he moved the cigar close to Rodriguez's cheek. He knew the prisoner felt the heat from the glowing tip barely a centimeter from his skin.

"I am not a Communist," Rodriguez insisted, his teeth clenched to keep them from chattering out of control. "I wrote a pamphlet protesting any effort to take land from the small farmers to put it back into the hands of the rich landowners. That's not communism or socialism. It's just believing the people should be allowed to own their own property without being controlled by a wealthy elite few...."

"It seems you use your tongue to say nothing but lies," Martillo commented. He looked at Ortiz and nodded. "Maybe it needs a lesson in misconduct."

Ortiz grabbed one of the alligator clips attached to Rodriguez's nipples and unfastened it. The captain held the clip in his gloved hand while Martillo jammed the burning cheroot into Rodriguez's earlobe. The captive cried out in fear and pain. Ortiz quickly raised the alligator clip and thrust it into Rodriguez's open mouth.

The metal clamp snapped down on Rodriguez's tongue. Ortiz held the clip down with his rubber-clad fist and switched on the generator with his other hand. More than a thousand volts of electricity poured through the metal clip into the prisoner's tongue. Rodriguez's eyes bulged, and his body pressed back against the chair as if cemented to the furniture. His muscles locked and his jaw seemed frozen, unable to offer any resistance to the assault of white-hot suffering that ripped through the nerves in his tongue to grip into his brain as if determined to pulverize it in a vise of pure agony.

Rodriguez jerked violently in the chair as Ortiz held the clip in place to continue the torture. When Martillo signalled him to stop, the captain removed the clip and Rodriguez slumped unconscious in the chair. Ortiz switched off the machine.

"Should I revive him, Colonel?" Ortiz inquired.

"No," Martillo replied with a sigh. "I don't think he knows anything. He's a stinking Communist sympathizer, but he doesn't seem to be connected with the FMLN.

Martillo grabbed Rodriguez's hair and yanked his head forward with one hand while the other drew the hammer from his belt. He pulled the prisoner's head down to expose the back of his skull. The colonel raised the hammer and swung the tool, smashing the steel head into the base of the unconscious man's cranium. He struck three times to be certain the junction of vertebrae at the skull was shattered.

"At least we have one less collaborator," Ortiz commented. He collected his generator and clips as he spoke. "If we include the peasant trash who ran this farm, we got rid of a number of collaborators today."

Martillo didn't reply. He pushed Rodriguez's head to one side. It wobbled loosely on the stem of a broken neck. The colonel grunted, satisfied the prisoner was dead. He located the man's shirt in a pile of clothes in a corner and used it to wipe the blood from his hammer. Martillo draped the garment over Rodriguez's shattered skull and returned the hammer to his belt.

"There's nothing else we can do here," the colonel said with a sigh. "Let's go."

The officers mounted the stairs of the basement. Martillo weaved slightly and clutched the handrail. Ortiz spread his arms, ready to catch the colonel if his commander lost his balance. Martillo clasped his free hand to the back of his head and gasped in pain.

"Do you need help, Colonel?" Ortiz inquired.

"Just another headache," Martillo hissed through clenched teeth. "I'll be all right, Captain."

The colonel slowly made his way up the stairs and entered a small kitchen in the farmhouse. He staggered to a chair and slumped into the seat. Ortiz quickly moved to a window and pulled the drapes shut. It would not do for the men outside to see their commander in such a condition.

Martillo took a small bottle of pills from his pocket and shook out two capsules. He gulped them down and waited for the painkillers to take effect. Ortiz found a glass and poured some water from the kitchen sink.

"I don't need that, Captain," Martillo assured him. "These migraines come and go. That damn Rodriguez brought this one on. I was so sure he was linked to the FMLN. Another false lead. It would not bother me so if we only killed Rodriguez, but the farmer and his family..."

"It was a proper firing squad," Ortiz stated. "They were collaborators and they were executed in a swift and humane fashion."

"I wish we didn't have to use Jinete's people," Martillo rasped as he rose from the chair. "They're scum. Hill bandits pretending to be freedom fighters..."

"We need them, Colonel," Ortiz said sadly. "For now. After this business with the United States government is finished, we won't have to deal with *El Jinete*."

"I should have put those two bastards in front of the firing squad and had them shot along with the farmer and his family," Martillo complained.

"We need Jinete's cooperation," Ortiz said with a sigh. "I admire your self-control and restraint, Colonel. It is not easy, but it is wise under the circumstances."

"Restraint?" Martillo said, and raised his eyebrows. "When restraint forces me to shoot a sixteen-year-old girl in the back of the head and allow two would-be rapists to live, I'm not so sure I approve of 'restraint.'"

"It was an act of mercy," Ortiz assured him. "You said so yourself. She had already been through a terrible ordeal when those two tried to force themselves on her, and you did not think she should be made to stand in front of the firing squad and face her own death."

"Or see her parents killed," Martillo said with a nod as he rose from his chair. "Of course, her mother and father witnessed their daughter's death."

"They were adults and actively supporting the Communists," Ortiz said with a shrug. "They did not deserve mercy. Besides, they were executed two minutes later, anyway."

"True," Martillo agreed. "They don't have to live with what they saw or what they did."

He turned to face Ortiz and added, "Unlike you and I." He had a look of suffering and martyrdom on his face, which prompted Ortiz to nod gravely, as though he understood perfectly.

In a little while they both emerged from the farmhouse. The corpses of the peasants still lay on the ground, their bodies rimmed by pools of their own blood. The farmer, his wife, daughter and four hired workers had been shot to death for allegedly assisting the Communist rebels. Martillo's men stood near the army deuce-and-half-ton truck. They still carried M-16 assault rifles used for the executions. At least one of them had had the decency to cover the girl's face with a canvas tarp.

"There is a tool shed behind the house," Martillo announced to his troops. "I want two men to go there and search it for paint and any sort of flammable liquid. Gasoline, kerosene, whatever. There's no need for us to use our own supply if these items are already here, and it will look more realistic if we use the materials available."

"Si, Coronel," Sergeant Lopez, the NCOIC of the unit declared. He pointed at two men and ordered them to carry out the commander's order.

The pair hurried to the rear of the house. Ortiz called out to them and instructed them to also look for rags and paintbrushes.

Martillo tried to avoid looking at the slain peasants as he faced his men once more. "Sergeant," he told Lopez. "I want you to set fire to the house. It is important the fire be started in the basement. I want that traitor's corpse burned beyond recognition. The walls are adobe and should survive the fire fairly well.''

Lopez saluted and confirmed that he understood. The NCO was a large bearlike man with a barrel chest and large belly. Though his rough and coarse features suggested a brutish intellect, it was an entirely false impression. Lopez was actually intelligent and less inclined to violence than most of the men in Martillo's death squad.

''I also want some rebel slogans painted on the outside of the walls,'' the colonel told the rest of his men. ''Big letters in red or green or whatever color we can manage. Just as long as it stands out clearly. I want someone who can spell, too. We'll see if we can't use the useless journalists who infest our country and whine and whimper with concern and sympathy for the damn Communists. It must be a requirement for a journalist to be a leftist Communist sympathizer.''

''The Jews run publishing in the United States and Europe,'' Ortiz commented as he finished the final touches on the mass execution of the peasants. ''Scratch a Jew and you find a Communist.''

Martillo didn't bother to respond. He knew Ortiz was violently anti-Semitic and never missed an opportunity to express his theory that all the world's ills were founded by the ''Zionist Communist conspiracy.'' Martillo considered that to be absurd. It was hard to believe Fidel Castro and Daniel Ortega were Jewish. The idea became even sillier when one considered Red China and North Korea were Communist nations. In the Middle East the Soviets had backed Arab nations, not Israel—which was supported by the United States.

Still, Martillo did not bother arguing with Ortiz's pet theory. The captain's personal prejudice didn't affect how he did his job. Ortiz could hate anyone or anything he pleased as long as he continued to carry out his duties as Martillo's second in command.

The soldiers returned from the shed with kerosene and some small buckets of paint. They had also found brushes and rags. Lopez took one of the cans and prepared to enter the house, but paused and turned to face Martillo.

"What about the ERP base, Colonel?" the NCO inquired. "Did Rodriguez tell you where it was before he died?"

"No, Sergeant," the colonel admitted. "His heart gave up under interrogation. He died before he could talk."

Martillo did not intend to tell his men they had tortured and killed the wrong man. He had doubts that any of the peasants were connected to the ERP—Ejercito Revolucionario del Pueblo—or any other rebel outfit. Still, the colonel figured they had no choice but to dispatch all witnesses. Most of his men wouldn't care if they had to slaughter innocent peasants, but Lopez was an exception.

"That is unfortunate, sir," the sergeant said grimly. "This whole business is unfortunate."

"We wouldn't have to use such tactics if the Communists didn't force us to do so," Martillo declared. "You've seen what these bastards have done to our people, Sergeant. A ruthless opponent must be dealt with in a ruthless manner."

"Si," Lopez said with a nod. *"Comprendo."*

The sergeant entered the house reassured he was doing the right thing. Others quickly set the stage for the improvised cremations and the painting of slogans on the adobe walls. Martillo took a fresh cheroot from his shirt pocket and watched his men carry out the orders. The scene disgusted him, and the fact that he was responsible for the slaughter did not sit well with him. Martillo wished he could ease his guilt by going to confession, but he could not even trust the priests with such information. Too many clergy sympathized with the rebel forces.

Still, he reminded himself, the end would eventually justify the methods he used. Martillo fired up the cigar and tried to find some comfort in the belief that he was a patriot carrying out his duty to save his country. El Salvador had suffered a great deal in the past ten years, and there was bound to be more suffering before the nightmare of civil war and terror ended.

Martillo himself would see to that.

5

The demonstrators effectively blocked the road from the San Salvador International Airport. Some carried placards with anti-American and anti-Cristiani slogans written in Spanish and English. Others waved signs that condemned communism and demanded the destruction of the FMLN and the death of Castro and Ortega. The two factions of left-wing and right-wing protestors had expected to encounter one another, and both sides were prepared for the confrontation.

The demonstrators threw rocks at each other. Some wore metal buckets with portions cut away to serve as improvised helmets, while others carried trash-can lids to use as shields. A number of people had sharpened the handles of their protest signs to use them as lances.

The National Police tried to keep both sides at bay. The presence of the uniformed men deterred total war between the protesters until the government limousine rolled into view.

The anti-Cristiani and anti–United States demonstrators tried to attack the long official car. The police struggled to fend them off, and the right-wing protesters charged at the opposition group. The rock throwing got worse. When the police stepped in to jab and slug with batons, the demonstrators stopped fighting each other and turned on the cops. Tear gas canisters sailed into the crowd, and warning shots were fired to restrain the violent mob.

That allowed the green-and-white minibus to drive past the demonstrators with little interruption. A couple of protesters beat the frame of the bus with their signs and spit on the passing vehicle, but they were more concerned with other matters to pay much attention to it. It managed to roll past with little more damage than a few dents and some gobs of spittle.

"I feel sorry for the dudes in that limo," Calvin James commented as he peered through the tinted glass of a window by his seat inside the bus. "They're catching a lot of heat just to make it easier for us."

"They're acting as a decoy," Ronald Sommers remarked, and fished a pack of cigarettes from his flowery shirt pocket. "It'd take us hours to get through the streets otherwise. Besides, everybody's attention is on the limo and not on us."

"I wouldn't count on distracting *everyone* with this tactic," Yakov Katzenelenbogen remarked. He gestured with the trident hooks at the end of his prosthesis as he spoke. "Professionals would watch for something like this. I wish we'd had enough time to put together a tactic with better security. Perhaps coming across the border by vehicle instead of using a plane."

"El Salvador is close enough to the United States that we could have done that," Gary Manning added. "It might have taken an extra few hours, but it may have been worth it."

"The guerrilla rebels are ignorant trash," Major Juan Ferrero stated. The Salvadoran military Intelligence officer was barely five foot five, but he seemed as tough as alligator leather. "I doubt they're intelligent enough to figure out even the most simple tactics."

"They've managed to remain at large for ten years during the civil war, and you haven't been able to stop them so far," Encizo commented wryly. "If they carried out the hit on the Embassy personnel, they obviously had some sources of information to know when and where to carry out the attack. It was also planned well enough to let them take out an army patrol car and flee the area without being captured. Seems to me that is ample reason not to underestimate them, Major."

Ferrero glared at Encizo. The Cuban met his gaze and held it. It would take more than dirty looks to intimidate Rafael Encizo or any of the other members of Phoenix Force.

"You say 'if' the rebels did the killing?" Ferrero remarked. "There is no good reason to doubt this. The Communists are responsible. Who else would do such a thing?"

Even the usually patient Gary Manning was getting irritable, but he answered the question reasonably.

"We don't know yet. That's one of the reasons we're here."

"Look fellas," Sommers began with a sigh. "I know El Salvador gets a lot of bad press back in the States. This country has had its problems. Nobody will deny that. Sometimes the government was at fault. I don't think you'll find too many Salvadorans who will cheer the decision to invade Honduras in 1969."

"We didn't lose," Ferrero said pompously. "We would have won if the OAS hadn't gotten involved and threatened El Salvador with economic sanctions and military force."

"Ain't it awful when they ruin a war before you can really get things rolling?" James commented dryly.

"My point is," Sommers continued, "that El Salvador hasn't exactly had a blameless history, but there are a lot of exaggerated claims about how bad the governments have been. The goddamn FMLN aren't a bunch of Boy Scouts. Forget that crap that they're just a bunch of peasants trying to gain freedom from a right-wing banana dictatorship. The Cubans and the Nicaraguans have supported the leftist terrorists. You'd better believe that."

"I recall that the FMLN actually claimed they got weapons from the Contras," Manning said. "Supposedly those so-called freedom fighters in Nicaragua started selling guns and supplies to the Salvadoran rebels to make a profit for their own movement.''

"And you believe them?'' Ferrero shook his head with dismay. "That's a stinking lie. The Sandinistas supplied them with those weapons. Not the Contras.''

"If we're talking about 1989,'' Encizo mused. "I remember there was some debate about that, but the guns the FMLN received were AK-47 assault rifles, which suggests the Communists were responsible. I also remember, in 1983 the Managua government tried to make a deal with Washington. The Sandinistas offered to end support of the rebels in El Salvador if the U.S. would discontinue military training of Contras in Honduras and El Salvador. That sounds almost like a confession of involvement by the Sandinistas.''

"You have a good memory, *señor*,'' Ferrero said with surprise. "And you don't sound quite as soft on communism as I feared.''

"Believe me, Major,'' Katz began with a sigh, "we've encountered many KGB conspiracies and support of international terrorism in previous missions. We've come across other Marxist and Maoist fanatic outfits that weren't connected with Moscow. Some were associated with other Communist countries or followed their own brand of extremist socialist doctrine. None of us have any sympathy for the fanatic left wing, but that doesn't mean the fanatical right is any better.''

"But the FMLN rebels killed McKeller and the Embassy security personnel,'' Sommers insisted. "That's obvious. Those poor bastards were killed because they were with the United States Embassy. Because they were *norteamericanos*.''

"So what?'' David McCarter snorted. The British ace searched through their luggage as he spoke and located his aluminum suitcase. "Didn't the boss of the ARENA Party make some comments about 'getting rid' of the gringos?''

"You refer to Major D'Aubuisson," Ferrero remarked. "He ran for president many years ago and said some foolish things. Of course, many Salvadorans agreed with him that the United States was carrying out social experiments in our country, and your American President did push for Duarte to be our leader."

"The United States supported the Christian Democrats because they seemed the most moderate political influence in El Salvador," Encizo stated. "With accusations that D'Aubuisson was the head of the death squads, it's no wonder Washington is suspicious of the ARENA Party."

"President Cristiani compares the ARENA Party to the Republicans in your country," Ferrero insisted.

"Don't expect the Republicans to thank him for that comparison," Katz replied. "Frankly we're less concerned with your country's politics than finding out who murdered those three Americans and why they did it."

The bus traveled to the heart of San Salvador and soon the National Palace was ahead of them. The Doric pillars and marble steps of the classically inclined architecture vaguely resembled the Capitol Building in Washington, D.C.—but without the massive dome. The El Salvador Legislative Assembly generally met at the palace. The building was surrounded by soldiers, and a tank was in sight. There were no demonstrators present in the area, but the military was obviously prepared for trouble.

The traffic was heavier in that part of the city. Some of the vehicles in the streets were television news vans from various countries, which wasn't good news for Phoenix Force. The media presented problems for security. The commandos needed to operate with a low profile and keep their activities unknown by anyone except the handful of Intelligence personnel Phoenix needed to carry out their mission. Television and newspaper reporters were scattered across San Salvador, but they seemed to be headed for the demonstrations at the airport. Emerald-green police cars streaked through the streets, their sirens screeching a warning for other traffic to get out of the way.

The driver of the bus pulled over to the curb to allow the police cars to pass. The guy behind the steering wheel was one of Ferrero's people. He was clearly a mestizo, like the vast majority of Salvadorans. The driver's mixed Spanish-and-Indian blood was shown by his features. Actually his heritage included more Nahuatl than Spanish.

Phoenix Force had reservations about working with the Salvadoran Intel forces. If the accusations against Major D'Aubuisson were true, high-ranking military Intelligence officers in El Salvador were running the death squads in the late 1970s. How much had changed in the last decade? Most observers felt the Christian Democratic Party leaders had been ineffective rather than evil, unable to cope with the fanatic factions on the far left and right. President Cristiani was still being evaluated. Washington would like to believe what the current leader of El Salvador said. He was educated at Georgetown, spoke English fluently and seemed to be an intelligent, thoughtful man. Certainly not a mad dog. Whether he could actually unite Salvadorans and end the turmoil remained to be seen.

Sommers seemed defensive of El Salvador, but the CIA case officer was obviously concerned with the possibility of a Communist takeover in Central America, and he didn't appear too worried about what sort of government any country had in the region as long as it was not left of center. The gruff, balding Company man was a veteran CIA operative who had spent most of his twenty-two-year career in Central America. He represented a mentality that had placed the United States on the side of right-wing dictators in the past.

The bus waited for the police cars to pass, then moved on. San Salvador was the largest city in El Salvador, and they passed a number of manufacturing centers as well as the José Simeón Cañas Central American University. The San Salvador Volcano towered in the distance beyond the city.

It seemed appropriate that a volcano stood near the capital of El Salvador, like a symbol of unpredictable forces that could erupt into incredible devastation.

They arrived at a textile mill near the outskirts of the city. A sliding door to a truck bay opened, and the bus pulled inside, where two uniformed figures stood, rifles held at port arms. They watched the bus come to a halt, and one man pressed the control buttons to close the door.

"We use this place as a safehouse," Sommers explained. "It's a joint operations project by the Company and the Salvadoran military Intelligence. We can work together easier this way on issues that concern the interests of both our nations."

"I see," Katz commented as he slid back the side door to the bus. If Sommers wanted to pretend the CIA and Salvadoran Intel were best buddies who respected and trusted each other, that was okay with the Phoenix commander.

Of course, Katz knew better. The Israeli had been involved in espionage and covert operations since World War II. He had worked with the OSS and British Intelligence before he left Europe to join Israel's struggle for independence after the war. Katz became a top Intelligence operative for Mossad and was occasionally attached to other Intel outfits, including CIA, the British SIS, the West German BND and the French Sûreté. He knew that Intelligence organizations never trust each other. Even allies spy on one another to try to get information the other outfit does not want to share.

The CIA and the Salvadorans no doubt only worked together when they both really needed help. The rest of the time they were most likely trying to steal information from each other. It was business as usual, Katz realized. Phoenix Force needed their cooperation, so there was nothing to be gained by antagonizing their reluctant allies.

They emerged from the bus and followed Sommers and Ferrero through the bay area. The armed soldiers watched Phoenix Force with distrust and undisguised hostility. Katz suspected they were just honestly expressing what both the Salvadorans and the CIA felt. They almost certainly resented the five-man team of specialists who had been sent by the President himself because he thought they could do a better job than the Salvadorans who lived in the country or the Company case officers who had years of experience in Central America.

Katz did not blame either group for feeling that he and his men were muscling in on their territory. As outsiders, though, they didn't have to work from a set of prejudices, which allowed them to be more objective and therefore more liable to do the job well. Phoenix Force had a mission to carry out, and Sommers and Ferrero would just have to suffer the wounds to their pride.

"This conference room is soundproof and quite secure," Ferrero declared as he escorted the visitors to a door at the end of the bay. "We can discuss our business better here."

The conference room was about the size of an average living room, with a long table surrounded by ten chairs. A cabinet held a coffee maker, bottled water and a small ice chest. Manning headed for the coffee and poured himself a cup. James followed his example while McCarter checked the ice box.

"No Coca-Cola," the Briton said with a sigh of disappointment. "Just some bottles of beer."

"That's okay with me," Encizo remarked as he reached around McCarter and plucked a bottle from the chest.

The British ace muttered something under his breath that wasn't intended to be heard by the others. He had acquired a fondness for Coca-Cola after serving with the British SAS in Oman during the Omani Dhofar conflict in the 1970s. The Communist rebels poisoned the water holes in the mountainous regions where the civil was fought. McCarter had developed a taste for Coke because it hadn't been safe to drink the water.

Ferrero closed and locked the door as Phoenix Force occupied chairs. Sommers stationed himself at the head of the table in an effort to claim some sort of symbolic sign of leadership even though he could not compete with the White House authority of Phoenix Force. Actually Katz didn't care if the CIA case officer wanted to sit on his head and whistle "Yankee Doodle Dandy." The Israeli got out his Camels and a Ronson lighter as Ferrero approached the table.

"We need to see the report forms on the terrorist attacks," Katz declared. "Autopsies, ballistics, forensics and eyewitness testimony, if any."

"A soldier with the patrol survived," Ferrero stated as he moved to the cabinets and opened a door to reveal a set of steel file drawers. "But I don't think his statement will be much help."

"We'd still like to see it," Katz insisted.

"It's in Spanish," Ferrero said with a sigh. He seemed reluctant to retrieve the statement from the files and was obviously stalling.

"I think I can manage to read it," Encizo assured him.

"One unusual item is the weapons used," Sommers declared. "Nine-millimeter Ingram machine pistols, American made. The FMLN generally use weapons of Communist manufacture. AK-47 assault rifles are the most common, but they also use a fair number of M-16s and other American-made firearms. Some are from black-market sources, and others have been confiscated from slain Salvadoran troops."

"A MAC-10 Ingram isn't a typical military weapon," McCarter remarked. He had carried an Ingram for years as a personal weapon. "It's compact, easy to conceal and carry. The Ingram is not very accurate and the range is limited, but it fires one hell of a rapid rate. Close to nine hundred rounds per minute. A real room cleaner. It has limited use and is something of a special ops weapon. I wouldn't imagine they'd have many MAC-10s in the Salvadoran military."

"Actually the United States government supplied us with a few hundred Ingrams in the 1970s," Ferrero explained. "I think they had some notion that the MAC-10 was going to be a cross between a pistol and a submachine gun. Six months ago a military base near Santa Ana was hit by ERP forces. They stole a large number of military arms, including two dozen MAC-10 machine pistols."

"I know the FMLN is the Farabundo Martí National Liberation Front," Calvin James commented. "But what's the ERP?"

"Ejercito Revolucionario del Pueblo," Ferrero answered. "The People's Revolutionary Army. It's actually the largest of the five terrorist groups that comprise the FMLN. We estimate that the entire FMLN may have more than ten thousand members."

"That's pretty big terrorist outfit," Manning said with a groan. "How big is your army?"

"Total military strength in El Salvador is approximately seven thousand five hundred members," Ferrero said grimly. "That doesn't include the National Police, but the terrorists may in fact outnumber us, nonetheless. You understand why we're worried."

"The ERP attacked a farm near Santa Ana this morning," Sommers added. "Men, women and children slaughtered. They burned the bodies and the house. ERP slogans were painted all over the walls."

"These were peasants?" Encizo asked with surprise. "Not landowners?"

"That's right," Ferrero confirmed. "The terrorists generally attack businessmen, military posts, landowners and members of what might be called the middle class."

"El Salvador doesn't have much of a middle class," Encizo stated. "You've got an upper-middle class, lower-middle class and downright poor."

"So you know my country better than I do?" Ferrero asked dryly, and gave Encizo a challenging look. "I find your insinuations insulting."

"I'm just stating a well-known fact," the Cuban insisted. "One of the reasons the FMLN has become so large and successful is because they've gotten a lot of support from the peasants. It seems odd they'd kill people from the ranks they count on for support. Especially leaving evidence behind virtually bragging about what they did."

"The farm was probably meant to serve as an example for what would happen to anyone who refused to help the ERP," Sommers suggested. "The victims were not known to be supporters of any political group in the past. I don't see why you're curious. What's this have to do with the McKeller killing?"

"It's too soon for us to say what may or may not be connected to the incident," Katz explained. "Certainly any terrorist activity or incidents that might seem bizarre or alarming are of interest to us."

Ferrero slapped a file folder on the table.

"Here's the report on the multiple murder in San Salvador. The one you were sent to deal with."

"Ballistics included?" Manning inquired.

"Yeah," Encizo confirmed as he examined the information. The Cuban handed the ballistics report to Manning and read the soldier's statement. "The terrorists were dressed in fatigue uniforms without insignia. No unit patches. The only one in civilian clothes was the man driving the sedan. That seems pretty strange."

"They were masquerading as soldiers," Sommers said with a shrug. "You'll notice they even shaved, and they cut their hair to be more convincing."

"But they didn't wear patches or insignia?" McCarter scoffed. "Some disguise."

"Maybe they didn't have any patches for a Salvadoran army unit," Ferrero said with a frustrated sigh. "Guerrillas in the Usulután province wear fatigue uniforms for training exercises. Maybe they were afraid they might encounter real troops with a specific unit who would have been suspicious of new faces they hadn't encountered before.

Maybe the terrorists simply overlooked that detail. Most of them are uneducated trash, anyway.''

"They were clever enough when they carried out the hit," Manning reminded him. "The ammunition used was 115-grain NATO 9 mm parabellum hardball. Government manufacture. Salvadoran military stamp on the shell casings."

"The terrorists stole the ammunition as well as the guns," Ferrero suggested. "You don't think my government ordered these killings? What would they have to gain?"

"The major is right," Sommers agreed. "El Salvador wants more support from Uncle Sam. The government wouldn't do something that could endanger their very survival. Aid from the United States has kept El Salvador from going down the tubes. When we cut off economic aid in 1980, they damn near fell apart."

"No one is accusing the government," Katz assured him, "but there are a lot of contradictory things about this hit. The terrorists were able to learn where McKeller would be and when the best time to hit him would be. They planned the attack well and obviously planned their escape just as well, yet they made some curious mistakes. Unfortunately none of those mistakes was big enough to help us much."

"So, you can't just snap your fingers and solve this mess?" Ferrero remarked. "What a disappointment. What do we do now?"

"We keep looking until we find the truth," Katz answered. "Whatever that might be."

6

The sun had gone down while Phoenix Force sat in conference with Major Ferrero and Ronald Sommers. The commandos left the safehouse with Sommers at the wheel of the minibus. The CIA man was less than happy with Phoenix and took advantage of the chance to talk to them in private.

"You guys could have used a little more tact in there," Sommers said as he drove the bus into the streets and headed for Delgado Avenue. "Ferrero is on our side, you know."

"He's on the side of protecting the Salvadoran government and military," Gary Manning replied. The Canadian sat with an aluminum suitcase on his lap and a rifle case at his feet. Phoenix Force had no trouble bringing the weapons from the U.S. to El Salvador because Brognola had arranged for customs to let them through at both ends.

"This is his country, damn it," Sommers declared.

"Charles Manson was born in the U.S.A.," Calvin James commented. "Just like you and me, Sommers. So what?"

"Maybe Ferrero knows more about El Salvador than you people do," the CIA agent replied with a sharp edge to his voice. "Could be I do, too. I've been here a lot longer than you have. White House authority or not, I've been in Central America before the present administration took over in Washington. I was here in '79 when the junta threw out General Romero."

"You and Ferrero aren't being objective," Katz told him. "You've both concentrated on holding back the Communists and covering up the dirty laundry of the far right."

"Do you know what the Communists have been doing in El Salvador?" Sommers demanded, glancing from the windshield to cast a hard stare at Katz. "You ever hear of Roberto Poma or Ernesto Liebes? They were murdered by the ERP. The terrorists held the bodies and claimed they had the men hostage so they could demand ransom money from the families. They abducted a Peace Corps volunteer named Deborah Loff in 1979 and tried to blackmail the United States into paying ransom for her release. She was more fortunate than most because she was still alive when they released her in 1980. Those are the 'poor oppressed peasant revolutionaries' the media likes to whine about back in the States. All those liberal celebrities who suck up to the Sandinistas are eager to kiss the FMLN's collective red ass...."

"Are you finished?" Katz asked. "None of us want to see the Communists take control of Central America. We don't have any sympathy for the FMLN or any other leftist fanatic organization, but you and Ferrero have already labeled this as a leftist terrorist assault. You've chosen to ignore anything that makes that theory questionable. Rather like the people who still believe in relics such as the Shroud of Turin. They're willing to accept computer 3-D hologram concoctions as evidence that it was the burial sheet of Jesus—although there is no scientific reason why that proved anything one way or the other—but they refuse to accept the carbon-14 tests that date the cloth to the Middle Ages."

"He's got a background in archaeology and linguistics," David McCarter told Sommers, explaining why Katz chose this unusual comparison. "He also doesn't make very many mistakes, because he tries to get as many facts as possible before making any decisions or theories."

"That's great," Sommers muttered. "You guys show up here with fancy guns and explosives or whatever the hell you've got in that aluminum luggage, and I'm afraid D.C. sent me a bunch of cowboy commandos or mercenary hitmen. Instead I get an intellectual who thinks he's a college professor, a couple of would-be social workers who belong in a classroom on civics and...I haven't figured out you other guys yet."

"Oh, man," Calvin James said with a laugh. "We've been described a lot of ways in the past, but I never heard anything even remotely like that before."

"It's pretty funny," McCarter agreed with a chuckle. The British ace had been compared to Charles Gordon, a young Winston Churchill and Attila the Hun, but never to a social worker.

Encizo leaned forward to pat the CIA man on the shoulder. "You want to know the truth, Sommers? We don't give a damn what you think of us. You're not in charge here. We are. Your control officer should have made that clear. If you fail to cooperate with us, we'll have you replaced by somebody who will. If you don't like it, go complain to the President of the United States."

Sommers growled something unintelligible as he steered around a pair of police cars parked along the curb of a narrow street. Two officers, armed with pump shotguns and wearing riot gear, blocked the bus and gestured for it to stop. Sommers obeyed. He got out his passport and U.S. Embassy identification as a policeman stepped to the window.

"La Embajada de los Estados Unidos," Sommers informed the policeman as he showed the officer the embassy ID.

"Si," the cop said with a nod. *"Su pasaporte, por favor."*

The company man handed him the passport. The policeman nodded again, handed it back and spoke briefly with Sommers. Encizo and James were fluent in Spanish, and the other three members of Phoenix Force understood the language to a lesser degree, but none of them heard enough of the conversation to be sure what it was about.

"¡No tiene su cédula!" a voice shouted from the street.

Another policeman in front of the official cars swung his shotgun and struck a young man dressed in cotton trousers and T-shirt. The blow knocked the youth to the pavement. The officer pointed the weapon at the guy's head while another one stepped forward with handcuffs. The policeman with the shotgun kicked the prisoner in the ribs before they hauled him to his feet and dragged him to the cars.

"Gracias, señor," the officer by the bus told Sommers and gestured for him to drive on.

The CIA man followed instructions, and drove past the police cars. Several other young men and a couple of women were spread-eagled against a wall. Some frisked the subjects while others barked orders and kept them in line with gun barrels. James grunted with disgust. He had formerly been a police officer in San Francisco, and he didn't like seeing anyone abuse the authority that came with a badge.

"What's going on?" Manning inquired as he glanced at the police with distaste.

"They're just checking for identification," Sommers answered. "Pretty standard. Especially after that riot we saw at the airport. Anybody out after dark without passport or a *cédula* will be hauled in for interrogation."

"¿Cédula?" Manning asked with a frown. "That's like a birth certificate, isn't it?"

"In El Salvador it refers to an official identification card," Encizo explained. "If a citizen doesn't have one, he or she is pretty much a nonentity here."

"It's how they do things here," Sommers said with a shrug. "You fellas have been out in the world enough to know other countries don't operate the same as the United States does. Things don't change overnight, either. We can't do anything about most of this stuff. Not our job, anyway."

"Our job is usually to try to keep things from getting worse," Katz replied, and that seemed to close discussion for a while.

Soon the bus pulled onto Alvarado Avenue. Sommers informed the passengers that they were approaching the U.S. Embassy. McKeller and his companions had been killed only a few blocks away. Phoenix Force had reservations at a hotel on the same street. They were using cover names and false identification. Officially they were UN observers, with Encizo and James listed as translators. The cover explained their international ethnic background and made it plausible for them to be met by a representative from the U.S. Embassy.

But there was the further consideration that the enemy might know Sommers's affiliation with the CIA. The case officer may have spent too much time in Central America. The old axiom that "familiarity breeds contempt" has more than a grain of truth. He was obviously on friendly terms with the Salvadoran government. Sommers had probably been invited to social functions, received gifts from officials and visited members of the Salvadoran upper classes at their homes. Since the enemy could be among the political right, they could very well know Sommers personally. If they were leftist extremists, they could have observed him for some time and strongly suspected he worked for the Company.

None of that gave Phoenix Force much reason for confidence that their mission was going to go fairly smoothly. The bus drew closer to the Embassy. A pair of Marines were posted in front of the building, clad in blue dress uniform with white saucer caps. Sommers grunted and tilted his head toward the Embassy.

"That's where I work," he remarked as if he were giving the passengers a tour of the city.

"I hope you have a nice office," Manning replied. He glanced down at the luggage at his feet. "We should have left these rifle cases at the safehouse. They're too obvious and will draw attention at the hotel.''

"Leave 'em in the bus and I'll take 'em back," Sommers assured him with a sigh. "I need to talk to Ferrero some more, anyway.''

The roar of an explosion from the street startled the men in the vehicle. The glare of the blast came from the U.S. Embassy. The Marines had vanished from view. They had either been taken down by the explosion or hurled themselves to the ground for cover. Automatic fire erupted from the Embassy grounds.

"Hell!" Sommers exclaimed as two armed figures appeared from a car parked by the curb.

The gunmen pointed short-barreled machine pistols at the bus. Sommers instinctively turned the steering wheel to try to swerve away from the threat. Encizo reached forward from the back seat and grabbed the wheel with one fist and pushed the CIA man toward the floorboards with his other hand.

"Down!" the Cuban ordered as he turned the wheel sharply to swing the bus back toward the gunmen.

Sommers had pressed down on the accelerator to try to flee. The bus bolted forward, which suited Encizo's tactics. He wanted to charge into the gunmen. The Cuban warrior intended to take the offense away from the enemy as quickly as possible and try to hit them with something they did not expect.

"*¡Qué la chigada!*" one of the gunmen cried as he dove out of the path of the charging vehicle.

The other man sprayed a salvo of 9 mm rounds at the windshield of the bus before he tried to jump aside. Bullets smashed a road map pattern of cracks in the thick glass. One slug pierced the windshield and punched into the backrest to the driver's seat. Fortunately for Encizo, the projectile had burned up all its energy and was embedded in the backrest.

The Cuban leaned around the front seat to hold the steering wheel with both hands. His spine shivered and his guts seemed to knot with fear, but Encizo had known fear all his life and it didn't cause him to freeze or panic. Encizo kept his head low and gazed up at the shattered windshield as he plowed the bus into the gunman.

A scream of terror and agony accompanied the ugly *whack* when the big vehicle slammed into the enemy triggerman. The guy's body appeared at the windshield as the blow knocked him off his feet and pitched him backward two meters to land against the car by the curb. The bus continued to plow forward and crashed into the side of the car. The unlucky gunman was trapped between the two vehicles when they collided. Blood sprayed the windshield like a spray of red paint.

"Put the brake on!" Encizo shouted to Sommers as he reached inside his jacket for the Walther P-88 holstered under his arm.

McCarter had already opened a side door to the bus and jumped out before it came to a halt. The Briton held an aluminum suitcase in one fist and a Browning Hi-Power autoloader in the other. He hit the ground on his feet, knees bent and body angled forward. McCarter lunged and rolled with the momentum. He tumbled across the pavement as the gunman who had evaded the charging vehicle pointed his Ingram subgun at the Briton's hurtling form.

Yakov Katzenelenbogen opened fire from the door of the bus. He held an Uzi machine pistol braced across his mechanical arm and aimed it at the terrorist about to waste McCarter. A trio of 9 mm parabellum rounds drilled into the gunman's chest. The impact knocked the man off his feet and hurled him backward before he could fire on McCarter. The terrorist's MAC-10 snarled a useless volley of full-auto slugs into the sky before he tumbled to the ground, his heart torn apart by two 124-grain Federal Hydra Shok rounds.

Another figure in fatigues appeared from behind the bashed-in wreck of the automobile at the curb. He was already bleeding from a scalp wound caused by flying glass, and his youthful features were distorted by pain and anger as he raised a bottle in his fist. The cloth jammed into the mouth of the bottle was already ablaze. He prepared to lob the Molotov cocktail at the minibus.

McCarter spotted the threat and immediately snap-aimed his Browning. The British commando was a former Olympic pistol team marksman in the 1970s, but he was called to duty by the SAS before he could participate in the games. He hadn't lost any of his uncanny skill with a handgun. The Browning cracked and its muzzle-flash jumped from the barrel.

The terrorist had presented a small target from his position of cover behind the car, but McCarter didn't need a large target. The well-aimed pistol shot struck the bottle in the enemy's fist. Glass shattered and gasoline spewed across the man's head and torso. The flaming rag immediately ignited the fuel, and fire shrouded the gunman. He uttered a scream that was transformed into a hideous wail as scorching heat raced into his open mouth and throat. He staggered away from the car, a helpless mass of flames.

McCarter triggered another shot and pumped a mercy slug through the fiery head of the tormented opponent. The burning figure collapsed to the pavement, probably welcoming death. Flames from the spilled gasoline continued to burn on the hood and roof of the car, and a sickly odor assaulted the senses.

Katz jumped from the bus and headed toward McCarter's position. The British ace had stationed himself by the iron bars and shrubbery of the Mexican embassy, which was located near its U.S. counterpart. Katz saw movement at the front of the American Embassy and assumed it was another terrorist. The Phoenix commander dove to the ground a split second before an automatic rifle spit out an angry burst of metal hornets.

The Israeli stayed on his belly and sought a target for his Uzi, but he could see little from his prone position and the sheet of rifle rounds above his head prevented him from moving. Katz was pinned down and had to rely on his teammates to take out the gunman.

Encizo pushed open the door at the driver's side of the bus and used it as a shield. He held the Walther pistol in both hands and leaned around the door. Aiming at the muzzle-flash of the rifleman, he triggered two shots. The double-action autoloader recoiled in his fists. One 9 mm Walther round hit the terrorist gunman in the right biceps muscle, and the other struck the steel frame of the man's M-16 assault rifle and ricocheted into his face. The bullet punched into a lower eyelid and squeezed the eyeball from its socket.

The terrorist wailed in agony and fell to his knees as blood streamed down his cheek. Another fanatic, next to the wounded man by the U.S. Embassy, glanced at his comrade. His stomach turned with repulsion when he saw his partner's face. Furious and terrified, the gunman raised his own M-16 and prepared to open fire.

He didn't notice Gary Manning at the opposite side of the bus. The Canadian had climbed out the other side door and crouchwalked to the end of the bus. An FAL assault rifle was in his hands, and he peered through a Bushnell scope mounted to the Belgian-made weapon. Scanning the Embassy grounds in search of opponents, he discovered the second rifleman about to fire on Phoenix Force. Manning lined up the cross hairs on the scope, centering on the target's head.

Manning squeezed the trigger. A 7.62 mm projectile hit the terrorist between eyebrow and ear, and the bullet knifed through his skull and wreaked havoc in his brain. The M-16 fell from lifeless fingers as the terrorist died on his feet.

A sudden flash of brilliant light from across the street drew Manning's attention. He whirled and swung his FAL toward the glare. The Canadian saw a slender figure at the sidewalk, crouched by a bench with a camera held at face level. The camera's flash burst another mininova of light. Manning moved his rifle back to the Embassy and sighed with relief that they were not being attacked from yet another direction.

"I almost shot that dude, too," Calvin James commented as he appeared beside the Canadian warrior. "That damn photographer has been taking pictures since Rafael steered us into that car. Gotta admit he's got balls to be out here with a camera instead of a gun."

"Balls, maybe," Manning replied. "I'm not so sure about brains."

A terrible moaning and cries for help echoed from the Embassy grounds. The terrorist who had been wounded staggered about, his right arm limp and useless and his left hand clasped over his injured eye. Phoenix Force watched warily, suspecting that it might be a trap. The man could be trying to lure them into the open to set them up for an ambush by unseen enemies.

Another burst of full-auto fire snarled. Orange flame from a muzzle appeared behind the wounded terrorist. The man's body arched in a violent back bend as bullets chopped into his spine. He dropped to the ground, and a man in fatigues stepped forward and shot the already fallen terrorist with a 3-round burst.

"Shit," James muttered. They wanted to take at least one opponent alive for questioning.

The white glare of the camera's flash flooded the streets again for an instant. Manning grunted with annoyance. It was an added distraction, and he didn't like cameras around during a mission, anyway. James was tempted to fire a warning shot at the shutterbug to try to scare the photographer away, but he recalled the fundamental police training that forbids the use of warning shots because they might endanger innocent people. Besides, he suspected the gutsy little photographer would not back off, anyway.

Automatic fire roared once more, and bullets hammered the rear of the bus. James and Manning ducked low as they heard slugs ricochet against metal. The barrage came from the Embassy. The man who had dispatched the wounded terrorist had directed his chopper on Phoenix Force. Katz and McCarter returned fire with Uzi machine pistols. The Briton had opened his suitcase and drawn the full-auto weapon for greater firepower than the Browning Hi-Power offered, and Encizo, still armed only with the semiauto Walther P-88 pistol, followed suit.

James, too, was wielding an Uzi. It wasn't his weapon of choice, but he hadn't managed to grab his suitcase before he bailed out of the bus. The rifle case with his M-16 was still in the vehicle. James also carried a pistol in shoulder leather. All the men of Phoenix Force, except McCarter, who stubbornly insisted on using the Browning, carried a Walther P-88 autoloader as a standard side arm.

"Cover me!" James told Manning. "I'm gonna try to get that bastard!"

He bolted from cover and ran for the Embassy, his back low and head down. The black commando held the Uzi close to his chest as he ran and counted on his fellow Phoenix commandos to keep the enemy busy as he rushed their opponent. Acting in concert was one of the reasons Phoenix Force had been successful for so many years. They operated smoothly as a team in any situation, each well aware of how the other would react in a crisis, and they had total confidence and trust in each other's ability and integrity.

The other Phoenix warriors effectively pinned down the gunman as James closed in. He reached the iron fence around the building before the terrorist realized what the commandos' strategy was. The gunman swung his weapon toward James and opened fire. Bullets sparked on the iron pickets of the fence. James stayed low and moved to the corner of the fence. The enemy fire ceased as he reached the edge of the barrier.

James hazarded a quick glance around the corner to check the gunman's position. He glimpsed the terrorist running for an alley, away from the Embassy, fumbling with the magazine of his box-shaped machine pistol. The man was armed with another MAC-10, James observed. He probably failed to appreciate the high rate of rpm fired by the Ingram and burned up all thirty-two rounds from the magazine.

The terrorist ejected the mag from the well to the pistol grip and reached for a fresh one for his MAC-10.

Like hell you're gonna reload, James thought as he pointed his Uzi at the fleeing figure and aimed low. The tough guy from Chicago triggered the Uzi and slashed a trio of 9 mm slugs across the terrorist's legs. The man screamed as bullets ripped into his thighs and left kneecap. His feet left the ground, and he slammed to the pavement hard. The Ingram chopper skidded from his fingers.

"Freeze!" James shouted as he approached the fallen figure. "Uh . . . ¡Alto, cachorro! ¡Sus manos arriba!"

The terrorist lay on his belly and raised his hands from the ground. James kept his Uzi trained on the guy, but he glanced about to see if there were any more opponents lurking among the shadows. An army patrol jeep appeared at the mouth of the alley. An officer, dressed in khaki uniform with a gold band around his service cap, jumped from the vehicle and jogged forward with a pistol in his fist.

"Easy, man," James urged as the officer approached. He gripped the Uzi by its stubby barrel and held it in one fist to assure the military man he was not a threat.

The officer suddenly pointed his pistol at the fallen terrorist and fired two shots. James gasped with surprise and outrage as he watched the big .45 pistol jump in the officer's fist. The terrorist's head split open from the large-caliber slugs, and his body twitched feebly in a weak death throe.

"What the hell did you do that for?" James demanded. He spoke English because he was angry, then immediately began to translate the question into Spanish.

"The terrorist was reaching for a gun," the officer declared in English. "I probably saved your life, *señor*."

"Bullshit," James muttered. He looked at the man's hard, lean face and noticed the twin silver bars on the epaulets of his uniform shirt. Salvadoran military ranks were similar to those in the American Army. "You didn't have to kill him, *capitán*."

"Es el comunista," the captain replied, and spit on the shattered skull of the corpse. "He's a Communist. Do you like Communists?"

"No," James said with a shrug, "but I don't care much for trigger-happy cops and soldiers, either. Thanks to you, we can't interrogate this bastard unless we can get a good medium."

He glanced at the captain's name tag, which read Ortiz. James considered lodging a complaint about the officer's behavior, but dismissed the notion as soon as it entered his mind. Complaints wouldn't mean much in El Salvador.

James walked back to the front of the Embassy. McCarter met him at the corner of the fence. The black commando told his British partner what had happened in a curt, bitter sentence. As they continued together back to the bus, Captain Ortiz called for them to wait, then jogged to them.

"Un momento," Ortiz said. "You men are armed with automatic weapons. Perhaps you're with U.S. Embassy personnel, but I want an explanation."

"Fine," James replied. "You can talk to our tour guide."

They drew up to the bus, where Sommers gingerly held a fire extinguisher and walked on shaky legs to the burning corpse. He had already put out the flames on the car, but he was too repulsed by the charred and dead man to get close enough to extinguish the blaze. The CIA man was obviously unnerved by the unexpected firefight. He wasn't accustomed to such violent encounters and he was still trying to come to terms with it emotionally.

Everything had happened so fast. Sommers had barely been able to think or comprehend what was going on, but the five-man team had instantly responded to the situation with cool professional skill and deadly efficiency. The Company case officer realized some of his previous opinions of the men of Phoenix Force had been far from accurate. They were not social-worker sissies or intellectual fence-straddlers. They were a superb fighting machine equipped with intelligence to search and destroy the correct target.

"I'll do it," Katz's voice volunteered.

Sommers turned to face the Israeli. Katz once more appeared to be a gentle, scholarly figure in a tweed sports jacket and gray turtleneck. The Uzi machine pistol hung from a shoulder strap over his left arm. He reached out with the hooks of his prosthesis to take the fire extinguisher from Sommers. The CIA man nodded gratefully and gave him the canister.

"The Salvadoran army has arrived," Katz commented as he aimed the nozzle of the fire extinguisher. "You'd better talk to them."

"Oh, yeah," Sommers said, still dazed by the experience, but aware that he was being given a graceful way out. "Right. I'll do that."

"Please do," Katz replied, and hosed down the flaming body as calmly as though he were watering a rose garden.

"You—you guys handled this pretty well," Sommers said lamely. He was also painfully aware that he hadn't been much use during the firefight.

"Unfortunately the attack on the Embassy means part of our reason for coming to El Salvador has already failed," the Israeli commented.

"How's that?" Sommers asked, confused by the remark.

"Things have already gotten worse," Katz explained.

7

It hadn't taken the El Salvador military and police long to charge onto the scene. More U.S. Marines also emerged from the Embassy to find their fallen comrades sprawled on the grounds. The Marine sentries had been torn apart by the explosion and their bodies riddled with bullets.

The soldiers and National Police began to argue about who had the greater authority. Captain Ortiz appeared to have the highest rank of any of the Salvadoran men in uniform. A senior lieutenant with the police complained that incidents within San Salvador were under the jurisdiction of his department.

"Would you care to tell that to my commanding officer?" Ortiz inquired. "His name is Colonel Martillo."

"No," the policeman answered, a trace of fear in his voice. "No, that won't be necessary."

Ortiz turned his attention to Ronald Sommers. Rafael Encizo stood nearby, arms folded on his chest to help conceal the Walther pistol he had returned to shoulder leather under his jacket. Gary Manning had quietly entered the bus and returned his FAL assault rifle to its case. The confusion created by so many jeeps and uniformed men was greater than that of the battle with the terrorists. Voices barked orders and questions in two languages. Headlights illuminated the streets as if the sun had risen.

"You say you vouch for these men, Señor Sommers?" Ortiz inquired as he took a notepad and pencil from a shirt pocket.

"Por cierto," Sommers assured him. "They are authorized to carry firearms, including automatic weapons. They have permits from the U.S. Embassy and the Minister of Defense of El Salvador, as well."

"I'm impressed," Ortiz commented as he turned to stare at Encizo. "You gentlemen must have friends in high places."

"I like to think God Himself looks on us with favor," Encizo replied with a thin smile. "From time to time, at least."

"Perhaps the Lord guided your bullets tonight," Ortiz mused, and glanced at two of the dead terrorists. "You must be very skilled fighters to get the better of an ambush such as Señor Sommers describes. *¿Con quién tengo el gusto de hablar?"*

"Just call me Cassias." Encizo answered the question with his current cover name. Ironically this had also been the name of a close friend of the Cuban, who had been killed in a previous mission.

"I congratulate you on your ability, Señor Cassias," Ortiz told him with a slight nod.

Their attention was drawn to a scuffle across the street as two soldiers struggled with the photographer for possession of the camera. Encizo hadn't paid much attention to the photographer before, but now that he looked closer, something about the slender shape of the camera buff seemed familiar. Clad in bush shirt, blue jeans and boots, the figure was obviously that of a well-built woman. Encizo saw long black hair that framed an oval face, the full lips with an angry, determined set and flashing large dark eyes.

"Maria," Encizo whispered in astonishment. "Maria Santo."

One soldier held the woman while the other pried the camera from her grasp. She struggled and swung a kick at the skin of the trooper who had the confiscated camera. The soldier grunted in pain and whipped the back of a hand across Maria's face. Her head recoiled from the blow, and she fell back against the other man, who held her from behind.

The soldier with the camera raised it overhead and prepared to dash it to the pavement, but a powerful hand suddenly seized his wrist. Encizo had bolted forward to rescue Maria. He gripped the soldier's wrist with one hand and wrenched the camera from the guy's fingers with the other. Encizo rammed a knee to his opponent's abdomen. The soldier groaned and started to double up, and Encizo lashed a backfist to the bastard's face and knocked him to the ground.

The other soldier shoved Maria to the ground and started to unsling his rifle. When he saw Gary Manning charge toward him, the soldier quickly swung the M-16 in that direction. Manning reached him first and swept a hand to the rifle barrel to push it toward the sky. His other hand drove a hard, short punch under the rib cage. The man gasped as the breath was knocked from his lungs, and Manning abruptly yanked the rifle from his opponent's grasp.

"Hey, man!" Calvin James's voice called out as he ran forward. "Toss it here!"

Encizo glanced at the black commando and saw James with his hands raised for a catch. The Cuban threw the camera to James, and the warrior from Chicago caught it. Another soldier rushed toward James and raised a rifle for a vicious butt-stroke to his skull. The black Phoenix pro glimpsed the attacker and turned sharply to deliver a powerful tae kwon do side-kick to the man's stomach. The blow knocked the wind out of the trooper and dumped him on his rear end.

"Stop it!" Sommers shouted.

"*¡Alto!*" Ortiz added with equal alarm.

The soldier who had taken Maria's camera and slapped her across the face started to get up. He reached for a pistol on his belt, but Encizo stepped forward and swung a hard uppercut under his jaw before he could draw the side arm.

The punch snapped the soldier's head back and seemed to straighten him. Encizo tagged him on the chin with a left hook and drove a right to his solar plexus. The trooper doubled up, and the Cuban slammed a knee into the man's already battered face. The soldier went down once more. This time he was unconscious, his jaw broken and nose smashed into crimson pulp.

Manning rammed the butt of the confiscated M-16 into his opponent. The man folded with a wheezing groan, and the Canadian warrior swung the rifle in his fists as if he were holding a steel bar. The frame smashed into the dazed man's face and knocked him almost two meters to land on the pavement in a dazed heap.

"What the hell is going on here?" a man in a dark blue suit demanded as he hurried from the Embassy to the street. "Sommers! I want some answers!"

"Yes, Mr. Ambassador," the CIA man said, barely glancing over his shoulder. "Things are still tense, sir."

Phoenix Force wouldn't have described the situation as tense. Soldiers pointed weapons at Manning, Encizo and James. They stood back to avoid the hands and feet of the commandos and watched them as if they expected the three warriors to attack regardless of the odds. McCarter and Katz still carried their Uzi machine pistols, and other troops stood near them, rifles held at port arms and ready to use if either man made a move to assist their teammates.

"Break the camera!" Maria cried out as she got to her feet. "It's not worth anyone getting killed...."

"Now you tell us," James muttered as he raised his hands, the Minolta camera still in one fist.

Ortiz ordered the troops to put down their guns, and they reluctantly obeyed. The Phoenix pros sighed with relief as the tension started to ease. Maria walked up to Encizo, and her eyes widened and her mouth fell open when she recognized him.

"Rafael," she said, as surprised to see Encizo as he had been to see her.

"Cassias," he told her, and raised his eyebrows to emphasize that it was the name he was currently using. "Roberto Cassias."

"*Si,*" Maria said with a thin smile. "You just look like someone I met in the Yucatán a couple of years ago."

A jeep rolled to a halt near the other vehicle, and a tall, athletic man in a khaki uniform stepped out from it. The soldiers snapped to attention as the officer approached. The gold laurel on the brim of his service cap and silver oak leaf insignia on his shoulders revealed his rank as a lieutenant colonel.

"*Capitán Ortiz,*" he said in a firm voice accustomed to command. He gestured at the soldiers and Phoenix Force. "*¿Qué es esto?*"

Ortiz reported to the colonel and Sommers explained the situation to the U.S. ambassador. A U.S. Marine lieutenant tried to get some information from anyone who was willing to talk to him. Katz took pity on the young American officer and gave him a brief explanation. James, meanwhile, returned the camera to Maria.

"*Gracias, señor,*" she said, then awkwardly repeated the sentence in English. "Thank you. I no speak English good...."

"*Está bien,*" James assured her. "It's okay. I speak Spanish. You and Cassias know each other from that business in Mexico?"

"Rafa—Cassias saved my life," Maria said. "I had been with a Mexican army patrol in the Yucatán, covering a story for my newspaper concerning our military. We were ambushed by 23rd September Communist League terrorists. I was the only survivor. The terrorists left me for dead. Alone in the jungle, I probably would have died if he...Cassias hadn't found me."

"Yeah." James glanced at Encizo. "He'd mentioned something about that. It's a pleasure to meet you, *señorita.*"

"Sí," Maria replied with a nod. *"Mucho gusto en conocerle."*

"Maria," Encizo whispered to the young lady from Mexico. "We need to talk, but right now there's a few things I have to take care of. Where are you staying?"

"Estoy en el Hotel Lujo," she replied.

"Bueno," Encizo said with a nod. "Good. We have reservations at the same hotel. You should get out of here for now. Nobody here is very happy you were taking photographs tonight."

"Does that include you?" Maria inquired, her eyebrows raised and her full lips performing a slight pout.

"That's one of the things we need to talk about," Encizo admitted. He raised a hand to her face and gently brushed the bruise on her cheek with his fingertips. "Are you all right?"

"I'm okay," she assured him, "thanks to you and your friends. Rescuing me seems to be a habit with you."

"Don't count on me being there in every crisis," Encizo warned. "From what I've seen of El Salvador, this country can be pretty rough and you have to be careful of the authorities as well as the terrorists and extremists."

"I noticed that, too," she said. "And you're right. I should get out of here before the troops decide they want to get their hands on this camera again."

"May I ask a favor?" Encizo inquired. "Please don't develop that film until we have a chance to talk."

Maria frowned, but she said, "All right. I owe you more than I can ever repay, so I'll agree to wait. You know I'm a photojournalist. This is my job, and I've taken a few big risks to do it."

"I'm not asking you to destroy the film," Encizo assured her. "Just wait until we can talk. Fair enough?"

"Fair enough," Maria agreed. "I'll see you at the hotel."

She turned and headed up the street. Encizo watched her leave, but he was aware Katz had stepped next to him. The

Cuban guessed what the Phoenix commander would say even before he heard Katz speak.

"That woman is a photographer for a Mexican newspaper, isn't she?" the Israeli inquired.

"She won't develop the film until I talk to her," Encizo assured him, but he realized it was a feeble reply.

"Her job is getting information for the public," Katz reminded the Cuban. "Our job is to carry out our missions with a low profile and maintain security as tight as possible. She's very dangerous to get involved with."

"I'll take care of it," Encizo promised.

"You could have gotten yourself killed when you rescued her," Katz stated, "or got the rest of us killed or thrown out of the country."

"What else could I do?" Encizo asked, fire in his dark eyes as he stared at Katz's face. "You saw how they treated her."

"The people we're looking for don't just knock women to the ground," the Israeli reminded him. "They murder them. They slaughter innocent men, women and children. There's too much at stake to let your emotions cloud your judgment. Too many lives at stake."

"I know," Encizo said, sighing. "I know you're right, but I still don't feel I'm wrong."

"If your actions endanger this mission," Katz told him, "you're wrong. Take care of it and be very careful how you handle it. Use your head and not your heart...or any other part of your anatomy that might influence your judgment."

Encizo opened his mouth to protest Katz's implication, but he remained silent as the tall Salvadoran colonel approached the pair. The Cuban was surprised to notice a hammer with a steel head hung from the man's belt as well as a holstered side arm. He remembered that Ortiz had mentioned "Colonel Martillo," and the police lieutenant had looked as if he might have a heart attack.

"Good evening, gentlemen," the colonel announced, and introduced himself to confirm Encizo's supposition. Martillo spoke English fluently. "Welcome to El Salvador. I'm sorry your first night here has been so violent and unpleasant."

"There's been a lot of violence and unpleasantness in El Salvador," Katz replied as he took out a pack of cigarettes.

"I know that better than anyone," Martillo assured him, and reached into a pocket to get his cigarette lighter. "I am the commander of a brigade of internal security forces. We patrol the entire nation of El Salvador in search of the Communists. Just this morning we encountered the terrible site of an ERP attack on a small farm near Santa Ana."

"We heard about that, Colonel," Encizo said. "Your people discovered it?"

"Oh, yes," Martillo confirmed as he flicked on his lighter and offered the flame to Katz. The Israeli nodded his thanks and used the fire to light his Camel cigarette. "I was there myself. So was Captain Ortiz. Truly terrible."

"Isn't it unusual for the FMLN or the ERP to attack peasant farmers?" Encizo asked.

"Not as unusual as you might think," Martillo replied. "We've seen more attacks of this sort by the Communists on innocent peasants. The murder of the Embassy personnel and now this attack on your Embassy seems to be a clear message from the FMLN. They're trying to frighten the peasants either into agreeing to help them or to remain silent about their activities, and they're trying to frighten away support from the United States, as well."

"Support for the Salvadoran government, you mean," Encizo commented.

"Of course," Martillo said with raised eyebrows. "You are a *norteamericano*, aren't you?"

"Naturalized citizen," Encizo replied.

"Then you should appreciate what your Administration is trying to do in Central America," the colonel declared. "The Communists are trying to take over this entire region.

Eventually they'll move on to Mexico and South America. In the end they'll try to attack the United States itself. Your government understands that. They support our country because they know we oppose the Communists, and the Contras have training bases here and launch operations against the Sandinistas in Nicaragua."

"Perhaps we should see this farm that was victimized by the ERP," Katz suggested. "We might be able to find some clues there."

"We didn't find anything except evidence the terrorists committed the atrocities," Martillo assured Katz. "They burned the house and the bodies, but they left slogans painted on the charred walls of the building...."

"We know that, Colonel," Katz assured him, "but we'd like to see it, anyway, and see the autopsy reports on the slain peasants and the ballistics reports."

"Autopsies and ballistics?" Martillo replied with a frown. "The bodies were too badly burned for autopsies, and the cause of death for these poor people is obvious. The bullets weren't removed because there is nothing to be gained by ballistics. The bodies have already been buried."

"So all that potential evidence was destroyed?" Encizo asked, and stared at the colonel with surprise. "Maybe we can have the bodies exhumed and perform the autopsies now."

"They were buried in a communal grave," Martillo explained. "I don't know where the burial site is. Perhaps I can find out."

"A mass murder was committed," Katz said. "You investigated it, reported it and evaluated the incident without autopsies or ballistics?"

"I can't say I investigated the incident," Martillo confessed. "That's not my field, you know. Military Intelligence was called in. If your clearance has a high enough security level, you can check with them. Mr. Sommers should be able to help you."

"Mr. Sommers has mainly done such a fine job at maintaining his own security," Encizo muttered with disgust.

"Thank you, Colonel," Katz told Martillo. "We'll look into this in more detail. For now, we have some other work to do before the night is through."

David McCarter approached the trio. He was shaking his head with dismay and carried the aluminum suitcase in one hand. The British ace had returned his Uzi to the container and his Browning Hi-Power was once again concealed in shoulder leather under his rumpled jacket.

"These bloody soldiers want to take the corpses of the terrorists off in a truck somewhere to the local Boot Hill," McCarter complained. "Ortiz won't let us keep them unless his colonel okays it."

"You want the dead terrorists?" Martillo asked with surprise. "What's the point of an autopsy here? You know how they died. You killed them."

"That's right," McCarter said with a shrug. "They're our kills so we should get to keep them. Ever been grouse hunting? Terrorists aren't out of season, are they?"

"Mr. Hill," Katz said sternly. He used McCarter's current cover name, and his tone warned the Briton to lay off the sarcasm. "I'm sure the colonel will cooperate with us."

"I don't see what's to be gained by doing an autopsy on a dead terrorist," Martillo repeated.

"You'd be surprised what information you can get from a dead man," Calvin James stated as he joined them. "If nothing else, we want fingerprints to try to identify them."

"They could be Cubans or Sandinistas," Martillo declared. "Terrorists certainly wouldn't wear dog tags or carry ID. Still, if you insist, I'll tell my men to surrender the bodies to you."

"We really do have to insist," Katz said. "Thank you, Colonel."

"I'm pleased to help any way I can," the colonel replied. "I trust you will keep me informed? We are all allies in this matter, are we not?"

"You will be kept informed of whatever information we can share with you," Katz promised. "Some data may have to remain classified on a need-to-know basis. I'm sure you understand."

"Of course," Martillo answered. "I've been a soldier all my adult life. You men must be veteran military also. You fight with great skill. Perhaps we can fight together against our common enemy. There are many battlefields in El Salvador. We may share one in the future."

Martillo turned and walked to his men to issue new orders. Sommers finished talking with the ambassador and joined the men of Phoenix Force. The CIA case officer glanced after the colonel and uttered a curt snort.

"I see you guys met 'Colonel Hammer,'" he remarked. "He's a very powerful man in this country. The soldiers say he has a backbone of steel. Just like his hammer. The FMLN tried to assassinate him about a year ago, before he was promoted to lieutenant colonel. He was shot twice, but that just made him mad."

"He might be mad already," Encizo said dryly. "I'm not so sure that guy's head is screwed on quite right."

"Martillo might be a little crazy," Sommers allowed, "but he's been more successful at hunting down terrorists than anybody I know about since I've been stationed in El Salvador. The Hammer might be a stuffed-shirt army pain-in-the-ass, but he's got a following among his men, and they figure he's some kind of god of war."

"If the god of common sense shows up, he ought to have a talk with you and Ferrero," Katz said with trace of disdain in his voice. "Half of El Salvador seems to know you're with the Company, and the good major didn't even bother to have autopsies performed on those peasants killed near Santa Ana. You two are part of a Central American vaudeville act."

"Damn it, I'm sick of this crap...." Sommers began.

"Yeah, we feel the same way," James told him.

"Sommers," Katz said, and pointed his prosthesis at the CIA man. "I want you to contact Ferrero and have him down here with a vehicle and personnel to collect these corpses. Then autopsies and examinations will be performed on the bodies. Mr. Johnson will be in charge of supervising the work, and they'd better do everything exactly as he says."

"Got that right," James added, who was going by the name "Johnson" for the mission. "I'm not in a good mood, man. Having people trying to kill me on an empty stomach tends to rub me the wrong way."

"You want to handle checking fingerprints with Interpol and other sources?" Manning asked Katz, having overheard the conversation. "I'll take ballistics and checking out the weapons used by the terrorists."

"Agreed," Katz replied. "Mr. Hill can try to determine the origin of the terrorists' vehicle and sweep it for any evidence the enemy may have left us."

"I hate that kind of work," McCarter complained. "It's boring. Still, I've done it before. Just get me some blokes who know enough about forensics to use the right end of a microscope."

"What about Cassias?" James inquired, hoping Encizo would be able to help him with the night's work.

"He already has an assignment concerning our security," Katz answered, and glanced at the Cuban. "You haven't forgotten?"

"I said I'd take care of it," Encizo replied.

"Sounds like we'll be up all night," Sommers said with a sigh. "The ambassador wants a complete report from me by eight o'clock in the morning. My control officer will probably want one two minutes after I contact him."

"You don't contact him until we take care of some of these matters," Katz instructed Sommers. "There's been too much concern for appearances and pacifying others for the sake of politics and policies. We have a real problem with real dead bodies on our hands, including two more Americans killed in the line of duty. We are going to find out who's responsible and why they did it.''

"Okay," Sommers agreed, nodding wearily. "By the way, the ambassador told me to thank you guys for saving the Embassy from being blown to bits."

"I'm not sure the terrorists had that goal in mind," Katz replied. "They could have set a large explosive charge instead of just lobbing a grenade at the front lawn and gunning down two Marine sentries. I don't think they intended to destroy the Embassy. They just left a very bloody calling card for the ambassador and the United States government."

"Some calling card," Sommers grunted. "What's the message?"

"Perhaps it's a warning," Katz said grimly, "of things yet to come."

8

Maria Santo sat in the lobby of the Luxury Hotel. The place hardly lived up to its title. The lobby was rather shabby, with old and badly treated furniture and faded ugly wallpaper. The windows were dirty and spotted with black specks. An overhead paddle-fan seemed to do little but stir hot air down from the ceiling. The desk clerk appeared to be going to sleep behind the counter, and a hotel security guard eyed Maria as if he thought she was a call girl waiting to pick up a customer in the lobby.

The guard made her nervous. He was built like a fireplug and carried a pump shotgun from a shoulder strap. Armed guards at hotels and restaurants were not unusual in El Salvador, but Maria wasn't used to a country that seemed like an armed camp. She had been frightened since she'd arrived in El Salvador, and she was certain she would feel that way until she left the country.

Of course, she had been frightened before and had still accepted previous assignments to troubled nations to cover news stories. The newspaper she worked for in Mexico City was reluctant to send a woman on such assignments, but the editors had been impressed by her handling of the story of the ambush sprung by the 23rd SCL in the Yucatán two years ago. That incident had led to more big features, more important stories and a few assignments that included an element of danger. Yet none of them had seemed as hazardous as the one in El Salvador.

Maria had been glad to see the man she had known only as Rafael when they met in Mexico. He now called himself Cassias, but she was certain Rafael was his real name because the group he'd been with in the Yucatán had used that name. They had been an odd assortment of Mexicans who assisted Rafael in search of the terrorists hidden somewhere in the jungle. The men who accompanied Rafael in El Salvador were very different. They were *norteamericanos* or perhaps Europeans. They seemed to face danger with cool efficiency and professional skill.

Encizo came in through the front entrance and met Maria in the lobby. The guard grunted with disgust and prepared to throw the stranger out of the building. The Luxury Hotel might not be a palace, but it was not a brothel, either. However, Encizo carried a suitcase and a valise as he marched to the front desk and asked the clerk if she had the name "Cassias" on the reservation list.

The clerk confirmed this information, and Encizo paid for the room in advance, covering the price for one week's rent. He indicated that the rest of his party would be coming in late to the hotel, but they had all arrived in San Salvador, so she should not cancel their reservations.

"They may not be here before dawn," Encizo added. "They're some sort of diplomatic investigators or whatever. I'm just one of the translators. Rather glad they decided they didn't need us both tonight, so I don't have to be at whatever boring function they're involved with."

"Si, comprendo," the desk clerk said with a weary sigh. "Here is the key to your room, Señor Cassias."

"Gracias, señora," Encizo replied as he accepted the key. "Is the restaurant still serving dinner?"

"Si," the clerk confirmed. "The kitchen does not close for two more hours."

"Bueno," the Cuban declared, and thanked her once again.

He turned back to Maria and escorted her to the dining room. A nervous young waiter showed them a table and menu. Encizo was familiar with Central American food, and experience had taught him the beef in most countries of the region tended to be tough and stringy. San Salvador was not a coastal city, so he didn't want to take a chance ordering fish. He decided to stick with chicken and rice. Maria followed his example and ordered the same. The waiter bowed and hurried off to the kitchen.

The restaurant was quiet and dark. Only one other table was occupied, and it was at the opposite side of the room. The candle at Encizo's table cast a soft glow across his companion's face. If anything, she was even more beautiful than Encizo remembered. Of course, she had been through a grueling and terrible ordeal in the jungle when he'd first met her. He had liked her and had admired her dedication to her work during their brief meeting. They had also felt a mutual attraction. Chemistry, some might call it. However, the Yucatán hadn't been the right time or place for romance. And, Encizo thought with regret, most likely the same would be true about El Salvador.

"It's been a while, Rafael," she remarked. "May I call you Rafael when we're alone?"

"Just don't say it too loud," the Cuban replied. "I spoke to Benito a few days after I completed my business in Mexico. He told me you got out of the jungle safely. I read your article about the 23rd SCL. It was very good. You have talent, Maria. That feature last year on the Mexican elections was also excellent. Both sides were fairly presented, and a great deal of insight was shown in your work."

"You're too kind," Maria said, smiling faintly. "I was also in touch with Benito after that business with the terrorists in the Yucatán. He still runs a leather goods store in Tijuana, you know. I think he's also part owner of a tavern and probably has some other business on the side. Quite a character. He likes to talk about the days when he was a matador."

"I remember," Encizo said with a nod. When he knew Benito Tillo, the ex-bullfighter had been a gunrunner, but he'd planned to retire from the shady business.

"He told me you went back to the United States," Maria went on. "He also said you were the only one of the group to survive. Your friend Manuel, Luis, Miguel and that Chinese-Mexican fellow who cut through the jungle vines like a machine with two machetes..."

"His name was Fong," Encizo reminded her. "If Benito told you they were all killed, he was correct. We were ambushed by the terrorists. They fought very bravely, but we were caught off guard and outnumbered."

The memory of that mission was very bitter and sad for Encizo. Manuel Cassias had been one of his closest friends, and the others had been good men—although they were not always exactly on the right side of the law. Encizo didn't tell Maria that the terrorists who attacked them had been led by a Cuban military adviser. Captain Raoul Encizo had been Rafael's younger brother, taken by the Communists at the age of five and raised to be a fanatical killing machine in Castro's army. Rafael Encizo had gone into the Yucatán to find his brother. He succeeded, but their reunion ended in tragedy.

"I'm sorry," Maria told him. "The authorities found the terrorist base in the jungle. The 23rd September Communist League killers and some Cuban soldiers had been wiped out. No one seemed to know who did it or why. I suppose you can't tell me now?"

"You're still a reporter, Maria," Encizo replied. "Better if I don't tell you so you won't be tempted to write about it." He gave her a rueful grin, then changed the subject. "When we met before, you were engaged to be married."

"I broke off the engagement," Maria answered. "Carlos was a good man, and I'm sure he'll make some woman a good husband, but my life changed after that experience in the jungle. You said at the time it would make me stronger because I survived. In many ways you were right."

"Maybe you became too strong," Encizo commented. "El Salvador is a dangerous place, maybe even more dangerous than the Yucatán. Here it is hard to say which hombres are good and which are bad. You already saw some evidence of that tonight."

"Definitely," she replied, and rubbed her bruised cheek. "But I wanted this assignment, Rafael. It's an important news story, perhaps the most important in Central America right now. That's why you're here, too. Isn't it? The men you're with are remarkable. Rather like you."

"They're probably the best four men I've ever known," Encizo admitted. "They're even more remarkable than you imagine. And that brings us to something we have to talk about, Maria. My friends and I are here on a covert mission. I can't give you any details, but I can say it concerns the well-being of Central America—including Mexico—as well as the United States."

"The *norteamericanos* have been supporting El Salvador for a long time," Maria remarked. "Just as they supported Somoza in Nicaragua. They'll back the worst types of banana republic dictators as long as the tyrants are opposed to communism."

"I'm not going to defend Washington policies," Encizo assured her, "past, present or future. That's not why we're here. Whoever is responsible for the murders of McKeller and his bodyguards and the attack on the Embassy tonight, they have to be stopped. We're here to find out just who they are and prevent their bringing things to a head. In order to do that, we have to maintain security and keep a low profile. We can't do that if you expose us in the newspapers."

"That's why you don't want me to develop my film," Maria ventured. "National security. Right? How often is that used as an excuse to cover up an embarrassment or outright corruption by a government? How often do they use the claim of national security to hide something from the public?"

The waiter arrived with their dinner. He had neglected to ask them what kind of wine they wanted with the meal or if they would rather have beer or coffee. Once again, Encizo's past experience in Central America taught him that it was not the best place in the world for wine, but the beer and coffee were usually exceptional. He ordered coffee and let Maria take her chances on whatever she wanted.

"Un poco de café," Maria told the waiter, confirming Encizo's judgment in these matters.

When the waiter departed to get the coffee, Encizo looked at Maria. He saw that fire of determination in her eyes and the firmness of the compressed line of her mouth. She wasn't a woman to back down easily. The Phoenix fighter admired that quality in her, but realized that her determination and stubbornness could become a problem at times.

"I'm not involved in politics, Maria," Encizo told her. "I won't argue that governments throughout the world use national security for an excuse to conceal their own misconduct. That has nothing to do with why I'm concerned about your photographs tonight. My partners and I can't have our faces on the front page of your newspaper. We're as good as dead if that happens. I'm serious, Maria. We've made a lot of enemies all over the world. Some of them have already put us on a death list and they've been trying to learn enough about us to find out who we really are. They already have descriptions of us and some information acquired over the years. If they have our faces on file, it would just be a matter of time before they'd catch up with us. One hit team already tried a few years ago."

"I owe you my life, Rafael," Maria said with a nod. "When I develop the photographs, I'll only use those that don't show your face or the faces of your four friends."

"We'd sure appreciate that," Encizo confirmed. "I also have to ask you for the negatives after you develop the pictures."

"You don't trust me?" she demanded.

"I do," Enzizo assured her. "But this doesn't concern just the two of us. My partners don't know you. Frankly they're worried about this, and I can't blame them. Under different circumstances, I'd feel the same way about a photojournalist with a roll of film that could ruin us. There's also the fact your newspaper could print other photos if they have the negatives. I trust you, but I don't trust the people you work for."

"I understand," Maria conceded. "So we can come to an agreement and make everyone happy? I get my story and you can keep your secrets. I don't suppose you can tell me anything you've learned since you arrived in El Salvador?"

"Unfortunately we haven't learned much," Encizo said honestly. "I can tell you the Salvadoran government is pretty sure the FMLN are responsible. They may well be right. You saw the way the 23rd September Communist League terrorists operate. The leftist fanatics in El Salvador are probably a similar breed, but the political extremists of the right wing may be just as bad. We don't know enough yet."

"How long have you been here?" Maria inquired.

"Not even a full day," Encizo answered. "We just happened to be passing by the Embassy when the terrorists attacked."

"I was on my way to the hotel," she stated. "It happens to be on the same street. Apparently we both came across the incident by chance."

"We can't count on coincidence," Encizo told her. "My friends are doing some investigative work right now. Maybe they'll turn up something."

"And meanwhile they sent you to keep me in line," Maria said dryly.

"Something like that," the Cuban admitted, grinning. "But I'd say it's the most pleasant duty I could have gotten. I am very glad to see you again, Maria."

"So am I," Maria replied, "even if you're still as mysterious and secretive as you were two years ago in the Yucatán. I used to imagine meeting you again and that you'd tell me you quit the CIA or DEA or whatever spy organization you belong to. Then you'd tell me your secrets and everything would make sense and things would be different for the two of us.''

''I think we all have secrets we never tell,'' Encizo remarked.

''And you're not going to quit, are you?'' Maria asked, well aware of the answer before she even asked the question.

''Not until they kill me,'' Encizo confessed.

A brief look of regret flashed in Maria's dark eyes. ''So much for pleasant daydreams,'' she said with a sigh.

As their dinner proceeded, the conversation changed to discussions of various countries and cities they had visited because of their careers. Maria had travelled throughout Central and parts of South America. She had also spent some time in the United States, mostly in Hispanic communities, and in Spain. Encizo only mentioned a few countries he had seen and gave no details about the activities of Phoenix Force. Some of their missions had secretly dealt with incidents that had received international news interest, so Encizo had to take care when he mentioned a country he was familiar with and never pinpointed what year or month he had been there.

Maria would certainly recall when more than a hundred terrorists took over the Vatican a few years ago or the killer gunmen at the Mardarjan embassy in London who murdered several innocent British citizens in cold blood. A dozen other incidents had captured the attention of the world for a short time, until they seemed to mysteriously ''take care of themselves.'' Only a handful of people knew an elite five-man team had been responsible for solving those crises. Even fewer were aware that team was known as Phoenix Force.

After dinner Encizo escorted Maria to her room in the hotel. They walked through the upstairs hallway, past several doors until they found the one with the number that matched the one on her key. Maria started to unlock the door, but Encizo placed his hand on hers and gently took the key. He gestured for her to step away from the door as he unlocked it.

The Phoenix commando turned the knob with one hand and slipped the other inside his jacket. He pushed the door open and glanced inside at the furniture in the unlit room. Encizo entered quickly and carefully, stepping around the door frame and away from the door. He drew his Walther P-88 and snapped on the wall switch. A ceiling light flicked on. Encizo didn't find anyone hiding in the room, and there was no apparent evidence anyone had searched Maria's quarters.

"Aren't you taking this paranoia thing a bit too far?" Maria asked in a tense whisper. She stood at the doorway and watched the Cuban search her room.

"Better to play it safe," Encizo insisted. "Don't come in yet. I want to check this place out a bit more."

He moved to the bed and looked under it but still kept an eye on the door. It was unlikely anyone was concealed behind it, because a person would probably have tried to jump him when he'd first entered. After he'd looked under the bed and behind a sofa, Encizo peered behind the door and found no one there.

Then he moved to the bathroom and found the shower stall empty. He next checked the closet and discovered it was empty as well. Only Maria's clothing hung from the rod inside. Finally Encizo checked the shelf above the clothes, aware that a cunning individual could climb up to it and lodge himself across the shelf. It was a hiding place overlooked during many searches by police and others who dismissed it as too unlikely. Encizo knew better.

"You can come in," Encizo told Maria.

"I'm so glad," she replied with a degree of sarcasm, then watched him return the pistol to shoulder leather under his jacket. "You generally check out a room this way."

"I always feel more comfortable when I do," the Cuban admitted. "You might think I overreacted, but don't forget the soldiers tried to take your camera tonight. Colonel Martillo made quite a show of being an apologetic gentleman who regretted the actions of his men. I suspect that the man is a shark, and I wouldn't be surprised if he told his men to come to your room to retrieve the camera or the film from it."

"Martillo?" Maria asked with surprise. "I've heard about 'the Hammer.' He's got quite a reputation. Rumors claim he even carries a claw hammer with a steel head."

"Those rumors are true," Encizo confirmed. "He arrived just before you left the scene to return to the hotel. You didn't get a good look at him, and I imagine he didn't see you, either. That's probably just as well."

"Did you know there are stories about Martillo being involved in a new death squad?" Maria inquired. "A lot of people are comparing him to D'Aubuisson in more ways than one."

"I don't think anyone actually proved D'Aubuisson was in charge of the death squads back in the late seventies and early eighties," Encizo reminded her. "Are you sure there is a new death squad in El Salvador? I know the military and police can be pretty heavy-handed here, but that doesn't mean..."

"The camera!" Maria said as she crossed the room to check the Minolta on top of a dresser.

The back of the camera was open, the film dangling from it. Encizo groaned softly and shook his head. Maria's photos of the incident at the Embassy presented a problem for Phoenix Force, but he realized how important it had been to Maria and he shared her disappointment.

"I'm sorry," he said gently.

"So am I," she replied as she removed the exposed film and tossed it into the trash can by the dresser. "A roll of 35 mm film costs five or six colones in El Salvador. Maybe I won't have to buy any here. I brought more than twenty rolls of film for this assignment."

"You're taking this in stride far too well," Encizo observed. "That must mean the film they destroyed wasn't the same film you had in the camera when you shot tonight's gun battle at the embassy."

"That roll of film is in my purse," Maria said with a smile. "I'm not stupid, Rafael. I want this film with me at all times. They just ruined a perfectly good roll of 35 mm that hadn't been used to take a single picture."

"The photographs you took tonight could still get you in a lot of trouble, Maria," the Cuban warned.

"Not if everybody thinks it's already been destroyed," she replied. "You're good at keeping secrets. This can be our little secret. Agreed?"

"I think so," Encizo answered. "Our previous agreement concerning the photos will still be honored?"

"Of course," Maria assured him. "I'll let you see the photographs, and we'll decide which are acceptable without endangering you or your friends. Then you can destroy the negatives. Meantime I'm going to complain to the governor of this department."

"What department?" Encizo asked, confused by the term.

"El Salvador is divided into fourteen states or provinces that are referred to as departments," Maria explained, pleased that she knew something about the country Encizo did not. "I'll tell the governor and the mayor of San Salvador that somebody broke into my room and ruined the film. I'll also complain about the behavior of those soldiers tonight."

"Do you want me to tell the Salvadoran authorities that I had walked you to your room and you had called after me to show what had been done to your camera?" the Phoenix pro inquired.

"I'd rather you didn't tell them we came up to my room to make love," she replied with one eyebrow cocked high. "You did have that in mind. Didn't you?"

"I didn't assume that," Encizo stated as he stepped closer and cradled her face with his hands. He caressed her cheeks and looked into her eyes. "But I admit I hoped it would happen."

She leaned forward and he lowered his head to hers. They kissed with warmth and passion. The mutual attraction they had known when they first met had sparked a desire that had smoldered for two years. They held each other close as the kiss continued, their hands touching, moving in gentle exploration.

Hungry for the touch of flesh on flesh, they shed their clothes. They fell onto the bed and continued feverishly to stroke and kiss. They couldn't seem to get enough of each other, and finally they were joined in that most ancient of rites. Encizo became lost in her, and they rocked together gently. Maria moaned with pleasure as he gradually increased the tempo and thrust faster and deeper.

Together they moved to the brink of ecstasy and reached the peak in unison. Their bodies trembled, and they clung tightly together. Encizo cherished these precious moments of closeness and gentle passion. He knew all too well that the harsh realities of his mission would soon bring him back to the battlefield and a world of intrigue and danger that left no room for the comfort of a woman's body or a lover's embrace.

He had learned that the sweet brief moments of life must be enjoyed, remembered and jealously guarded. As he smoothed the damp hair from her face, he thought that they had just shared a memorable experience—the kind that life, all to short and often hard, does not always offer.

9

The army jeep drove off the dirt road to travel through the tall tropical grass. The headlights knifed through the darkness and provided enough visibility for Sergeant Lopez to avoid any pitfalls. The terrain became steadily more difficult, and the jeep bounced across the uneven ground. Monkeys started to chatter among the branches, and birds cried out in alarm. The mechanical beast had disturbed the nocturnal creatures of the jungle.

Colonel Martillo ignored the sounds of the night. Even the ominous angry growl of a jaguar didn't worry him. *El tigre* was the biggest predator in Central America, but for all its strength and speed the jaguar avoided contact with man. Besides, even one and a half meters of spotted power and fearsome claws and teeth were no match for automatic weapons.

"This is far enough," Martillo told the sergeant.

Lopez nodded and stopped the jeep. Both men emerged from the vehicle and walked deeper into the jungle. Martillo carried an M-16 in addition to his side arm and steel hammer. The big NCO held a flashlight in one hand and a pump shotgun, canted on his shoulder, with the other. Lopez pressed his thumb on the button of the flashlight to blink out two long dashes, the Morse code for the letter *M*.

They approached the dense wall of foliage and vines. Leaves rustled as furtive creatures scurried away at the approach of the men. Lopez swung the flashlight beam toward the noise and raised his shotgun. A couple of monkeys stared down from the branches, eyes wide and bright, mouths open to expose their small but menacing teeth.

"I've spent too much time in the city," Lopez muttered as he lowered his weapon.

A blinking light in the shadows caught their attention. The light flashed a message. One dot and three dashes signaled the letter *J*. It was Martillo and Lopez's signal to head toward the light. Two figures materialized from the shadows and met the soldiers. They were attired in green fatigue uniforms and camouflaged with trailing twigs and leaves and boonie hats. Both were armed with M-16 assault rifles.

"Buenas noches, Coronel," one of the men greeted. "Good evening, Colonel. *El Jinete* has been expecting you."

"Take us to him," Martillo replied gruffly. *"¡Ándate!"* The colonel and his NCO followed their guides into the jungle. The foliage was not as thick as it appeared in the darkness, and they made their way through the rain forest faster than Martillo had expected. Some of the vines and bushes were actually part of a net set between trees to help conceal the camp located at a partial clearing in the jungle.

Half a dozen tents with camouflage-print canvas were set up at the camp. Two army trucks were concealed under some coconut trees and giant ferns. Armed men waited for Martillo and Lopez to arrive. They were young, tough characters. Some were scruffy-looking with long hair and beards, while others had short-clipped hair and clean-shaven faces. The green uniforms had no insignia of rank or unit, but Martillo could easily tell which men were members of his private army of Salvadorans. They still shaved and conducted themselves as if they were regular army under his command.

The others were followers of *El Jinete*. The rebel leader sat on a wooden crate, chewing a leg of mutton and sipping bottled beer. Jinete was a short, fat man whose ammunition belts crisscrossed his chest as if he were an extra in a movie about *banditos*. In fact, Martillo knew that Jinete had been a hill bandit in Nicaragua before the fall of Somoza.

Then he had "embraced" patriotism and joined the counterrevolutionaries, better known as the Contras.

Martillo regarded *El Jinete* with secret contempt. Though the rebel leader called himself "The Horseman," Martillo doubted the Nicaraguan thug had ever been on a horse in his life. The title was meant to conjure romantic visions of dashing highwaymen of legends long ago. There was nothing dashing or romantic about the Nicaraguan slobs in Martillo's opinion. Jinete's fatigue uniform was stained with grease marks and spilled beer. He carried two .38 Special revolvers in hip holsters and wore a low-crowned sombrero instead of a cap or boonie hat. Martillo thought Jinete looked like a cheap *bandito* out of some terrible Hollywood Western.

Martillo hated working with the man. Jinete was not directly connected with the Contras, although he claimed he and his men were legitimate freedom fighters against the Communist regime in Nicaragua. They had used this claim as an excuse to enter El Salvador with the Contra training camps, but it hadn't taken them long to break away from the genuine Contras and head into the jungles to adopt their former trade as common bandits.

Colonel Martillo had learned about Jinete's band and decided to form an uneasy alliance with them. Jinete and his men had connections with gunrunners, dope smugglers and other shady characters. They were also experienced with living in the hills and jungles and hiding from the authorities in their native land. Martillo could deliver supplies and money to the bandits and protect them from the Salvadoran military. Both had something the other wanted, so their pact was formed.

Jinete looked up at Martillo and smiled. His opinion of the colonel was no more flattering than was Martillo's of him. Martillo was a tin soldier, a political fanatic who was pumped full of righteous bullshit and protected by his field-grade rank in the Salvadoran army. Another stinking *federale* who thought he was God because he had some authority over the lesser mortals, who were powerless to oppose him. Jinete had spent most of his life trying to avoid *cabróns* like Martillo. It was a bitter pill for Jinete to swallow, but he needed Martillo's cooperation as much as the colonel needed his.

"I got your message," Jinete told Martillo, and belched from the last gulp of beer. "You say the men who attacked the American Embassy won't be coming back. What happened?"

"They're all dead," Martillo replied with a sigh. "None of them were captured, but none survived, either."

"*¡Cristo!*" Jinete cursed as he tossed the empty bottle aside. "I thought you and that snotty captain of yours would see to it only your people were patrolling the area when the attack took place."

"We did," Martillo assured him, "but we didn't expect a group of foreigners to be driving along, jump out of their vehicle and chop down our people like a farmer at harvest time."

"Foreigners?" Jinete asked with a frown. "What kind of foreigners? *Yanquis? Norteamericanos?*"

"I'm not sure what their nationalities are," the colonel admitted. "They were with a security adviser with the United States Embassy named Sommers. The man is actually CIA. Whoever these strangers are, they must be working for the *norteamericanos* and probably the CIA. They seem very professional. Intelligent, well trained and obviously dangerous. Our people actually ambushed them on the street. Everything was in their favor, but these five specialists went through them like a pack of wolves against a group of lapdogs. None of them even got a scratch in the battle, but they wiped out our assault team."

"Three of those men were my *compañeros* from the old days," Jinete said angrily. "Where are these five foreign bastards? I'll kill these gringo scum myself!"

"And what would that accomplish?" Martillo demanded. "You might claim some revenge, but if we kill them, others will be sent to replace them. These strangers have the support of the United States government and that of El Salvador. If we get rid of them, everyone will be hunting for us and besides, killing these men wouldn't be easy."

"I'm not afraid of any man," Jinete declared. "So, what do you suggest? We do nothing?"

"Exactly," Martillo said with a nod. "I'll be able to stay informed about their investigations. I'll know if they're getting close to the truth. We'll deal with that when and if it happens. Meantime you stay here with the men and don't launch any actions without my approval."

"For how long?" Jinete demanded. "These bastards might be in El Salvador for months."

"It won't take that long," Martillo promised. "You admitted that you sold some guns to the ERP before I met you. The Communists are obviously planning an offensive. We need only let them make the next move. After what we've already done, the ERP and the FMLN will be obliged to retaliate. The Communists have been planning to make a move against the government. Now they will be goaded into taking action too soon. They won't be prepared to carry out their attack successfully, but we will be ready for them when they try."

"Are you a *brujo*?" the bandit asked with a snort of disgust. "You can sit down and stare into a crystal ball or at some chicken bones on the ground and foresee the future?"

"Of course I'm not a sorcerer," Martillo said, "but I am a military strategist and I can predict how the enemy will respond to a set of situations. Don't forget, I've been fighting the FMLN terrorists for years. I know how they think."

"You never make any mistakes, eh?" Jinete muttered. "I don't like this, Colonel. I don't work this way."

"I know how you and your men work," Martillo said with disgust. "I saw two of them try to rape a young girl at that farmhouse near Santa Ana. Rape, pillage and loot. That's how your kind works.''

El Jinete stiffened, offended by the remark. Martillo met his gaze and stared back, unafraid of the bandit. He still held the M-16 canted to a shoulder, and Sergeant Lopez remained by his side. Nearly half the men at the camp were Jinete's followers, but the rest were loyal to Martillo. If the Nicaraguan tried to call a showdown with Martillo, he wouldn't win. Perhaps both sides would be wiped out, but he wouldn't win. Martillo knew his man well enough to feel confident the bandit wasn't prepared to sacrifice his life to defend his honor—if he had any such conception at all.

Jinete had decided on his response.

"Si," he said in a loud voice, and laughed so hard his belly trembled. ''You are a man of such high moral virtue that you were offended to see my men have a little fun with this little peasant wench. Yet *you* shot the girl in the head.''

''It was necessary,'' Martillo insisted.

''If you see her ghost, you can tell her that,'' Jinete replied. ''Somehow I don't think you'd convince her you are such a pillar of morality because you saved her from being raped and then killed her. I don't think she'd thank you for wiping out her family, either, Colonel Hammer.''

''They were Communist sympathizers,'' the colonel said stiffly.

''That's what you said about that fellow Rodriguez,'' Jinete snapped back. The bandit sensed he was jabbing through Martillo's emotional armor and delighted in the success of his verbal barbs. ''I heard on the radio that the police are still looking for Rodriguez and suspect the FMLN may have abducted him because he had written criticisms about the political left as well as the right. Rodriguez was not a Communist, Colonel. He was just stupid enough to write a pamphlet criticizing land reform that would return ownership of farmers' property to big landowners. All those peasants at the farm you killed were probably innocent, as well.''

Sergeant Lopez saw the fury in Martillo's eyes. The NCO realized his commander and Jinete hated each other's guts, but now they seemed determined to goad one another until one man finally lost his temper. It was foolish, Lopez observed, yet both Martillo and Jinete were proud and concerned with machismo. Both were accustomed to commanding others, and each of them considered the other man to be inferior.

"Jefe," Lopez said in a loud voice, and both Martillo and Jinete turned when they heard the word for "leader." Each of the two thought he was being addressed. "It may not be my place, but I feel I should caution you that this is not a wise time to destroy the unity between our forces and *El Jinete*'s group. There are other matters that must be dealt with first."

The voice of reason helped cool Martillo's anger, and he nodded. He realized Lopez was right. What bothered the colonel was the fact he had started the verbal confrontation with Jinete. He knew better than to act in such a manner. Martillo became aware of a throbbing pain in the base of his skull that seemed to reach across his scalp and claw into his forehead with viselike force.

"This isn't the proper time to concern ourselves with these personal matters," Martillo agreed as he turned away from the bandit leader. "We can settle this after our mission has been accomplished."

"I'll look forward to that," Jinete assured him.

Martillo headed from the camp, followed by Lopez. The NCO urged his officer to slow down and turned on the flashlight to help them find their way back to the jeep. He noticed the colonel had taken out a small bottle of pills and hastily gulped down two capsules.

Colonel Hammer had suffered from migraines for almost a year. Sometimes the pain was too great for his medication to cope with. Martillo's head felt as if it might explode as he followed Lopez to the vehicle. He managed to reach the jeep before he threw up.

The migraine was similar to a monstrous hangover. Martillo was gripped by nausea and the hot agony in his skull. The colonel vomited in the grass and clung to the side of the jeep, afraid he might topple forward to the ground. His backbone seemed to vibrate from the pain, and his stomach again forced him to double up and eject its contents.

Few of Martillo's followers knew he was plagued by such merciless headaches. Lopez was well aware of it, of course, but he also knew the colonel had taken on a great amount of stress and responsibility since he started to put together his own plans for saving El Salvador. Such pressures were bound to take their toll, the NCO allowed.

He didn't question whether or not the migraines affected Martillo's judgment. Lopez trusted the colonel to lead him. Martillo had been educated, trained to be a leader and promoted to field-grade rank in the military. Lopez had little education and had chosen to make the army his life. He had served under Martillo so long he couldn't imagine not following the colonel's orders.

Martillo climbed into the jeep and assured the NCO he was all right. Lopez started the engine and drove back to the road. Colonel Hammer took some more medication, and his migraine subsided. The wind in his face helped revive him. The image of *El Jinete*'s grinning face finally faded from his mind's eye. Martillo sighed with relief as the pain in his head ended.

"Are you feeling better, Colonel?" Lopez inquired.

"Si," Martillo assured him. "I'm much better now, and I may be lucky so that it won't last so long this time. Perhaps these headaches will stop after this business is over and El Salvador is safe once more."

Lopez could not recall any time their country had been safe.

"The migraines can be very bad, Sergeant," Martillo said as he leaned back in his seat and tried to relax as they headed back for San Salvador. "Sometimes the pain seems enough to drive one mad."

10

Yakov Katzenelenbogen pulled back his sleeve and adjusted the straps of the prosthesis attached to the stump of his right arm. Ron Sommers stared at the device with fascination. The padded socket for the abbreviated limb was perfectly fitted for the Phoenix Force commander's arm and was held firmly in place by the straps. The wires and cables that operated the hooks were concealed in the thick plastic shell that formed the artificial forearm. It was a high-tech plastic alloy developed by NASA. Resistant to extreme heat or moisture, the plastic was harder than most metals.

The steel hooks were attached to a metal base at the end of the artificial arm. The base could turn to adjust the position of the hooks for grasping objects. The two larger hooks were about ten centimeters long, with a smaller, thicker hook that served as a thumb. Sommers was intrigued by the ease with which Katz used the prosthesis. The Israeli didn't seem to have any trouble handling weapons or more conventional devices one uses on a day-to-day basis. Of course, Sommers didn't know that Katz had lost his arm on a desert battlefield during the Six Day War. He was also unaware that the same explosion that maimed Katz also killed his only son.

Rafael Encizo entered the conference room to join Katz, Sommers and David McCarter. The British ace seemed in a surly mood as he reached inside his ill-treated sports jacket for a pack of Player's. He barely glanced up at Encizo as the Cuban took a seat across from Katz.

"How'd things go with the lady reporter?" McCarter inquired. He fired up a cigarette and added, "If that's not too personal?"

"You mean the photos she took last night?" Encizo replied with an innocent shrug. "While I was talking to her about it over dinner, someone broke into her room at the hotel and yanked the film out of her camera. It was exposed and ruined."

"Really?" Katz looked at Encizo. "I'm surprised a professional photographer like Maria Santo would be that careless with a roll of film that was so valuable for her coverage of news in El Salvador."

Encizo knew damn well Katz had already figured out what had probably happened. Sometimes the Israeli fox seemed to be telepathic. Trying to slip a lie past Katz was like trying to sneak a Sherman tank through a metal detector.

"I think she had other things on her mind," Encizo said with a suggestive smile.

"You mean you seduced her and managed to destroy those photos when she wasn't looking?" Sommers asked with a chuckle. "Goddamn, Cassias. James Bond would give you an A+ for that one."

"I didn't do it," Encizo stated. "If your CIA chums aren't responsible, I figure it must have been Ferrero's people or even Martillo's troops. I wouldn't be surprised if Captain Ortiz would take care of a little project like that for his commander."

"Whoever did it, did us a favor," Sommers declared. "You sound as if you're offended by this. That cute little reporter could blow the lid off your security. Your people are the ones facing the most risk if those pictures appear in print. Luckily we don't have to worry about that now."

"Lucky us," Katz said with a sour grunt. "We put in some time and effort in fingerprinting the dead terrorists, taking dental X rays, photographs and such to try to identify them. Ferrero patched us through with the National Police and Military Intelligence in San Salvador, and we used CIA computers at the U.S. Embassy to link up with the Company nerve center in Langley as well as Interpol offices with the Justice Department in Washington D.C."

"Any luck?" Encizo inquired.

"We got positive ID on two of the terrorists," Katz confirmed. "Both ex-convicts who served time in Salvadoran prisons for crimes committed while still juveniles. One was a thief, and the other stabbed another kid in a fight when he was fifteen."

"Did they serve time in the same joint?" Encizo asked. "Could be they met each other in prison and joined a youth gang of political extremists associated with either the far-left terrorist rebels or the far-right factions possibly associated with the government or, perhaps, just the ARENA Party."

"No," Sommers answered. "One punk was in a prison in San Vicente, and the other served time in San Francisco."

"San Francisco?" McCarter asked with surprise.

"San Francisco Gotera," the CIA man explained. "That's here in El Salvador. Not San Francisco, California. Anyway, wherever and whenever they got together, it wasn't when they were serving time as teenage hoodlums."

"Neither served a full year behind bars," Katz added. "What's curious about these two characters is there's no record that either spent the compulsory one-year term of duty with the Salvadoran military, as required for every male between the ages of eighteen and thirty. Yet both men were in their mid-twenties, until they stopped aging after last night."

"So, they could have run off to the hills or the rain forest to join the FMLN," Encizo mused.

"They could have," Katz agreed, "but Ferrero called in a few minutes before you arrived, Cassias. His people met with the families of the deceased. They were asked what they knew about their relative's activities in the past year or so. None of the families had heard much from their misguided offspring for the last six or seven months. In fact, both families mentioned that they had had very little contact with these lads *since* they left the army.''

"You mean they served in the army but there isn't any record of their time in the service at all?'' Encizo inquired, surprised by the news. "I could understand if there was some classified material that wound up in a shredder, but to have no trace of them at all . . .''

"That's right,'' Katz confirmed. "Unless the families are lying about their sons being in the army—which seems pretty unlikely—somebody wipes out their records. Not just military service records, either. One of the young men was supposedly a truck driver for a coffee company a couple of years ago. There's no record he ever received a driver's license. Both of them were supposed to have *cedulas*, but there's no record they ever applied for or got their certificates. In fact, their birth certificates also vanished. Someone tried to wipe from the face of the earth the proof that either man ever existed.''

"They almost succeeded,'' McCarter commented. "Aside from the knowledge of the families, the only proof left was their brief time as jailbirds when they were teenagers. Obviously whoever did this cover-up didn't know about their early troubles with the law. My guess is, the blokes responsible didn't know about this because our dearly departed excons didn't mention it.''

"You'd think if they were left-wing rebels trying to pull down the Salvadoran government they would have been proud of serving time as outlaws against the establishment,'' Encizo remarked.

"It is curious,'' Katz admitted. "It also suggests there's a high-level connection with access to top secret information associated with the terrorists.''

"That doesn't mean they're part of the government or the ARENA Party,'' Sommers insisted. "We can't start crying for the head of the president of El Salvador unless we've got a ton of solid evidence.''

"No one is suggesting anything of that sort," Katz assured him. "President Cristiani has nothing to gain by causing friction with the United States and El Salvador. No doubt he's hoping to reestablish increased foreign aid from Uncle Sam. After his first two months in office, the economy in El Salvador took a drastic plunge under Cristiani."

"That can't all be blamed on the Salvadoran government," Sommers declared. "Coffee prices plummeted after Cristiani took over. Seventy percent of this country's export earnings come from the coffee trade."

"As I understand it," Encizo began, "Cristiani's advisers want to raise interest rates, tighten credit and carry out some other economic changes which are going to be hardest on the poor. Since eighty-seven percent of the population in El Salvador fit that category, you can expect to see a hell of a lot of unhappy people here in the future."

Major Ferrero entered the conference room. The military Intel Officer did not appear to be glad to see the three Phoenix commandos at the table. He marched to the coffeepot and poured himself a cup before he asked if Katz had shared the information his people had learned about the slain terrorists.

"Yes," the Israeli assured him. "Did you find out anything else?"

"I'm still hoping to hear from some of my forensic personnel," Ferrero answered as he slumped into a chair. "One of your men worked with them on chemical analysis of dust and other particles found in the hair and under the nails of the terrorists. I believe your black friend even insisted on analyzing the stomach contents of the dead men to try to find out what they had eaten recently."

"Sounds disgusting," Sommers muttered. "What does Johnson figure he's gonna learn by examining the contents of a dead man's stomach?"

"That's part of how Mr. Johnson handles an autopsy," Katz explained. "He checks the contents of the stomach to learn what an individual has been eating, possible use of drugs and chemical substances. The type of food a person eats can reveal a great deal about what locale he's been living in recently. Fresh fish might suggest the person was living near the coast, while a diet of canned food might mean the individual was previously at a site where other sources of food were scarce. Dust and other residue in the hair and skin can give similar clues."

"I certainly hope Johnson learns something from such efforts," Ferrero commented. He turned to face Encizo. "You were with the Mexican woman? Santo? The photographer?"

"She was pretty upset about her film," the Cuban told him. "Maria thinks I took her to dinner last night to distract her while somebody broke into her room and yanked the film out of her camera to destroy the photos taken during the gun battle at the Embassy."

"You didn't do it intentionally," Ferrero said, shrugging, "but it worked out that way."

"So, you had it done?" Encizo asked.

"Of course," the major admitted without a trace of regret. "That film was a threat to our security. An even more serious threat to you and the other members of your team."

"So I've heard," Encizo said dryly.

"Have you learned where those peasants were buried after they were discovered near Santa Ana?" Katz asked. "Martillo gave us the impression military Intelligence was responsible for that."

"There were no autopsies," Major Ferrero said with annoyance. "The cause of death was obvious, and the bodies were badly burned. The ERP slogans on the walls of the farmhouse..."

"We've heard all this before, and it doesn't sound any less incompetent now than it did the first time," Katz informed the major. "That still doesn't explain why no one seems to know what happened to the dead bodies at Santa Ana."

"There was no family to claim them, so they were buried in a communal grave," Ferrero explained. "This isn't uncommon in El Salvador. I'm sorry if that offends you, but we are not a rich country like the United States.''

"Sorry I didn't bring my violin," McCarter snorted. "Well, what do we do now?"

"Where are Johnson and Connors?" Encizo asked, using the cover names for James and Manning.

"They were up late working on the autopsies and ballistics tests last night," Katz answered. "They're trying to catch up on their sleep now."

"The chemical analysis of some of the data from the autopsies Johnson supervised hasn't been completed yet," Ferrero said. "Nothing in the autopsies so far has been very valuable, from the reports I read."

"The ballistics weren't too surprising, either," McCarter added. "Salvadoran government issue 9 mm and 5.56 mm ammo. All hardball projectiles. The weapons were U.S. manufacture, supplied to the Salvadoran military."

"It has already been confirmed that the FMLN broke into a military base and stole weapons and ammunition," Ferrero stated.

"But we don't know that the terrorists were using weapons from that cache," Katz reminded him. "I think we should try to learn more about the two terrorists we were able to identify. Perhaps the families know what company and battalion the young men served in during their military hitch. If we can learn that, we may be able to contact officers, NCOs and enlisted men who knew these two when they were in the service."

"Maybe Captain Ortiz will uncover some useful clues," the major suggested. "He's having some suspicious characters interrogated."

"Suspicious characters?" Encizo asked with a frown. "What does that mean, Major?"

"Suspected political enemies of the state," Ferrero answered. "Individuals who have been under surveillance for some time in the past, due to their radical leftist views."

"That sounds like a brilliant exercise in social justice," Katz said, and shook his head with dismay.

Calvin James entered the conference room. The tall, lanky black man seemed well rested after getting some sleep. He caught only the tail end of the conversation and asked who Katz was talking about.

"Ortiz is conducting 'interrogations' of 'suspected' radicals," Encizo answered. He made no effort to conceal his disgust.

James stiffened. He and Encizo had once been interrogated by terrorists who seized control of the Vatican. The pair were captured and taken to a torture chamber. The physical damage had been minimal, although Encizo still carried a circular scar in the center of the palm of his hand from a red-hot coin that had burned into his flesh, and the end of James's little finger on his left hand had been savagely abbreviated by a pair of pliers. The memories of that session in hell would always be with the Phoenix Force commandos who had endured the ordeal.

"Do you know where Ortiz is?" James asked. He glanced down at the clipped end of his finger as he spoke.

"I believe he's set up a temporary base here in San Salvador in the basement of the Veaga Clock and Watch Shop," Ferrero answered.

"Well, I'd better go help him," James announced as he turned toward the door. "I've used scopolamine in the past, and I can also tend to any injuries these fellas might have suffered."

"Johnson," Katz said, a slight edge to his voice warning James to keep his temper in check.

"My driver will take you there," Ferrero offered.

"Great," James replied. "I'm on my way."

"I'll go with you," Encizo offered and started to rise from his chair.

"No, you won't," Katz told him. "You and I need to have another little chat."

"That leaves me," McCarter announced, and headed for the door after James.

The British commando and the black warrior from Chicago hurried into the bay section to find Ferrero's driver. Encizo reluctantly stayed in his chair and glanced at Katz. The Phoenix commander fixed a hard stare on the Cuban's face as he reached into his shirt pocket for a pack of Camel cigarettes.

"Mr. Cassias and I are going to take a little walk and talk about a couple of private matters," the Israeli told Sommers and Ferrero.

"I need to go to the Embassy anyway and talk to the ambassador," the CIA man stated. "I'm sure the major would let you use this conference room. It's secure."

"There's no such thing as a room that's totally secure," Katz told him. "Mr. Cassias and I could use the exercise, so we'll take a stroll and discuss our business."

"Yeah," Encizo said glumly. "I can hardly wait."

11

The Zoological Park provided a pleasant, tranquil setting in a city plagued with turbulence and violence. Yakov Katzenelenbogen and Rafael Encizo strolled past some park visitors and moved toward a group of llamas from Peru housed in an enclosure with a tall fence. Exotic birds called out from other portions of the park, and the scent of wildflowers contributed to the relaxed, unusual atmosphere.

Encizo, though, wasn't feeling very relaxed as he watched Katz take a small black plastic box from his pocket. About the size of a pack of cigarettes, the device was a miniature radio scrambler. If anyone tried to eavesdrop on their conversation with a rifle microphone, the scrambler would jam the receiver unit of the surveillance equipment. The llama would serve to block the view if CIA or Salvadoran Intelligence sent a skilled lip-reader to try to keep tabs on them with a pair of binoculars from a distance. Such precautions were standard procedure for Phoenix Force.

"All right, Rafael," Katz began with a sigh. "I know you have quite a way with the ladies, but I doubt that even you could convince a female photojournalist to let you spend the night with her after she discovered a roll of film so valuable to her career had been destroyed."

"Not much slips by you," Encizo commented. "I wondered how you figured out I was less than honest back there."

"It wasn't too hard," the Israeli replied. "Sommers and Ferrero didn't catch it, because they have such a low opinion of journalists in general, and they probably underestimate the intelligence of women, as well. From what little you told me about Maria Santo, I guessed she was too professional to leave that film in her camera unattended while she had dinner with you. You or I wouldn't make that sort of mistake, so I assume she wouldn't, either.''

''I wasn't lying to you and David. I just wanted to keep Ferrero and Sommers off her back.''

''Chivalrous but foolish,'' Katz remarked. ''Those photographs could ruin us, Rafael. All of us in Phoenix Force are in jeopardy because of that roll of film. Sommers and Ferrero don't have nearly as much to lose as we do if those pictures appear in print.''

''I talked to Maria,'' Encizo insisted. ''When she develops the photographs, she'll only use those that don't show our faces, and she'll give me the negatives to destroy.''

Katz shook his head and looked Encizo in the eye.

''Will you be realistic?'' he asked. ''Her job is to cover news stories with as much detail as possible and make them interesting and exciting to her readers. That includes using the most dramatic photographs with the story. You don't know her very well, Rafael.''

''But you don't know her at all, Yakov. I realize you have to be suspicious of everyone and everything. I know you have to think like that because the survival of Phoenix Force depends on being suspicious and forever on guard. But the world isn't divided into us and them. Everybody who doesn't belong to Phoenix Force isn't our enemy.''

''Sommers and Ferrero are on our side—more or less,'' Katz stated, ''but we can't trust them very much, either. That's why we're conducting this conversation in a zoo with a scrambler turned on. I'm actually not as concerned about the terrorists eavesdropping on us as I am about the CIA or the Salvadoran Intelligence personnel. You knew Maria Santo for less than twenty-four hours two years ago. She had been through a terrible ordeal, she was lost in the jungle and you were her great savior and protector then. This is a different situation. People don't act the same when they have to depend on you for their very survival."

"She won't betray us."

"You'd better be right," Katz warned. "If you can't get those photographs and the negatives, we'll have to take them."

"By whatever means necessary?" Encizo asked, and raised an eyebrow in a mute challenge.

"If it comes to that, yes," Katz admitted.

"What if I won't go along with you on that?" the Cuban asked.

Katz stared at the llamas for a moment and shook his head slowly. He again turned to face Encizo.

"Phoenix Force has been through quite a lot over the years," he began. "We've fought a lot of battles together and we could always rely on each other. I don't know how many times we've saved each other's lives."

"I know," Encizo said in a soft whisper. "I remember when a bullet creased my skull when we raided that Nazi stronghold in France. I was laid up in the hospital for months. I would have died if you guys hadn't been there for me. When I recovered, I was back on the team as if nothing had happened. When I went down to Mexico on my own to find my brother, you all came to the Yucatán to help me even though it was an unauthorized operation without Presidential sanctions. You risked your lives and your careers for me. Believe me, Yakov, I haven't forgotten."

"The woman is important to you," Katz stated. "I understand that. Julia was important to me, too, but I lost her because Phoenix Force had to come first. Try to work this out with Maria, but if she doesn't deliver those photos and negatives, you'd better be sure what side you want to be on. Like it or not, it *is* a matter of us against them. If you stand against Phoenix Force on this, the other three will back me."

"I know," Encizo said, nodding.

"You're very good, Rafael," Katz told him. "One of the best men I've ever worked with. You're very intelligent, cunning and extremely dangerous. That same description fits Gary, David and Calvin. They're all very good, too."

Katz didn't mention his own ability. He didn't have to. Encizo was well aware of the fact Katz was the most experienced member of the team, and in actual fact one of the most experienced combat veterans and espionage agents in the entire world. Katz was as lethal as any of the younger members of Phoenix Force, and he possessed a genius-level IQ and a vast reserve of knowledge and talent. Encizo had never considered the possibility that he might be pitted against the other four members of the Force. Any one of them would be his equal in a fight, but there was no doubt what the outcome would be if he had to take on all four.

"I never thought we'd have a conversation like this," Encizo said, and shook his head. "We've been closer than family for years. We've almost been living in the same skin since the Force was put together."

"That's true," Katz agreed. "And like a single living unit, we can all be destroyed if one member's face appears in Maria's newspaper. We can't allow that to happen, Rafael."

"No, we can't," the Cuban agreed. "You don't have to worry about my loyalty, Yakov. I'll stand with you guys regardless of what happens, but I still want to try to work this out with Maria. I think I can do it."

"I hope you're right," Katz replied. "I also hope Calvin doesn't fly off the handle with Captain Ortiz."

"I can understand if he does," Encizo said. "Especially after what he and I went through during that mission in the Vatican."

"That's why I didn't want you to go with him," Katz admitted, and sighed. "It's pretty bad when I figure Mc-Carter should accompany someone to keep them from losing control."

"You figure he'll be good at that?" the Cuban asked.

"McCarter?" the Phoenix Force commander repeated, but it sounded more like a groan.

IT WAS an innocent-looking small establishment located at the outskirts of San Salvador, not far from an army post outside the city. The Veaga Clock and Watch Shop was owned by a former army officer and an influential member of a committee of San Salvador businessmen who supported the ARENA Party.

He was also a personal friend of Colonel Martillo and willingly allowed the army officer to use the basement of his shop any time he wished and for virtually any purpose Martillo desired. Since Captain Ortiz was Colonel Hammer's trusted aide, the same courtesy was extended to him when he asked to use the basement as an unconventional base for the so-called interrogation of suspicious individuals.

Calvin James and David McCarter arrived at the shop in a Ford Galaxy 4-door with Ferrero's driver at the wheel. A sign, shaped in a circle with the face of a watch painted in the center, bore the legend of the establishment. The front windows displayed an assortment of mantle clocks and quaint, miniature grandfather clocks. A sign in the door read *Cerrado*.

"Closed, my ass," James growled as he emerged from the car and read the sign.

"Watch how you handle this, mate," McCarter suggested. The Briton joined the black commando on the sidewalk. "We're already on bad terms with the military after last night."

"They ain't on such good terms with me, either," James replied, and headed into an alley next to the shop.

McCarter followed him, and they walked between the buildings to the rear of the shop. Two army jeeps were parked behind Veaga's establishment, with a pair of Salvadoran troopers posted next to the vehicles. They stared at the two men dressed in civilian clothing. One soldier

grabbed his rifle and started to point it at James and Mc-
Carter.

"*¿Dónde está el Capitán Ortiz?*" James demanded.
"Where is Captain Ortiz?"

"*¿Quién es Usted?*" the man with the rifle replied.

"My name is Johnson," the black warrior answered.
"This is my associate, Mr. Hill. The captain met us last
night."

"*Si,*" the other soldier said with a sneer. "I was there,
too. You and your friends beat up two soldiers because of a
damn *mexicano* bitch with a camera."

"I didn't exactly beat anybody up," James said with a
shrug. "I just kicked a *cabrón* in the gut. Now, quit wasting our time and get Ortiz out here."

"No," the soldier with the rifle in his fists snapped as he
stepped closer and almost jabbed the muzzle of his M-16
into James's stomach. "You go away, *negro mono*. Take
your *yanqui* friend with you and go while you still can."

"I'm not a Yankee," McCarter complained. "I'm British, you ignorant goat-brain, son of a whore."

The soldier hissed with anger and swung his M-16 toward McCarter. That gave James the opportunity he
needed. The tough guy from the Windy City slammed a
palm under the barrel of the man's rifle to shove it upward,
pointed at the sky. He rapidly delivered a snap-kick to the
soldier's groin before the guy could attempt a butt-stroke or
swing his rifle away from James and step back to get beyond the Phoenix warrior's reach.

The blow forced the soldier to double up with agony.
James abruptly wrenched the M-16 from his opponent's
grasp and swung a leg in a high roundhouse kick. His boot
hit the trooper hard at the jawbone, just below the earlobe.
The soldier collapsed to the ground.

"Don't try it!" McCarter warned. The Briton had drawn
his Browning Hi-Power from shoulder leather and pointed
it at the other trooper before the startled man could grab his
weapon.

The soldier raised his hands and stepped away from his M-16. His rifle was propped against the frame of a jeep, and he realized he couldn't hope to grab it before McCarter could blast him. James reached down and grabbed his dazed opponent by the hair and the back of the collar. He hauled the man to his feet and rammed a knee to his abdomen.

"This is for that 'black monkey' remark, idiot," James announced, and punched the guy on the point of the chin.

The man's knees buckled, and his head snapped back from the blow. He fell against the side of a jeep and slid unconscious to the ground. James turned his attention to check the other soldier.

"Ortiz is in the shop," James remarked. "Isn't he?"

"I can't answer that," the man replied stiffly. His eyes darted nervously from James to McCarter.

"I think you just did," the black commando told him. "Drag your *compañero* out of the alley."

"Si, señor," the soldier replied with a nod.

He bent over the unconscious man, scooping his arms around the upper torso from behind. McCarter stepped closer and pressed the muzzle of his pistol against the back of the soldier's skull. The frightened trooper gasped and froze in place, eyes squeezed shut as he expected the Briton to pump a bullet into his brain.

James removed a set of unbreakable plastic riot cuffs from the small of his back and knelt beside the soldiers. He made certain the conscious soldier had both arms under the other man's armpits and bound the guy's wrists together. The startled trooper opened his eyes when he felt the plastic strip tighten around his wrists. He was surprised and embarrassed to discover he was locked in an embrace with the unconscious soldier. He held the man in a bear hug from behind and could not get loose.

"Now," James began as he pulled another set of riot cuffs from his belt. "You two just stay here and keep your mouths shut. You yell a warning to Ortiz and whoever's in there with him, and we'll come out here and make sure you never yell anything to anyone again."

He used the second strip of durable plastic to bind one of the unconscious man's hands to the other soldier's already shackled wrists. This would prevent either man from slipping out of the cuffs. James gathered up their M-16 rifles and checked to make certain they were not carrying side arms. He also confiscated their bayonets and pocket knives.

"If you get bored," McCarter suggested, "you might check the tire pressure on those jeeps.

The Phoenix pair moved to the back door of the Veaga Watch and Clock Shop. James carried one M-16 by the pistol grip, the stock braced at his hip. The other rifle slung across his shoulder and the Walther P-88 in shoulder leather under his jacket supplied him with plenty of firepower. It was more than he ought to need. McCarter held the Browning in one fist and tried the door knob with his other hand. The door wasn't locked. The Briton pushed it open.

He entered, both hands around the butt of the pistol in a Weaver's combat grip. James stood at the doorway, an M-16 ready to back up the British ace. Two more Salvadoran soldiers and a short, balding man with glasses stared at them with surprise. The civilian and one trooper sat at a small table with a pot of coffee and three cups. The other soldier stood near a workbench, surrounded by shelves loaded with boxes of parts to clocks and watches. Diminutive tools, a magnifying glass with mounted lights and equipment for Veaga's work were laid across the table.

"*¡Quédate!*" McCarter ordered. "Stay!"

"*¿Qué es esto?*" the civilian demanded. "What is this? I am Señor Veaga, the owner of this shop, and I have friends in the government...."

"*¡Cállate!*" James snapped as he pointed his rifle at the man. "Shut up! Where's Ortiz?"

None of the men answered, but a wail of agony drew James's attention to a door near a small icebox. The black commando tossed one M-16 to McCarter and told him to watch the three men in the room. He unslung the other rifle and moved to the door.

"Try not to overreact too much," McCarter urged, his attention still fixed on Veaga and the two soldiers.

"You know how diplomatic I am," James replied, and slammed a hard kick to the door.

The lock broke from the blow. James charged down the cellar steps. An NCO appeared at the foot of the stairs with a .45 pistol in his fist, but he had wasted a precious half second getting the side arm out of a button flap holster. He was still working the slide to chamber a round when James slashed the rifle barrel across his wrists to strike the Colt autoloader from his grasp.

The black commando stood on the third riser from the foot of the stairs and swung a kick to the startled NCO's face. His boot heel slammed into the sergeant's jaw. As the soldier fell back into a corner and slumped to the floor, James jumped to the bottom of the stairs and swung his M-16 at the two remaining figures in the basement.

Captain Ortiz stood beside a naked man strapped to a chair. The helpless figure was covered in sweat and stained with his own blood. His mouth was cut and bleeding, his nose broken and one eye swollen shut. Alligator clips were attached to his nipples and wired to the generator near Ortiz's right hand. The captain reached for his side arm, but James had already trained his weapon at the officer's chest.

"Do it and I'll blow you to hell, Ortiz," James warned as he slowly approached the pair. "Loosen that gun belt and no tricks."

"This is none of your business, Johnson," Ortiz told him, but he unbuckled the gun belt and lowered it to the floor. "I was interrogating a suspect. You have your methods and I have mine...."

"I don't want to hear it, Ortiz," James declared. "Now, get that shit off that man you've been torturing."

"You're going to regret this," the captain said with a sigh.

Ortiz removed the alligator clips from his victim's chest and started to unbuckle the restraining straps. James glanced about the basement. The single naked bulb in the ceiling cast a harsh light across the room. The room was almost empty, aside from some old crates and broken furniture stored in the corners of the reddish-brown brick walls. It was disturbingly similar to the improvised torture chamber James had been a victim of four years earlier.

"Here, Johnson," Ortiz announced as he hauled the semiconscious, battered figure of the unfortunate naked man from the chair. "Take him!"

He shoved the torture victim into James. The Phoenix pro moved the rifle to avoid the man's hurtling form and caught the guy with one arm to ease him to the floor. Ortiz suddenly charged and swung a boot to the M-16. He kicked the rifle from James's hand and lashed a solid left hook to the commando's face.

James's head turned sharply from the blow, and he staggered two steps backward. Ortiz followed and drove a hard right to the black warrior's abdomen. James grunted from the punch and his stomach ached from the pain, but he managed to grab Ortiz's forearm in both hands before the captain could draw back his fist. The Phoenix fighter held the guy's wrist with one hand and shoved the other into the crook of Ortiz's elbow. James turned sharply and swung his opponent into the nearest wall.

Ortiz's back hit the brick barrier hard. His face twisted with pain, and a moan escaped from his lips. James closed in and threw a snap-kick to the captain's abdomen. Ortiz moved abruptly, and James's boot slammed into the wall. The ball of his foot screamed a message of pain through the nerves up through his ankle to his hip. Ortiz lunged and hooked a fist under James's ribs. The black commando groaned, and his lungs ached from the blow. Ortiz grabbed his jacket lapel with one hand and slapped the other palm at the back of James's head.

The Phoenix veteran knew what Ortiz planned to do. The Salvadoran intended to haul him into the wall and smash his face and forehead into the bricks. James quickly raised a boot, placed it against the wall and shoved hard. The kick drove him backward into Ortiz, and both men stumbled backward across the room. They collided with the armchair that had been used for the torture session. The furniture tipped over, and both men crashed to the floor.

The naked man said something and crawled away from the struggling pair. James and Ortiz started to rise. The Phoenix pro swung a right cross to his opponent's jaw, sending Ortiz staggering into the pile of crates and junk. The captain snarled with rage and hurled a wooden box filled with old clothes and a broken lamp. James ducked, and the unorthodox projectile sailed above his bowed head.

Ortiz attacked and swung a kick for James's head before the black warrior could straighten. The boot struck James on the cheekbone. His head recoiled from the kick, and his face seemed to catch fire. He fell back into a wall as Ortiz closed in. The captain rammed an uppercut to James's stomach, but the black commando responded with a left hook to the jaw. Ortiz's head turned sharply, and James drove a heel-of-the-palm stroke under the captain's nose. The blow snapped the cartilage and caused blinding pain in the center of Ortiz's face.

The captain staggered from the assault, clutched his smashed nose with one hand and swung a wild punch at James. The black hardass easily dodged the fist and swung a kick to Ortiz's midsection. The Salvadoran doubled up with a gasp, and James hit him with a hard right cross. Ortiz's knees buckled and he fell to all fours. James closed his fist and hammered it between his opponent's shoulder blades. Ortiz sprawled across the concrete floor in a dazed heap.

"*¡Alto!*" a voice shouted at the foot of the stairs.

James turned to discover the NCO he had knocked out was back on his feet, but his hands were raised in surrender. His .45 Colt autoloader lay by his feet, and his body trembled with frustration and helpless rage. David Mc-Carter stood on the stairs with his Browning Hi-Power pointed at the sergeant.

"I wondered what the hell was going on down here," the Briton remarked. He glanced at Ortiz and the naked man curled up in a corner. "Doesn't look so good."

"Could be worse," James replied as he struggled to catch his breath. "What did you do with the three upstairs?"

"I found a length of rope about ten feet long," Mc-Carter explained. "Had those blokes stand facing a wall with their hands behind their backs. Then I tied the wrists of the first man and wound some rope around his ankles. Wrapped up the second chap's wrists and ankles the same way, and wound some rope around the last one's ankles before I tied his wrists and knotted some line around his belt. Figured that would hold them for a little bit."

"Yeah," James agreed as he gingerly touched the welt on his cheek and fingered his jawbone, glad that nothing seemed to be broken. "Let's find this dude's clothes and get him out of here."

"Right," McCarter said. He stepped to the third riser and suddenly lashed out a boot. He kicked the unlucky NCO in the face. The guy went down once again, his jaw in worse shape than before. James found a pile of clothes in a corner and handed them to the torture victim. The man accepted the clothing and managed to thank James. He looked very weak and trembly from all he had undergone.

"I got a feeling Colonel Hammer won't be too happy with us," James commented.

"A lot of people might be a bit upset with us after this," McCarter said, then shrugged. "But, what the hell. We're not in this business to make friends."

12

"Are you guys crazy?" Ronald Sommers demanded when he met Calvin James and David McCarter at the bay doors to the textile mill they were using for a safehouse.

"A lot of people have that opinion about us," McCarter answered as he stepped from the Galaxy and shut the door.

"Hey, man," James told the Briton, "everybody who knows *you* has that opinion."

"I bet Ortiz wouldn't say that," McCarter replied.

"Then you admit you went to the Veaga Clock and Watch Shop and beat up Ortiz and two of his men?" Sommers demanded. "You also threatened Mr. Veaga at gunpoint and tied him up, as well as three other soldiers?"

"You might say we had a full morning," James answered.

"Jesus," the CIA man moaned. "Are you aware Martillo has already found out about this stunt, and he's complained to Ferrero, the U.S. Embassy and the president's office? Veaga issued complaints to the mayor, the governor and God knows who else. The National Police have a warrant out for your arrest. I just got off the phone with the ambassador. He thinks you guys should hide out in the Embassy while he arranges to get you out of the country before you wind up in a Salvadoran prison...."

"That's very nice of him," McCarter remarked, "but we haven't finished our mission yet, so we're not ready to leave."

Another Ford 4-door sedan pulled up to the bay doors and rolled inside, behind the car McCarter and James had been in. Two Salvadoran Intelligence operatives sat in the front seat, side by side. Both wore civilian clothing and they were attached to one another by a set of handcuffs snapped around their wrists. The driver wore another pair of cuffs, which were attached to the steering wheel. Their faces were bruised, and one man had a black eye. They seemed weary, humiliated and embarrassed.

The rear door of the car opened and Gary Manning emerged from the vehicle. The big Canadian looked at his Phoenix Force partners and shook his head. He pulled a .45 autoloader from his belt and removed the magazine. Manning placed the magazine on the roof of the car and pulled back the slide to eject a round from the chamber.

"I finished having lunch at the hotel and stepped outside," the Canadian began as he placed the empty pistol on the roof next to the magazine. "These two tried to place me under arrest. We had a chat, and they told me they were acting on orders from Major Ferrero."

Manning pushed back his jacket to reach to the small of his back. He drew another Colt .45 from his belt and began to unload it.

"So I convinced them to bring me back here," he concluded, "because I'd like to know what the hell is going on."

"It's a long story," James replied.

"Somebody tell me the abridged version," Manning said as he slapped the second empty pistol on the car roof. "I'm not very happy about this. Something about being harassed by the people I'm supposed to be working with tends to rub me the wrong way."

"Your partners here barged in on Captain Ortiz while he was interrogating a suspected terrorist sympathizer," Sommers answered.

"Oh," Manning said with a nod. "He was 'interrogating' a suspect, huh? Does that mean torture?"

"Ortiz was fryin' this dude with an electrical generator," James answered. "The guy admits he's a socialist and made the mistake of having a copy of the *Communist Manifesto* in his house when Colonel Martillo's boys came a-calling."

"That sounds like great grounds to determine somebody is assisting the terrorists," Manning commented as he fished a pair of handcuff keys from his pocket. "If the two guys in the car will promise to behave themselves, I'll give them these keys."

"Goddamn it!" Sommers snapped as he snatched the keys form Manning's hand. "Your friends beat up Ortiz and two other men—one of whom has a broken jaw. They also threatened and humiliated a leading citizen of the business and political community here in San Salvador. That sort of stuff just isn't done here!"

"Why don't we get on the phone and ask President Cristiani if he approves of his military personnel resorting to torture?" McCarter suggested. "Then we can talk to the President of the United States and see what he thinks about having us thrown out of El Salvador because we stopped that bastard Ortiz from torturing some bloke."

"That's not how we do things here," Sommers insisted. "You don't come into El Salvador and make an enemy of one of the top military men in the whole damn country. Martillo can makes things awfully damn hard for you."

"His flunky was sure makin' things hard for that fella in the basement of the Veaga shop," James commented.

"Let's discuss this in the conference room," Sommers told the others. He glanced down at the keys in his hand and tossed them to the handcuffed men in the Ford.

The three Phoenix commandos followed Sommers to the conference room. Major Ferrero was inside, seated at the table with a cordless telephone in his hand. He glared at James and McCarter as he spoke into the phone, then he pushed down the antenna and placed the phone on the tabletop. "You two are lucky you're not in a prison cell," he declared.

"You're lucky I've had a chance to calm down since your men tried to arrest me," Manning told him.

"They were told to arrest you and bring you here," the major replied.

"I was coming here, anyway," the Canadian told him, "so why did you send them?"

"You can thank your friends for that," Ferrero answered. "Surely you know what they did. I wanted to make certain you didn't carry out some similar act of foolishness."

"You're not in charge here, Ferrero," Manning reminded him. "Maybe you forgot that, or you don't quite believe it."

"Perhaps we'll see about that," the major replied. He turned his attention to Calvin James. "And you lied to me, Johnson. You said you were going to help Ortiz interrogate suspects. Even mentioned scopolamine. You didn't say anything about stopping his interrogation and giving him a thrashing."

"It wasn't interrogation. It was just sheer brutality," James answered. "Ortiz wasn't trying to get information. He was trying to force confessions. You can get anybody to confess to anything if you cause enough pain. A person will say anything just to get the pain to stop."

"I don't approve of those tactics, either," Ferrero assured him, "but it isn't your job to correct the behavior of Captain Ortiz or anyone else in the Salvadoran army. Whatever his methods, he was trying to get information about the terrorists."

"By rounding up people considered to be on the political left?" Manning asked, and shook his head. "That only serves to make the military and the government appear to be repressive and brutal and actually builds sympathy for the very political forces you're opposed to. El Salvador has received assistance from the United States in the past, and you want it in the future, as well. When men like Ortiz commit these types of outrages, your government appears to be the villains and the U.S. suffers from guilt by association."

"It's sure happened enough times in the past," James added. "Nicaragua, Iran, the Philippines and plenty of others. Maybe the United States deserves a certain amount of blame for supporting some of these dictators. Maybe Uncle Sam should tell these tyrants to clean up their act, pay some attention to human rights and just plain decency, or we're cutting off the foreign aid and military hardware. Doesn't make much sense to support a government that's going to piss off its people until they get ready to revolt. Look at what happened in Iran. We supported the Shah and let him get away with that stunt he pulled with the SAVAK secret police and all the rest. When the revolution came there, the United States of America was labeled as the Great Satan of the West because we were so closely linked with the Shah."

"El Salvador isn't Iran," Ferrero insisted, clearly insulted by the comparison.

"But you've sure as hell had some problems here about how the government and the military handles the civilian population," McCarter told him. "A lot of countries have bands of would-be revolutionaries running about, but not many have rebel forces that are estimated to be larger than the nation's entire armed forces. That bloody well suggests there's something wrong with how this country is being run—or at least how it's been run in the past."

Ferrero looked huffy, and he squared his shoulders defensively.

"I don't really appreciate this lecture about my country. You don't have the right to judge us."

"We have the right to judge people who use torture like Ortiz," James insisted. "Everybody with any sense of decency has a right to be opposed to that sort of behavior. Maybe it's not just a right, but a *duty* to be opposed to it. You said yourself you don't approve of it, Major. Assholes like Ortiz are giving your country a bad reputation. If

President Cristiani is serious about improving El Salvador, he has to bring a halt to brutal methods, and he needs decent men like you to help him do it.''

"A decent man?" Ferrero raised his eyebrows and almost smiled. "I didn't think you men had that high an opinion of me."

"You've been sort of a pain in the arse to us," McCarter told him, "but I'm sure we've been pretty much the same for you. Still, I don't imagine you'd set up torture chambers and throw people in prison just because you don't like some of their politics."

"Speaking of people getting thrown in prison," Manning began. "Our other two teammates are missing. Is there a warrant out for their arrest, too?"

"No," Ferrero assured him. "Goodman and Cassias are with some of my people questioning family members of the two slain terrorists we were able to identify. They're trying to learn more about the dead men and some of their more recent associates. Hopefully they'll find something useful."

"I hate to say this," Sommers began, "but everything isn't all chummy and nice. Martillo still wants you guys to pay for what you did to Ortiz. You're still in trouble with the National Police, the mayor of San Salvador and a whole bunch of other pretty powerful people here."

"Tell Martillo to go to hell," James replied. "He must be as bad as Ortiz if he's willing to endorse the form of interrogation his dear captain was using."

"In all fairness and to give the man the benefit of doubt," Manning stated, "the colonel might not know what his captain did. I don't imagine Ortiz would admit he was torturing suspects if Martillo was in the dark about his methods."

"I wouldn't bet Martillo doesn't know about Ortiz," James said grimly. "That sucker walks around like he owns everything he sees, and he carries that steel claw hammer on his belt like it was a baton. He's probably used that thing for more than drivin' nails with.''

"Martillo can probably be kept at bay by a phone call to the right government officials," Sommers remarked. "We can call off the National Police, as well. The U.S. ambassador has already filed a complaint to the State Department about you guys causing damage to U.S. relations with El Salvador. Can't really blame him. I don't know enough about you men to give him ample reason to defend your presence here."

"The fact we rescued the U.S. Embassy doesn't mean anything to him?" McCarter inquired dryly.

"Unfortunately," the CIA man began, "you fellas already presented a pretty convincing argument that the terrorists didn't intend to destroy the Embassy. You said the attack appeared to be violent harassment and that the goal was to create fear rather than destruction."

"Yeah," Manning, the demolitions expert, agreed. "They would have concentrated the attack on the building itself and either used a large explosive charge or lobbed grenades and Molotov cocktails at the windows if they intended a serious attack on the Embassy."

"Whose side are you on?" McCarter complained.

"I'm simply stating the logical facts," Manning insisted.

"This is no time for your imitation of Mr. Spock," the Briton muttered with disgust.

Sommers waved his hands in the air to get everybody's attention. "The fact is," he began, "based on our own evaluation of the terrorist attack, they largely succeeded in what they attempted to accomplish. Of course, the ambassador is glad that you stopped the enemy from getting away with their assault, but he also noticed you didn't manage to take any of them alive."

"We would have if one of the terrorists hadn't finished off a wounded comrade and Captain shoot-first Ortiz hadn't killed the dude I wounded," James said bitterly.

"I know," the CIA man assured him. "I was there, too. Believe me, I've tried to convince the ambassador you men are doing the best you can, but so far there hasn't been much positive evidence to support that claim, and now plenty of complaints are rolling in concerning how you gentlemen are handling this situation."

"We've been here less then twenty-four hours, and he's pissed because we don't have enough results so far?" James said, and rolled his eyes toward the ceiling.

"I'm just glad this mission isn't in the middle of the bloody ocean," McCarter growled. "They'd probably be upset if we couldn't walk on water and talk to the dolphins."

YAKOV KATZENELENBOGEN and Rafael Encizo returned to the safehouse later that afternoon. Major Ferrero and Ron Sommers had left the mill to meet with officials concerning the turmoil created by the complaints about recent actions by James and McCarter. Katz and Encizo were unaware of these events until their fellow Phoenix Force members reluctantly explained what had happened.

"Couldn't you have handled this matter with a little more tact and a little less force?" Katz asked with a weary sigh.

"Hey, I didn't kill Ortiz or his storm trooper pals," James replied. He touched his cheek and discovered the swelling was gradually going down. "I'll say this for the captain—the son of a bitch is no pushover. He put up a pretty good fight."

"Weren't you supposed to help keep things from getting out of control?" Encizo asked McCarter.

"I was?" the Briton replied with surprise. "Well, I'd say it didn't get out of hand, really."

"No, you wouldn't," Manning growled as he poured himself a cup of black coffee. "Did you get any useful information from talking to the family and friends of the deceased terrorists?"

"Some of it is interesting," Katz confirmed. "Although Mr. Cassias can probably explain better, since he and the Salvadoran Intelligence personnel actually handled the questioning because their Spanish is obviously much better than mine."

"Cassias?" Manning began with raised eyebrows. "We're—"

Katz flashed him a warning look, and Manning immediately understood that even when they considered themselves to be in private, they had to maintain their cover. For all they knew, the safehouse was bugged.

"As I was saying," the Canadian continued, "we're anxious to hear what you learned."

"Well, I don't know if we learned enough to settle things down," Encizo began. "But one of the families we talked to recalls their boy Juan had formerly served under a Major Martillo when he was in the army. Supposedly he thought the major was a great man and a true patriot opposed to communism."

"Doesn't sound like a likely recruit for the FMLN," McCarter commented. "But it's sort of interesting how Colonel Hammer keeps popping up all over the place."

"Yeah," Manning agreed, "but it doesn't prove anything. What else did you find out?"

"Every family member and associate of the dead men we were able to contact insisted the deceased were never involved with revolutionaries, leftist politics or anything that might suggest they'd join any sort of terrorist outfit," Encizo added. "Of course, I doubt they'd say anything different even if they suspected something shady about their misguided and departed relatives and friends. That might not be wise in El Salvador."

"No kidding," James remarked. "I saw what Ortiz did to a guy he considered to be left wing. Well, I guess the fella is a socialist, so he must be left wing, but . . ."

"Yeah, yeah," Manning said, and bobbed his head. "The problem is we still don't know a damn thing. The terrorists may have been right-wing fanatics or left-wing nuts who pretended they were to the political right, or the people who knew them are lying to protect themselves. There's so much fear in this country it's hard to tell what the truth is."

"One thing is certain," Katz declared. "We'd better get some positive results soon. This mission hasn't gone too well. So far we've done a better job at aggravating the authorities and the military than finding the terrorists."

"What was I supposed to do?" James demanded. "Stand by and let Ortiz torture that man today?"

"It's not just that," Katz insisted. "We clashed with the army last night when Mr. Cassias came to the rescue of Maria Santo. A lot of influential people want us out of the country. Our security, as well as the success of our mission, may be in extreme jeopardy."

Encizo glanced down at the floor. He knew what Katz was talking about. He hoped his trust in Maria wouldn't prove to be misplaced. If she failed to keep her word about the photographs and negatives, Phoenix Force could be on its last mission.

13

Larry Convy mopped his brow with a sweat-soaked hand-kerchief. The climate seemed to get hotter and more humid north of San Salvador. He had spent the past year and a half with the network's European office, and he was unaccustomed to the tropical climate of the small Central American country. He wished he hadn't carried a backpack stuffed full of penicillin, quinine and other medical supplies concealed among the spare clothing, shelter half of a pup tent and other innocent items.

Chet Nado, Convy's cameraman, carried a similar pack, in addition to his video camera. He had less trouble handling the burden in the heat. Nado was more experienced with Central America than Convy, and had worked with other TV reporters and journalists in El Salvador in the past. He'd become acquainted with Hector, a terrorist unit commander, during his coverage of the civil war in El Salvador. The acquaintance would be fruitful, apparently, since Hector was to be their connection and their lead to a great story.

Convy considered himself very lucky to have Nado on his team. The guy was not only a veteran newsman, a skilled camera expert and familiar with the country, but he also spoke Spanish fluently and he had actually met Hector on two previous occasions. Convy and Nado could get an inside scoop on the terrorist attack on the U.S. Embassy and beat everybody else to the story.

"Rebels, not terrorists," Convy muttered as he trudged behind Nado through the high grass and giant ferns.

"What's that?" the cameraman inquired, and glanced over his shoulder at the reporter.

"Just reminding myself not to refer to Hector and his boys as terrorists," Convy answered. A sizable insect flew into his face, and he yelped in surprise, then batted at it disgustedly.

"Try to keep it down, Larry," Nado urged. "The army knows the FMLN has a base somewhere near Cojutepeque and sometimes they got patrols out here. If they catch us, they'll haul our ass back to town. If they find these medical supplies in our gear, we could be in a lot worse trouble."

"We've got medicine and antibiotics, not guns," he declared. "We had to bring something to negotiate with Hector to tell us his story. At least the FMLN can't use the stuff we give them to kill people with."

"Giving any sort of assistance to these guys isn't appreciated by the Salvadoran government," Nado reminded him. "Besides, the fact that we're carrying these medical supplies and that we've got press cards, a camera and microphones is pretty strong evidence we had some idea where Hector's cell is located. The authorities won't be very happy with us if they figure we've been keeping that sort of information secret."

"They can kiss my ass," Convy replied. "We're members of the American press corps, and the American public has a right to know the truth. The Salvadoran gestapo isn't gonna do shit to us. We're American citizens...."

"El Salvador considers itself to be part of America," Nado told him. "Central America. Remember? These folks figure they're Americans, too. We're from *los Estados Unidos*. The United States. That makes us *norteamericanos* down here."

"I thought Canada was North America," Convy remarked.

"They never taught you the difference between a continent and a country when you went to school as a kid?" Nado asked.

"What difference?" the reporter replied.

Nado shook his head and turned his attention to the tangle of vines and tall grass under the coconut palms. He swung a machete at the brush and chopped a path through the rain forest. Convy followed. He could hardly believe they were only a few kilometers from Cojutepeque. Hell, El Salvador was no larger than the state of Massachusetts, and it was the most densely populated of any Central American country. How the hell did it have enough room for so much goddamn jungle?

"*¿Adónde va?*" a voice shouted from a grassy knoll behind the pair. " *¿Qué hace?*"

Convy glanced over his shoulder and saw three soldiers at the knoll. Two carried assault rifles slung on their shoulders. The third man in uniform wore a service cap and side arm. He stood in front of the troopers and was shouting at the two newsman.

"Where are you going?" the officer demanded, this time in English. "What are you doing?"

"Goddamn it," Convy rasped under his breath.

"Let me talk to them," Nado whispered. "These guys usually go easy on television news personnel because they know we belong to bigger, more powerful media than the newspaper journalists. Maybe we can get past them without being searched. If they find the medical supplies..."

"*¡Señores!*" the young officer called out. "*¿Es usted el norteamericanos?*"

"*Si,*" Nado replied. "We just wanted to get some footage of the jungles for our news report about the terrorist activity in your country and why you men of the armed forces have such a great task to hunt down these butchers in such difficult terrain."

"This area is dangerous," the officer told him. "Come with us back to the road, and we will escort you to Cojutepeque. You will be safe there."

"What's he saying?" Convy inquired. Nado and the soldier spoke Spanish, but the reporter only understood a few words in the language.

"He just pulled the plug on our exclusive interview with Hector," Nado explained with a sigh.

The unexpected eruption of full-automatic weapons exploded from the bush like bolts of lightning screaming from a cloudless bright sky. Nado cried out as high-velocity rifle rounds smashed into his back. A bullet struck and shattered the video camera. Bits of metal and plastic showered down on Convy's head and shoulders.

"Oh, God!" the reporter exclaimed, and threw himself to the ground.

Nado fell beside him. The cameraman's body twitched as blood oozed steadily from a bullet hole under his left shoulder blade. The crimson flow splashed the face and shirt of Larry Convy. He turned away and buried his face in the grass. The reporter trembled in fear and revulsion as blood continued to pour from Nado's punctured heart.

The army officer had also been hit by the treacherously swift assault. Three slugs tore into the soldier's chest and hurled him backward into his men. The troopers dropped low behind the knoll and unslung their rifles. More enemy bullets plowed into the ridge and punched clods of dirt from the earth.

Convy remained on his belly and wiped the blood from his face and eyes. He saw a pair of boots appear near his head. The reporter gazed up at a figure clad in tattered fatigue uniform with a rifle in his fists, muzzle pointed as the reporter's head. A smile appeared in the center of the man's shaggy black beard.

"Get up, *yanqui*!" he ordered, and kicked Convy in the ribs.

More armed figures emerged from the foliage under the palms. Some fired at the soldiers' position at the knoll. One man reached down and grabbed Convy by the seat of his pants and shirt collar to haul him from the ground. He shoved Convy toward the trees and poked him in the spine with a gun barrel.

"*¡Ándate, yanqui!*" the man snarled. "Move, Yankee!"

Convy staggered forward, dazed and disoriented by the unexpected violence and death that had occurred around him. The reporter had come to El Salvador for a major news story, but he hadn't counted on being in the middle of a gun battle. He heard one of the ambushers scream and glanced over his shoulder to see the gunman collapse, his torso bisected by a trio of bullet holes. The man's assault rifle clattered to the ground beside him.

Another member of the hit team rushed forward and reached for the fallen weapon. He failed to notice he had exposed himself to the soldiers' line of fire and two bullets crashed into the side of his skull. His head split open, and brain tissue gushed from his shattered head as he fell across the corpse of his slain comrade.

The attack force quickly retreated into the rain forest. Some withdrew more slowly and continued to fire at the soldiers' position at the knoll. Two men stayed close to Convy and roughly escorted him through the jungle. They shoved him along and jabbed him with rifle barrels. Convy tried to catch his breath as they force-marched him through the trees and dense foliage.

"Who—who are you?" he managed to gasp. "Where are you taking me?"

"You find out soon enough, *cabrón*," one of the gunmen snapped. "Keep moving or you wind up like your friend back there!"

Convy felt as though he had been dropped into a nightmare. Stunned, he fixed his eyes on the ground and kept moving, not knowing which step would be his last.

RAFAEL ENCIZO KNOCKED on the hotel room door and announced himself as Cassias. Maria Santo opened the door and smiled at the handsome Cuban commando. He hoped she would still have reason to smile after he talked to her.

Encizo entered her room, and Maria closed the door. She wrapped her arms around his neck and kissed him.

"I was hoping you'd see me today," Maria whispered, but she noticed his body was rigid, and his expression revealed his thoughts were centered on serious matters rather than romance. "I see. This visit is business and not pleasure?"

"Have you developed the film yet?" Encizo inquired.

"I should have guessed that was on your mind," she said, and disengaged herself from the Cuban. "I should have known you didn't come here to see me...."

"Maria," Encizo began as he stepped forward and placed his hands on her shoulders. "You know how serious this is. If you've developed those photographs, I have to see them."

"No, I haven't developed the damn film yet," she replied.

"When you have photos this important do you usually wait to get them developed?" Encizo asked, a trace of suspicion in his voice.

"Sometimes I wait until I return to Mexico City to do it in a professional darkroom under the best possible conditions," she replied.

"Not this time," he told her.

Maria pushed his hands away.

"That sounds almost like a threat, Rafael. I haven't seen this side of you before, and I don't think I like it."

"I don't like having my life and the lives of my friends and partners on the line because of a roll of 35 mm film that could get us all killed," he answered in a hard voice.

"So you don't trust me," she accused, and started to turn her back to him.

Encizo grabbed her by the shoulders and spun her around to face him. Maria swung a slap aimed at Encizo's face, but he caught her wrist. She felt his body tense as the survival instincts trained inside his nervous system began to respond to an attack. He had to keep his body from responding with the reflex action that had become second nature after years of being in an extremely dangerous profession and that often made the difference between staying alive or being dead.

Maria gasped when she saw Encizo's eyes. The gentleness and understanding she had seen there vanished, and Maria caught sight of the hard ruthlessness that was also part of the personality of Rafael Encizo. They were the eyes of a man who had killed many items in the past and wouldn't hesitate to do so if he had to. Maria's mouth fell open and she trembled. Suddenly she was terrified of a man she thought she was falling in love with.

"If I didn't trust you, we wouldn't be talking now," he assured her. "But trust is relative, and you can't ask a great deal of it from me. There's too much at stake for me to wait for those photos and simply hope you will keep your word."

"If I questioned your word, you'd probably knock me across the room," Maria stated. "Or kill me."

"Of course I wouldn't," the Cuban replied with a sigh. "I know how to develop film. I can probably get a professional darkroom for the evening, too. Are you willing to let me develop the photos for you, Maria?"

"No," she answered, offended by the suggestion.

"Does that mean you don't trust me?" he inquired.

"That's not fair," Maria told him.

"Not many things in life are fair," Encizo said. "It's not fair that you and I have to be adversaries because we both have a job to do, jobs with different goals. It's not fair that three Embassy personnel were murdered on the street after paying a visit to a museum. It wasn't fair that two Marines were killed just for being on duty in front of the U.S. Embassy last night."

"I'm aware of that, Rafael," she said softly, and shook her head. "I also know that whatever sort of work you do, it's top secret and very important. My career is important to me, too."

"You'll have the damn story," Encizo insisted. He spread his arms apart, palms turned up. "But I can't let you take us down in the process."

"I intend to develop the film tonight," Maria told him. "It's easier to use the bathroom as an improvised darkroom if I wait for the sun to go down."

"It's almost twilight," he observed as he glanced out the window. "There's time for us to have dinner before you work on the film."

"I don't think so," Maria replied. "Things have changed for us, Rafael. They'll never be the same now."

"We had a wonderful illusion," Encizo told her. "Unfortunately that's just what it was. We never could have any sort of relationship that could last. What future could you have with a man who can't even tell you his real name or any details about himself? Every time I told you anything, you'd know it was probably a lie. Every time I left on a mission, you'd have no idea where I was going or what I was doing. Eventually there will be a mission that's my last. That's the one I won't return from."

"You can't quit?" Maria asked sadly.

"Somebody has to do it, and I'm one of the few men around who can," Encizo said. "A small group of men with the right skills, connections and determination really can change the world, or, more important in most cases, keep the world from changing. Hard to believe, sometimes, but things really could be a hell of a lot worse than they are now. You'd be astonished if you knew how many times cities were nearly destroyed, wars almost occurred and other actions that could have cost hundreds or thousands of lives were prevented. I have to do it."

"You mean you want to," she said, accusation in her voice.

"I won't deny it," the Cuban admitted. "Besides, I can't quit even if I wanted to. Sooner or later, my past would catch up with me, and so would the enemies I've made over the years."

"You're beginning to make me nervous just being in the same room with you," Maria remarked.

"Frankly you may have good reason to feel that way," Encizo told her.

A knock at the door startled Maria. Encizo moved to the hinged side of the door and reached inside his jacket to touch the grips of the Walther P-88 holstered under his arm. Maria looked at him and swallowed nervously. He nodded and tilted his head toward the door.

"Who is it?" Maria called out.

"It's Mr. Johnson," a familiar voice replied.

Encizo sighed and grabbed the doorknob. He opened the door and looked up at Calvin James in the hallway. The tall black commando grunted. "I figured I might find you here," he said.

"It's not what you think," Encizo stated.

"Doesn't matter what it is," James told him. "Something has come up. We gotta move, man."

"Now?" Encizo began, but he realized the answer was obvious. "All right. Just a minute..."

"We don't have a minute," the badass from Chicago stated. "Come on."

Encizo said a hasty farewell to Maria and followed James down the corridor. They entered the elevator and pressed the down button. As the elevator descended, James informed Encizo that another terrorist attack has taken place less than half an hour before.

"This time they hit a couple of television guys from the States," James explained. "The cameraman was killed, and so was a lieutenant who was the Salvadoran army patrol in the area. The other newsman was apparently kidnapped and hauled off into the jungle."

"What were they doing there?" Encizo wondered.

"We don't have any other details so far," James answered. "I sure didn't want to mention any of this in front of your lady reporter friend. Did you get those photographs and negatives?"

"You know about that, too," Encizo said, sighing deeply.

"My ass is on the line here, too, you know," James reminded him. "I take it you didn't get the stuff from her."

"She's going to develop the film tonight," the Cuban answered.

"Hey, you've been all grown up and dealt with women longer than I have," James remarked. "Have you really discovered they're all honest and trustworthy? Women can be as treacherous as men. A couple of 'em I've known could teach most guys a lesson in the fine art of lying."

"This lecture sounds familiar," Encizo commented. "I'm taking care of this, Cal. In fact, I was going to stay in her room until she developed the photos and handle everything personally tonight."

"If you don't take care of this," James began with a shake of the head, "David and I will."

"What's that mean?" the Cuban demanded.

"It means Mr. McCarter and I have discussed the matter, and neither of us want to wind up on the front page of a Mexican tabloid next week," James answered. "By the end of the month we'd all be on Wanted posters for the KGB Mokrie Dela assassination department. I'm not bettin' they're out of business since *glasnost*. Even if we didn't have the Russians to worry about, there's still ODESSA Nazi outfits, terrorist organizations with and without state sponsorship, criminal syndicates and probably a lot of other dudes who want us dead."

"I know," Encizo assured him. "So, what did you two decide to do if I fail to get Maria to cooperate?"

"We'll toss her room and destroy every roll of film she has to make sure we get the one that could ruin us," James admitted. "If we have to, we'll search her also. I may even give her a dose of truth serum and question her under the influence to make absolutely sure we got the film."

"No bamboo under the fingernails?" Encizo said dryly.

"Don't lay that junk on me," James snapped. "We're talkin' about survival, man. You're like a brother to me, Rafael, but so are all the other guys in Phoenix. I'm not going to let that woman drag us down because you've got a thing for her."

"Neither am I," Encizo assured him as the elevator doors slid open.

14

The minibus arrived at the army post near Cojutepeque. The headlights of dozens of trucks, jeeps, armored cars and a few civilian automobiles filled the motor pool and parade field with harsh white light. Soldiers were everywhere. They stood in formation while officers issued orders. They double-time marched from their barracks to the headquarters building to be issued rifles and ammunition.

Phoenix Force and Major Ferrero emerged from the bus. The five commandos wore camouflage uniforms, paratrooper boots and headgear. They carried Uzi machine pistols with shoulder straps, the weapons hung at hip level for immediate use if needed. Each man carried a Walther P-88 in shoulder leather—except McCarter, who still favored his single-action Browning autoloader—and ammo pouches, grenades, knives and other combat gear hung on their belts.

"Bloody hell," McCarter muttered as a familiar figure approached the bus. "What's he doing here?"

Colonel Martillo greeted Phoenix Force with a curt nod. He was accompanied by Captain Ortiz and an officer in the National Police. Ortiz cast a short, hate-filled glance at Calvin James. The captain still carried bruises on his face from his encounter with the tall black warrior. James smiled at Ortiz, though that did not seem to improve the captain's attitude.

"*Buenas noches, Coronel,*" Ferrero declared with a salute.

"Let's speak English for the sake of our visitors from the United States," Martillo replied as he returned the salute. "I was told you gentlemen would be here. We can use all the help we can get."

"What's going on?" Katz asked as he gestured with the hooks of his prosthesis to indicate the activity on the base. "Looks like they're getting ready to go to war."

"That's correct," Martillo confirmed. "The troops are going to organize a sweep of the rain forest and surrounding area in an effort to locate the terrorists. You know they kidnapped a television reporter from the United States? A man named Lawrence Convy."

"Yeah," Gary Manning answered. "We heard. He was in the area with a cameraman. Right? Any idea why the two of them were up here by themselves? They should have realized it was dangerous."

"The cameraman has been identified as Chester Nado," the National Police commander replied. "He had been in El Salvador before and had connections with some of the terrorist leaders in the FMLN. We believe the ERP unit commander known as Hector was one of them."

"Hector and his group have been terrorizing this area for almost a year," Martillo explained. "Nado was carrying a backpack with medical supplies needed by the terrorists. He and Convy probably intended to trade these supplies for information and perhaps an interview with the ERP."

"They wanted to beat everybody else to an exclusive story," Rafael Encizo remarked. "That's why they were alone."

"They got what they deserved, in my opinion," the colonel stated. "Unfortunately an army patrol had discovered the two *norteamericanos* and tried to bring them back to town. That's when the terrorists attacked. A young lieutenant was killed, and one of his men was wounded, but they exchanged fire with the enemy and managed to take two terrorists out of the battle."

"Did you bring the bodies here?" James asked. "Have they been examined?"

"My people have the corpses at the police morgue," the police officer answered. "They haven't been identified yet, and I doubt anything will be gained by autopsies."

"We'll arrange autopsies in the near future," Ferrero told him. "Does anyone have an idea where the terrorists might be located?"

"Forensics discovered traces of red clay and copper at the bottom of the dead men's boots," the police officer said. "This suggests a definite area that was formerly a site for copper mining a couple of years ago. It's about eight kilometers from where the abduction and gun battle took place."

"Sounds promising," McCarter mused. "What were the terrorists armed with?"

"AK-47 assault rifles," Martillo answered. "Soviet manufacture. I'm sure you're no strangers to the weapon. Probably supplied by Cubans or Sandinistas from Nicaragua. Hector's people may even be Sandinistas. We don't know enough about them to say one way or the other."

"All right," Katz began. "We have a likely location for the terrorist base. We can only speculate as to how large the enemy forces might be, but it seems unlikely it would be beyond forty or fifty men. More than that would be difficult to conceal even in a rain forest. We'd better assume they're well armed and well trained."

"Well, it's not a good idea to send all these troops to go mucking about in the jungle," McCarter announced. "They'll be more apt to alert the ERP to danger than to find the enemy by some sort of wide sweep of the area. If the terrorists are at the site you mentioned, finding them might not be a major problem."

"The ERP knows the area and we don't," Encizo added. "That can be a big advantage. I suggest you send the majority of the soldiers in a mock operation about twenty or twenty-five kilometers from the old mining area. If the terrorists have scouts scattered throughout the rain forest, they'll report the largest troop strength is quite a distance from their base. That'll give the enemy the impression that we don't have any idea where they're located. Give them a sense of false security."

"That's not a bad ploy," Martillo said with a nod. "We can distract them and launch the real attack on their base. Of course, that means we can't use a large assault force for the actual attack on the enemy base. That would warn them, anyway, and a large number of men won't be able to approach the site undetected. If we use twenty men, it would mean we'd probably be outnumbered by two to one. Perhaps more if the terrorist base is larger than Mr. Goodman's estimate."

"There's no way we can be sure of anything," Katz told him. "Still, we'll have a better chance to succeed if we use a small number of men for the strike force. In fact, I'd say fifteen would be a better number for the group than twenty."

"They'd be less apt to be detected in the jungle," Ferrero agreed, "but fifteen men against fifty or more? That's pretty bad odds."

"Well, that's just too bad for the terrorists," McCarter replied with a wolfish grin.

"Oh, shut up," Manning told him.

"The odds aren't really as poor as they sound," Katz assured the major. "If we have the element of surprise and we can hit the enemy base at its weak points and keep the terrorists from spreading out—granted it's a lot of 'ifs'—then the size of the opponents' manpower won't be that great an advantage for them."

"We've handled far worse odds in the past," Encizo stated. "Colonel Martillo, you've confronted terrorists before. Do you have ten men who can accompany us? Ten very good men who can handle this sort of assignment and follow orders."

"I'll select nine of my best men," Martillo answered.

"Do us all a favor and don't include Captain Ortiz," James suggested.

Ortiz glared at him. "This isn't a personal matter, Johnson," the captain spit out contemptuously. "You may not like me, but that doesn't mean we can't work together."

But Martillo had already made his decision.

"You should remain with the rest of the men, Captain," he said. "If anything happens to me, you'll have to take command."

"If anything happens to you?" Ferrero asked with surprise. "You don't intend to take part in this operation? You're a field-grade officer and one of the top military commanders in El Salvador. Your expertise and experience makes you more valuable in command position than in the front lines...."

"I am a front-line commander," Martillo declared. "And I am also one of the best choices to participate in this mission. I certainly have the training and the experience. Besides, I wouldn't want to order men into a combat situation I myself would not be willing to do. Considering the odds, this operation does sound almost like a suicide mission."

"I wouldn't say that," McCarter commented. "We've handled a lot of operations like this against bigger odds, and we're still alive. You can only commit suicide once, you know."

"Don't get overconfident," Katz warned. "We can't afford to take anything for granted or assume this is routine. You can only get killed once, too."

PHOENIX FORCE and the men selected from Martillo's troops traveled as far as possible into the rain forest by truck. The driver wore a pair of night-vision goggles with special fiber optics in the lens that magnified reflected light. This allowed him to see in the dark without using the headlights. The truck couldn't travel far before the dense foliage and thick tangled vines and low-hanging branches formed a solid wall that blocked the way.

They emerged from the truck and continued on foot. Colonel Martillo carried an M-16 in addition to his .45 side arm and ever-present steel hammer. He noted that the five commandos had acquired even more weaponry for the raid on the terrorist base. Martillo would have considered that excessive had they not already displayed considerable ability as fighting men. They were certainly expert with every weapon they carried, and Martillo realized they had extra firepower because they were accustomed to taking on greater numbers in combat.

Rafael Encizo and Calvin James were also toting M-16 assault rifles with folding paratrooper-style stocks and thirty-centimeter-long silencers attached to the barrels. Both men also carried fighting knives as well as their compact Uzi machine pistols and Walther autoloaders. Encizo's Cold Steel Tanto was in a belt sheath in a cross-draw position, and the handle of a Gerber Mark I fighting dagger jutted from a sheath clipped to the top of his boot. James carried a Blackmoor dirk in a sheath attached to his Jackass leather shoulder holster rig under his right arm.

Gary Manning had a Belgian-made FAL assault rifle with a silencer and a Starlite night scope mounted to the frame. The Canadian also had a small backpack at the small of his spine. It contained Composition-4 RDX plastic explosives. His pockets were stuffed with special blasting caps and detonators. David McCarter held a Barnett Commando crossbow instead of a rifle. A modern version of a centuries-old design, the Barnett crossbow was lightweight with its skeletal frame, a mounted scope and a cocking lever to allow the archer to load, cock and fire more rapidly than one could manage with a traditional crossbow. Attached to the British ace's belt was a quiver of bolts for the Commando bow. The feathered ends were green and red. The former color labeled the bolts as standard target quarrels with steel tips. Red feathers indicated the bolt was equipped with cyanide in the fiberglass shaft above the point.

Yakov Katzenelenbogen was the only member of the Phoenix team who didn't carry a long-range weapon. Before he'd lost his arm, Katz had been right-handed. He had adjusted to using his left hand and the prosthesis, but certain problems with hand-eye coordination remained. Trying to aim a rifle with an artificial limb while using the right eye to focus through the sights was simply too awkward for Katz.

Occasionally Katz used a rifle under special circumstances, but generally he favored an Uzi on the battlefield. The machine pistol version of the famous submachine gun was smaller than its big brother. It was also less accurate and had a shorter range, but at close quarters when rapid fire was needed, the Uzi minichopper was superb. The Israeli commando also carried a Walther P-88 in shoulder leather and a ballistics knife in a metal tube-scabbard on his belt.

The Phoenix Force commander watched Sergeant Lopez quietly assemble the other eight men from Martillo's unit. The big NCO seemed quite competent, Katz observed as he watched the men line up in formation. Most of the troops carried M-16 rifles, but Lopez and two other soldiers were armed with Winchester pump shotguns. They were young, eager for battle and willing to risk life and limb for the thrill of combat. Katz supposed that they were either too inexperienced to appreciate the horror of the battlefield or their former confrontations had been with opponents who couldn't fight back.

Katz had reservations about working with Martillo and his men. They were hardly on the same level as the American Rangers, Special Forces or SEALS, the British SAS, the West German GSG-9 or many of the other elite military units that Phoenix Force had previously worked with. Nonetheless, Martillo's outfit was what they had, and Phoenix Force would have to make the most of the situation.

"Colonel," Katz began, "before we reach the enemy base, we should establish an understanding with your men.

We may have to separate the unit into two or possibly four smaller teams.''

"How would we break up the command?" Martillo asked with a frown. He clearly didn't like the idea of letting foreigners give orders to his men.

"If we break into two groups, you and I would command one team, and Mr. Cassias and Mr. Johnson would command the other, due to their expertise in the field and their ability to speak fluent Spanish," Katz answered. "A four-way division would consist of three soldiers under your command, three with Cassias and three with Johnson. The other two members of my team, Connors and Hill, will go with me."

"Very well," Colonel Hammer reluctantly agreed. "I'll explain it to my men and make sure they understand that they are to follow orders from you and your partners as if the commands came from my own lips. Each man will know which team he should join if and when it is necessary to divide our unit."

"Do any of them know this terrain?" Encizo inquired.

"Two have patrolled here before and know where the copper mining used to be," Martillo confirmed with a nod.

"Tell one of them to come with me and we'll take point," the Cuban volunteered. "After a while the other man and Connors can take over."

"I'm beginning to see why your team is regarded as being so special," Martillo remarked. "You all have unique skills, and each of you can supply specialized expertise to the unit. The way you handled the terrorists at the Embassy shows you function well as a team. Of course, this time the challenge will be considerably greater than what you faced on that occasion. I'm curious to see how you manage."

"I hope we don't disappoint you," McCarter said dryly.

"Just remember we all have to cover each other's ass when we find these bastards," James added. "You may not feel any sympathy for the TV reporter the terrorists kidnapped, Colonel, but he's not one of the enemy. He may be dumb as a house brick, and I'm sure you're pissed off that he intended to give medical supplies to the FMLN in exchange for a story. But Convy is still a victim of the terrorists. He doesn't deserve to die for what he did. That's true whether the terrorists kill him or your men 'accidentally' blow him away in a firefight.''

"That's not our method of operation," Martillo said, offended by the suggestion. He put a hand to his head, and his eyes squeezed shut briefly. "Isn't it enough that we're crushing the Communists? Now you expect us to worry about protecting some left-wing journalist pig who is trying to undermine your country as well as my own?"

"Colonel," Sergeant Lopez began as he approached his commander, "I need to talk to you privately for a moment."

"Si, por cierto," Martillo replied, and stroked his throbbing head as though he were in pain. "As for you *norteamericanos*, don't worry about that damn reporter. If the terrorists haven't killed him, my men won't unless the *imbécil* panics and runs into the line of fire when the shooting starts."

The colonel followed Lopez to the front of the army deuce and a half. Phoenix Force watched Martillo and his NCO head for the cab of the truck. Manning whistled softly.

"Do you think the good colonel has a problem dealing with criticism?" the Canadian whispered. "That migraine seemed to come out of nowhere."

"Usually a migraine is a vascular problem that can be triggered by a number of things. But for it to happen that fast and that severely when there was some tension and anger suggests it might be a genuine physical problem or a deep-seated psychological one with some strong psychosomatic side effects," Calvin James added. "In other words, it's possible the dude is literally not right in the head."

"Bloody wonderful," McCarter muttered. "And we have to work with this lunatic."

"We've been working with you for years," Manning told the Briton.

"Sod off," McCarter growled.

"Seriously," Encizo said grimly, "this could be a real problem. We already knew Martillo wasn't the sort we would have requested to work with, but if these headaches affect his ability to take action or make decisions..."

"I'm aware of the risks," Katz assured his partners. "The fact is we can't go back now. Try not to antagonize the colonel, and keep an eye on him. Sergeant Lopez seems to be used to Martillo's condition. Whatever else happens, I want that NCO to stay with Colonel Martillo until this operation is over."

"Has it been your experience that most lieutenant colonels are willing to listen to their first sergeants?" Manning remarked, and shook his head.

"Not really," Katz admitted. "But I'm willing to try anything that might help at this point."

15

The rain forest sprawled across rolling hills to the north of Cojutepeque. The abandoned copper mining operations had been conducted at two of the hills, but only one had an actual mine shaft built into the side of one of the hills. El Salvador had not had much luck with mining industries in the past, and these ventures were no exception to the rule.

Trees, shrubbery, bushes and tall grass grew along the hillside around the mouth of the mine shaft. The foliage helped conceal the improvised base within the mine and outside it. Lean-to shelters had been set up under nearby trees. Some men slept under the lean-tos, while others sat by the hill, drinking coffee and eating canned food and tortillas. A few cleaned and oiled their weapons.

Gary Manning peered through the Starlite scope mounted on his FAL rifle. He recognized the arms the men at the base carried. The guns were Soviet AK-47s, with banana-shaped magazines and wooden stocks. The Soviet military was still in the process of replacing the AK-47 with the AK-74 version of the famous Kalashnikov rifle, but thousands of the older models were still in circulation throughout the world. Manning had a lot of respect for the AK-47. It was a well-made rifle, and each magazine held thirty rounds of hefty 7.62×39 mm and fired at a rate of 600 rpm.

Four sentries patrolled the area, each armed with a Kalashnikov and a walkie-talkie radio. Manning observed the guards carefully. They seemed to pay more attention to the activities at the center of the camp than to the surrounding rain forest. A man dressed in camouflage trousers, a green undershirt and a beret sat behind a small field desk with a kerosene lamp and some papers before him. Another man knelt in front of the desk, his hands bound behind his back. Two burly guards stood next to the prisoner.

Manning watched the camp through the Starlite scope as he leaned against a coconut palm tree and peered through a gap in the wall of leaves and bushes. He estimated the camp was less than half a kilometer away. The Canadian warrior lowered the FAL rifle and withdrew to join his teammates. He quietly reported what he saw.

"The captive must be Convy unless they've got somebody we don't know about," Manning explained. "The guy at the desk doing the Che Guevara imitation is probably Hector."

"How many do you reckon there are?" McCarter inquired.

"About twenty are obvious and awake, if not totally alert," Manning answered. "There may be just as many asleep under the lean-to shelters or inside the mine shaft."

"That mine hasn't been used for some time and hasn't been maintained," Colonel Martillo stated. "I wouldn't think the ERP would use it except for an emergency shelter. Besides, the mining company discontinued digging after they determined the copper deposits were too small to be worth the effort. The shaft is only twenty-five or thirty meters deep."

"The timbers used for supports in the shaft probably wouldn't rot within less than two years unless there was an unusual degree of moisture," Manning replied. "The mine might not be that dangerous, and it's possible the terrorists don't appreciate the risk even if it is."

"Primary concern has to be dispatching the sentries and the other terrorists who are most likely to be an immediate threat," Katz stated. "Since Hector is close to the mine shaft, he'll probably try to reach it for cover and use Convy for a hostage. Make sure he doesn't succeed."

"He won't," McCarter promised.

"Now, we don't want a massacre," the Phoenix commander insisted. "If we can take prisoners, do so. This cell is part of a larger movement involving the ERP and the FMLN. They may be able to give information about those organizations and hopefully answer some of our questions about the attacks on U.S. citizens in El Salvador."

"I don't want any of my men to get killed because we're handling these scum with kid gloves," Martillo complained.

"No one is using kid gloves," Encizo assured him. "Some people aren't going to survive this encounter. We'll try to have all the casualties among the enemy."

"Divide the unit into two groups," Katz instructed. "We'll approach the camp from both sides with the men in a wide horseshoe formation. We'll flank the enemy and block any effort to escape. Also, radio Ferrero and tell him to order more troops to start moving into this area. If we have a prolonged firefight, we should be able to keep the enemy pinned down until reinforcements arrive."

"They probably won't arrive in time to save us," Martillo commented. "If we have a prolonged battle with superior forces, we'll probably be wiped out."

"Nobody lives forever, Colonel," Katz replied with a shrug.

A BORED SENTRY propped his AK-47 against a tree trunk and watched the prisoner stand by the desk to have his wrists untied. Hector handed the *yanqui* reporter a pen, and Convy began to write what the ERP leader ordered. The sentry grinned as he took a pouch of tobacco and some rolling papers from a pocket. It wasn't hard to break the *norteamericano*, he thought. Hector had said *los Estados Unidos* was filled with cowards and weaklings.

Something moved behind the guard. He heard an object brush against the grass and thud on the ground. The man turned, crushing the makings of a cigarette in his fist. He sighed with relief when he saw his rifle lying on the ground at the base of the tree. It must have slipped, the sentry thought as he bent over to retrieve his weapon.

He hadn't seen Rafael Encizo hidden behind the tree trunk. The Cuban's hand grabbed the sentry's lower face to cover his mouth and bash his skull against the side of the tree. Encizo's other hand held his Cold Steel Tanto in an icepick grip, the six-inch blade extending from the bottom of his fist. The Phoenix pro struck hard with the high-quality fighting knife. The reinforced, slanted steel point point punched behind the sentry's right ear.

A modern version of a samurai *tanto* knife, the Cold Steel blade pierced the mastoid bone and punctured the sentry's brain. Encizo held the guard as his body twitched. The convulsions were brief as the sentry died almost immediately from the lethal knife wound. Encizo hauled the corpse behind the tree and placed it out of view of the camp. The Cuban commando then low-crawled to the bush where the other members of the team waited, concealed among the foliage. One of Martillo's men kept Encizo's M-16 and Uzi while he carried out the stealthful removal of the sentry. Encizo was relieved to get his other weapons after he returned to the bush.

Another guard noticed that one of his fellow sentries had disappeared. He stepped closer to the area where he had last seen the man. The sentry frowned as he stared at a tree trunk. He was reasonably sure the other guard had been near the tree a moment ago. Perhaps he had simply stepped from view for a call of nature. The guard was uncertain if he should contact the others by radio, or if that would only embarrass his comrade.

The sentry's attention was still centered on the spot where the other man had vanished. His back was turned to Calvin James as the tall black man emerged from the bush. James's back was arched and his head low, and he walked silently on the balls of his feet. He had left his rifle and Uzi machine pistol with the other members of the strike team for the same reason Encizo had earlier. The more one carried, the greater the risk of making noise.

James held the Blackmoor dirk in one fist. He also used the icepick grip, with the sixteen-centimeter double-edged steel ready to strike with deadly force. James gripped the black handle and raised the AUS-8A stainless steel blade as he stepped behind the sentry and extended his empty hand.

He swiftly grabbed the man from the rear and clasped his free hand around his mouth. James simultaneously rammed a knee to his opponent's kidney to keep him off balance, then swung the Blackmoor with lethal accuracy. The point stabbed between the target's collarbone and shoulder. The force of the stroke drove the blade deep into the soft flesh and tissues between the bones and severed the subclavian artery.

James felt his opponent struggle as the sentry's rifle clattered on the ground. The Phoenix warrior pulled the guard backward and jerked at the knife handle. He didn't do that because he was sadistic or cruel—exactly the opposite. The sentry was already as good as dead, and James wanted him unconscious to allow him to die as swiftly and painlessly as possible.

The man's body went limp, and James dragged the corpse to the bush. He heard a voice cry out in alarm and realized someone had heard the sentry drop his rifle and had possibly seen James take out the man, as well. James yanked the dirk free from his slain opponent's flesh. He dumped the body on the ground and headed for the bush as fast as possible.

"Hell," he rasped under his breath as he dove to the ground and started to low-crawl toward the others. "It's comin' down now!"

A third guard had seen James take out his comrade and shouted an alarm as he raised his AK-47. He heard the sizzle of something slicing through air and suddenly felt a burning pain in the left side of his chest. A crossbow bolt had pierced his rib cage and punctured his heart. Cyanide was immediately released in his bloodstream from the split fiberglass shaft.

David McCarter watched his bolt strike the intended target and saw the sentry stiffen from the lethal dose of poison. The man died before he could fire his AK-47. He toppled lifeless to the ground, the unfired rifle still in his fists. The British commando worked the cocking lever to the Barnett crossbow and moved to a new position behind the tangled weeds, bushes and vines surrounding the enemy base.

The fourth sentry saw his comrade collapse and glimpsed the feathered shaft of the bolt in the man's chest. He glanced about for any sign of the enemy, but saw nothing. Others within the camp were already alarmed by the warning shout uttered by the guard who now lay dead with a crossbow quarrel in his heart. The last sentry swung his AK-47 toward the bush, unaware he had already been marked for death.

Gary Manning was positioned on the hillside above the camp. He peered down at the remaining sentry through the Starlite scope of his FAL assault rifle. The cross hairs found the man's head. Manning squeezed the trigger. The silencer attached to the FAL coughed harshly, and a 7.62 mm slug crashed into the guard's skull. The bullet hit just above the ear, near the temple and split bone to drill into his brain. The Canadian marksman saw his opponent fall, confident the man was dead.

Manning climbed higher on the hillside as the ERP rebels began to react to the unexpected threat that had descended on them. The Canadian commando had noticed a cluster of weeds around a hole in the hill. He moved to the position and examined the gap. Manning had hoped it would lead down into the mine shaft below, and he discovered that it was indeed an air shaft dug when the mining operation had been in use.

Finding it was a stroke of luck and offered to make Manning's task easier. He crouched by the hole and slipped off his backpack. The Phoenix commando removed a packet of C-4 and took a special blasting cap and detonator from his pockets. He fitted them into the white doughlike plastic explosives and set the detonator timer. Manning slid the packet into the hole and moved away from the site to the cover of a cluster of trees.

Two terrorists threw down their coffee cups and cigarettes to grab their weapons. Another ERP flunky, who had just finished assembling his rifle after cleaning it, shoved a magazine into the well and pulled back the operating handle to chamber the first round. One of the men guarding Convy swung his weapon toward the foliage, while the other pointed the barrel of a Soviet-made PPSh-41 submachine gun at Convy's head.

Yakov Katzenelenbogen aimed his Uzi machine pistol at the gunmen who had pointed their weapons in the direction of the assault unit. The Israeli expertly triggered a 3-round burst into the closest opponent and punched the 9 mm parabellum slugs through the center of the gunman's chest. The first opponent tumbled to the ground as Katz fired another trio of Uzi projectiles into the second terrorist. Two 124-grain Federal Match-Nine slugs slammed into the ERP triggerman's sternum and throat, and the third parabellum finished him off.

The terrorist who had just readied his AK-47 swung the weapon at the muzzle-flash of Katz's Uzi. Colonel Martillo aimed his M-16 and fired before the ERP man could trigger his weapon. The terrorist's head recoiled from the impact of the 5.56 mm slugs that smashed through his face. The Kalashnikov rifle hurtled from the man's fingers as his body convulsed, then his body fell beside a trio of other gunmen who hastily assumed a prone position.

Rafael Encizo trained his M-16 on the guard who was threatening to shoot Convy. The Cuban raised the barrel and triggered a 3-round burst. The guard's skull burst open in a bloodied shower, and Convy cried out in terror and dropped to the ground. His actions saved his life, as a harmless salvo flew above the reporter's head.

"*¡Mierda!*" Hector exclaimed as he drew a .45-caliber Obregon pistol from his belt and swung his arm across the desktop to aim it at Convy's prone form.

David McCarter was also watching the men by the field desk. He had prepared to deal with Hector before the shooting erupted. The Briton held the Barnett Commando crossbow, the skeletal buttstock braced against his shoulder as he looked through the scope and chose his target with as much care as the need for rapid action allowed.

McCarter squeezed the trigger. The bolt hissed from the Barnett, and the bowstring hummed near his ear. Hector shrieked as the steel tip of the projectile slammed into his forearm. The bolt punctured flesh and muscle and pierced bone. Hector's hand popped open, and the Mexican-made Obregon autoloader hopped out of his fingers. The terrorist leader stared at the crossbow bolt lodged in his arm. The bloodied tip jutted from one side of his forearm, and the green-feathered butt of the quarrel extended from the other side.

"*¡Qué la chigada!*" Hector cried, and clutched his wounded arm.

The roar of an explosion came from within the mine shaft. Clouds of rock dust, chunks of stone and shards of timber spewed from the mouth of the mine. The ERP followers cried out in terror as the unexpected blast further confused and frightened the terrorist forces. Hector and the surviving guard were thrown to the ground by the explosion. Others threw themselves flat on the ground and covered their heads for protection against the shrapnel.

Phoenix Force and Martillo's troops fired on the ERP camp. Terrorists rolled from their lean-to shelters and grabbed rifles, only to be riddled with bullets before they could use the weapons. A Salvadoran soldier broke cover to charge forward and fire on the enemy. A terrorist gunman staggered forward, dropped to one knee and pointed the

AK-47 at the trooper. The soldier's rifle fire tore up a trio of dirt geysers next to the terrorist but failed to strike the opponent. The enemy returned fire and hit the soldier in the stomach with at least one round.

The soldier screamed and tumbled to the ground. His M-16 fell beside him as he wrapped his arms around his bullet-torn abdomen. The terrorist prepared to finish off the wounded man with another burst of AK-47 lead. Calvin James triggered his M-16 and nailed the enemy gunman with a trio of 5.56 mm slugs in the upper torso. The terrorist fell backward, and his rifle snarled a wild salvo in the direction of his comrades.

"Somebody cover me!" James exclaimed, and charged from the bush to run toward the fallen soldier.

He held the M-16 by the pistol grip in one fist and fired it like an enormous handgun as he dashed to the wounded man. James didn't attempt to hit any of the terrorists, but simply fired the weapon to discourage the enemy and keep them at bay for a moment. The black badass reached down and grabbed the injured trooper with his free hand. He gripped the back of the guy's collar and dragged him to the shelter of the nearest tree trunk, still awkwardly firing at the enemy position.

"You're not making our job any easier," James growled as he hauled the wounded man to the relative safety of the tree.

GARY MANNING HAD FIRED at the enemy from his vantage point on the hillside. He caught sight of a flash of movement among the trees along the hill. Three ERP hitmen advanced toward the Canadian's position. They tried to make the most of the surrounding foliage to conceal their movements, but Manning was adept at spotting quarry among camouflage. He had first acquired the ability as a hunter in the Canadian woods and later perfected his skills at such specialized detection in Vietnam and on previous missions with Phoenix Force.

The commando moved to the largest available tree trunk for cover and waited for the enemy to climb higher and closer. The most ambitious of the ERP gunmen pushed through a cluster of ferns and scanned the area for Manning. He found the Canadian, but not on the terms he had intended. Manning thrust his FAL rifle around the trunk of the tree and opened fire. The terrorist cried out and tumbled lifelessly down the face of the hill.

The surviving ERP pair responded with twin streams of AK-47 projectiles. Bullets spewed bark into the air near Manning. He removed a concussion grenade from his belt and pulled the pin. Manning held it for one and a half seconds before he released the grenade and allowed it to roll downhill. The Canadian kept his back to the tree trunk and held the FAL in one fist while he gripped the Uzi machine pistol in the other.

The grenade exploded. Manning heard the howls of his opponents when the concussion blast tore into their cover. Eardrums burst and blood flowed from their nostrils as they were thrown several feet by the explosion. The pair landed hard, weapons still clutched in their fists.

Manning swung around the tree trunk and opened fire with his weapons. The FAL and Uzi spit full-auto fury. Bullets ripped into the stunned terrorists and sent their bloodied corpses rolling down the hillside. Manning grunted with grim satisfaction and turned his attention to the remaining opponents at the enemy base.

The terrorists were virtually defeated. Most were dead or wounded. A pair of fanatics, driven beyond reason by anger, frustration and fear, charged the assault force's position with empty AK-47 rifles held as clubs. It was a suicide attack, since their opponents were clearly well armed with plenty of firepower. Other more rational yet still-determined terrorists tried to stay low and shoot at their elusive adversaries.

"Crazy bastards," McCarter muttered as two of the frenzied men charged straight for his position.

A soldier prepared to fire point-blank on the pair, his shotgun aimed at chest level. McCarter shouted to the trooper to hold his fire and stepped forward to meet the attackers, Uzi machine pistol held low. The pair crashed through the wall of foliage and slashed at the vines and low branches with the buttstocks of their AK-47s.

"Now that's no way to treat a firearm," McCarter muttered with disgust. "What do you think you have there, mate? A bleedin' ax?"

The first opponent spotted McCarter and his eyes swelled with lunatic rage. As the man attacked, aiming the buttstock at McCarter's head, the Phoenix warrior triggered the Uzi. A short burst of 9 mm rounds slashed across the terrorist's legs. The man screamed as the tibia and fibula bones splintered in both shins. His legs were chopped out from under him, and he sprawled facefirst to the ground. The terrorist slid two meters and slammed into the base of a tree. Bone crunched on impact as the terrorist's shoulder was dislocated, and the man uttered a moan and passed out from the pain and shock.

The second terrorist suddenly hurled his AK-47 at McCarter. The tactic caught the British warrior off guard because it was generally a foolish move to throw one's only weapon at an opponent. The rifle struck McCarter across the forearms and knocked the Uzi from his grasp. The half-berserk opponent snarled and charged the Briton with both arms extended, his hands aimed at the Phoenix warrior's throat.

McCarter met the charge and thrust his fists upward to drive his forearms into the wrists of his attacker. The twin blows knocked the terrorist's hands away from McCarter's throat and forced the man's arms apart. The Briton's right hand snaked out and clasped his opponent at the back of the head as his left hand grabbed his shirtfront.

The Phoenix pro turned sharply and pulled the terrorist forward to haul the opponent over his hip. The judo throw hurled the fanatic to the ground. He rolled with the impact and started to rise, but McCarter stepped forward and kicked him in the ribs. The terrorist grunted but still rose and managed to swing a wild roundhouse at the Briton.

McCarter easily dodged the uncoordinated move and swooped a sly left hook to his opponent's skull. The man staggered backward and swayed unsteadily on legs that were about to buckle. McCarter slashed a cross-body karate stroke and chopped the side of his hand under the guy's heart.

The blow lifted the terrorist off his feet and dropped him on his back in a dazed lump. McCarter nearly leaped forward to finish off his opponent with a commando stomp. He resisted the impulse, aware that his reflexes and training could get the better of him. The terrorist was already beaten, and stomping both heels into the fallen man's chest would probably kill him. McCarter instead reached for a set of plastic riot cuffs to bind the unconscious opponent's wrists.

ENCIZO LOBBED a stun grenade among the terrorist gunmen who were attempting to hold out against the assault force by staying low and firing from a prone position. The explosion sent one opponent two meters in the air to crash-land with a machete in one hand and a rifle in the other. Dazed and bloodied, the man lay motionless on his back. The other enemy gunmen thrashed on the ground, their hands clasped to their ruptured ears, blood streaming from mouths and nostrils.

Katz, Encizo, Martillo and Sergeant Lopez approached the vanquished ERP camp. Colonel Martillo paused by the stunned terrorist and kicked the AK-47 beyond the man's reach in case he started to regain consciousness. The terrorist suddenly sprang up from the ground and slashed the machete at the colonel. The heavy blade clashed against the barrel of Martillo's M-16 and struck the rifle from the officer's hands.

"*¡Cristo!*" Martillo exclaimed as he jumped away from the flashing machete.

The terrorist raised the big jungle knife in both hands and prepared to deliver a deadly overhead stroke. Martillo moved in and grabbed his opponent's forearms to hold the machete at bay. The colonel whipped a knee between the other man's legs and twisted the terrorist's arms, making the knife man let out a high-pitched whimper and leaving him unable to resist Martillo's effort to wrench the machete from his grasp.

The big knife fell to the ground near Martillo's feet. The colonel swiftly rammed another knee into his opponent's abdomen. The terrorist doubled up with a violent cough, and opened his mouth to vomit. Martillo suddenly drew the hammer from his belt and raised it high. His other hand also grasped the handle, and Martillo swung the tool in a vicious overhead stroke. The steel head of the hammer smashed into the base of the terrorist's skull. Bone cracked and the man collapsed, his skull fractured and spinal column broken above the nape of his neck.

Encizo saw the colonel take out his opponent and knew that Martillo did not need any help. The Cuban commando had previously guessed Colonel Hammer was a very dangerous individual, and the Salvadoran officer's ability in combat had confirmed his suspicions.

Suddenly Martillo glanced at Encizo and hurled his hammer at him. Encizo hissed through clenched teeth, surprised by the colonel's actions. The Phoenix commando ducked low and pointed his M-16 at Martillo. The sound of a hard object striking flesh and bone, followed by a loud groan, drew Encizo's attention to a figure, who it appeared, had been standing behind him, ready to attack.

He turned to see a terrorist weaving in a drunken manner as he stumbled about on unsteady legs. Blood poured down the man's face from his forehead. The bone had been bashed in by Martillo's hammer, which lay at the terrorist's feet. The man's PPSh-41 submachine gun was still clasped in his fists. Encizo swung his rifle at the opponent and fired a 3-round burst through his heart, bringing him down for keeps.

Rafael Encizo returned his attention to Martillo. The colonel smiled at him, and the Phoenix warrior nodded his thanks to the officer. Martillo returned the gesture and drew his .45 autoloader as he advanced toward the enemy camp.

Although his right arm had been crippled by the crossbow bolt, Hector crawled toward his fallen pistol and reached for the gun with his left hand. Bullets ripped into the ground near his fingers and kicked clods of dirt into the terrorist commander's face. He gasped with surprise and fear as he drew back his hand and glanced up at the man who stood in front of him with an Uzi machine pistol braced across an artificial arm.

"Try that again and I'll shoot some fingers off, as well," Yakov Katzenelenbogen warned.

Hector glared at Katz, but he raised his hands in surrender and assumed a kneeling position. Larry Convy still lay on his stomach, both arms wrapped around his head, afraid to look at the carnage surrounding him. The reporter whimpered with fear as Sergeant Lopez knelt beside him and tried to assure Convy he was safe.

Katz kept his attention fixed on Hector as the ERP boss slowly got to his feet. The Israeli noticed a slight gleam in Hector's eye and a mere hint of a smirk on the terrorist's lips. He seemed too cocky for a man who had just seen his forces defeated in a one-sided battle. Katz suspected Hector still had one final trick up his sleeve.

The terrorist's left hand suddenly swooped to a Soviet-made F-1 grenade on his belt. Hector was grinning with triumph as he reached for the pin. If he had to die, Hector intended to take one or two opponents with him.

Katz could have shot Hector, but he wanted the ERP leader alive. The Phoenix veteran lunged forward and thrust his prosthesis at Hector's left arm. The terrorist screamed as the steel hooks clamped around his wrist in a deadly vise and prevented him from reaching the grenade. Katz increased pressure with the metal talons and twisted hard. Bone snapped in Hector's wrist, and his fingers convulsed in a spasm of pain.

The Phoenix commander slammed the frame of his Uzi down on Hector's other arm. The right limb was already broken and severely injured by the crossbow missile still lodged in the forearm. Hector uttered a feeble sound of pain as his eyes rolled up. His knees buckled, and he slumped to the ground in a senseless heap.

"Now, behave yourself," Katz remarked dryly.

16

The Salvadoran troops that had been called in for backup arrived at the site. Phoenix Force, Colonel Martillo and his men had rounded up the surviving members of the ERP camp. The terrorists were already bound, disarmed and frisked by the time reinforcements arrived. Calvin James was busy treating the wounded. The Phoenix medic did as much as possible with the limited supplies from his kit and the unfavorable conditions. He dealt with the injured terrorists as well as the wounded soldiers.

Larry Convy was emotionally shaken by the ordeal but, aside from a few bruises, unharmed. Phoenix Force avoided contact with the reporter as much as possible. They didn't want Convy to be able to make a detailed description when he finally got around to writing about his brush with death.

The new arrivals helped march the terrorist prisoners through the rain forest to the trucks and jeeps where yet more soldiers waited. Convy was hustled into a jeep by Captain Ortiz, who had commanded part of the reinforcements. Ortiz spoke briefly with Martillo, nodded and climbed into his jeep, next to Convy. Martillo watched the vehicle pull onto the road and roll from view before he turned and headed for the deuce and a half truck. Rafael Encizo waited for the colonel by the rear of the rig.

"I ordered Ortiz to escort the reporter because he speaks English and he knows better than to answer any questions the Anglo might ask," Martillo explained. "If that's what concerns you, there's no need to worry. You and your friends have a low opinion of the captain, but Ortiz is a very intelligent and competent officer.''

"That's not what I wanted to talk to you about," Encizo said with a sigh. What he had to say next would not be easy. "You saved my life in the gun battle. Thank you, Colonel."

"De nada," Martillo replied with a smile. "For a moment, you thought I threw my hammer at you. Correct?''

"It startled me," Encizo admitted. "You're very good with that hammer, Colonel."

"I used a hammer long before I used a gun, Señor Cassias," Martillo explained. "My family name came from the trade practiced by my ancestors. They were carpenters for centuries, and my father was a carpenter before he became a businessman. He participated in trade agreements and sales with merchants in Central and South America as well as the island nations in the Caribbean and the West Indies. He still taught me the fundamentals of carpentry when I was a boy. He didn't know I'd become a soldier. If things had been different, perhaps I wouldn't be in the military today."

"I suppose we'd all be doing something else if things had been different," the Phoenix commando replied. He hoped this would end the conversation so he could join his teammates and return to San Salvador.

"My father handled a large amount of trade between his company in El Salvador and certain businesses in Cuba when Batista was in control of the country," Martillo continued. "Cuba was a thriving, economically prosperous and happy nation under Batista. True, it had casinos and prostitution, but the people were free and life was good."

Encizo did not comment. He recalled Batista's regime as oppressive and corrupt. Cuba was a police state under Batista, and dissenters were seized at night and later found murdered, the corpses discarded in gutters outside Havana and Santa Clara. Maybe Martillo's father thought Cuba was a West Indies version of Las Vegas or Disneyland, but Encizo remembered his homeland quite differently under Batista's rule.

"Then Castro and the Communists took over," Martillo said grimly. "My father had the misfortune of being in Cuba for a business deal on New Year's Day in 1959 when Batista was forced to flee the country. The Communists seized businesses and arrested the owners or murdered them on the spot. They mistook my father for a Cuban capitalist and killed him that afternoon on the first day of 1959."

"I didn't know that, Colonel," Encizo said. "You must have been very young when that happened. It's very hard for a boy to grow up without his father."

"I'm sure you understand," Martillo said as he glanced down at the ground. "Your Spanish still retains a slight Cuban accent, and I suspect you're originally from Cuba, but you've picked up some colloquialisms from the Spanish-speaking people of other countries."

"You have a keen ear, Colonel," Encizo informed him.

"So I am right," Martillo said with a nod. "That's why I bored you with my story about my father. I assume you, too, lost family when Castro took power."

"I did," Encizo confirmed. "It was a long time ago, but I'll always remember it. My family wasn't political, but they were caught in the middle of the revolution and suffered because they were taken to be supporters of Batista."

"You must hate the Communists as much as I do," Martillo declared. "It seems to me you must also understand why I will do anything to keep those Marxist butchers from taking control of my country. Fortunately we've dealt with the ERP cell responsible for the terrorism against the *norteamericanos*. Now the President of the United States and the Congress will increase aid to El Salvador to help us protect our country and protect citizens from *los Estados Unidos* in the future.

"That's not up to me, Colonel," Encizo answered. "Washington makes decisions without much regard to what somebody like me thinks."

"But your team will give a detailed report to the President?" Martillo asked with a frown. "You will advise him that we need more assistance here."

"We don't report directly to the President," the Cuban explained. "We've got a chain of command just like you do. Our superiors will be fully informed about the outcome of our mission, but our little organization doesn't have anything to do with policy-making or any other decisions that come out of the White House."

"So, your President is willing to give millions of dollars of aid to a Communist country like Poland, but he's unwilling to help El Salvador in our fight against Communist domination," the colonel said with disgust. He placed a hand to his head as he spoke. "Excuse me. I should see to my men now."

Martillo turned and walked to a formation of soldiers with Sergeant Lopez in command. The colonel rubbed the back of his skull, and his stride was slightly unsteady as he approached the men. Encizo grunted and sighed. Martillo had struck a nerve with the conversation about Castro and the Communist takeover in Cuba, yet Encizo had even greater doubts whether Colonel Hammer was fit to command his troops.

The Cuban climbed into the back of the truck. Katz, McCarter and Manning were already inside the rig. James had already left with another vehicle loaded with injured personnel. Encizo sat beside McCarter and placed his M-16 on the floorboards.

"Had a nice chat with the colonel?" the Briton inquired.

"Yeah," Encizo replied. "He told me the story of his life. What I wonder about is how many chapters he skipped over and why."

"CONGRATULATIONS," Ron Sommers said with a broad grin as he placed two bottles of champagne into a large bucket of ice in the center of the conference table. "Mission accomplished."

Phoenix Force had returned to the covert safehouse at the textile mill in San Salvador. Major Ferrero had already radioed a brief report to confirm the ERP terrorist base had been put out of action, Convy safely rescued and Hector taken captive. Sommers was ready to celebrate when the commando team arrived.

"That might be premature," Katz warned as he took a seat at the table. "We're not so certain our mission is finished here."

"*¡Madre de Dios!*" Ferrero exclaimed, and rolled his eyes toward the ceiling. "Hector and his band are notorious in the north. We have been hunting them for more than a year. They are fanatic Communists and they killed one *norteamericano* newsman and kidnapped the other. There is no doubt about it. It is clear they are the terrorists responsible for the attacks on the United States Embassy personnel, and now the U.S. media personnel, as well."

"They certainly were responsible for the terrorist attack at Cojutepeque," Katz agreed. He fired up a Camel and took a deep draw on the cigarette before he continued. "The fact Convy was held captive there is positive proof of that. Hector was trying to get the reporter to write a ransom note. The terrorists intended to blackmail the television network for a million dollars to return Convy or they'd murder him."

"They sure as hell don't sound too innocent to me," Sommers commented.

"Nobody said they were innocent," Gary Manning assured him. "Hector and his men are indeed terrorists, but we're not convinced they were responsible for the earlier incidents involving U.S. Embassy personnel. There was no attempt to kidnap anyone on the previous occasions. No demands for ransom money or payoffs to discontinue attacks on the Embassy or U.S. citizens."

"So, they decided to make some money with their terrorist activities," the CIA agent suggested. "You know how Communists are. They hate capitalists, but they love capital—especially when it helps pay for their operations against us."

"How about the fact they were all armed with Communist Bloc weapons?" David McCarter inquired. "Not a single American-made firearm or grenade among Hector's group. A few of their handguns were made in Mexico or Brazil, but none were made in the U.S.A. The blokes responsible for the previous incidents used M-16 rifles and MAC-10 Ingrams."

"Maybe they only had a few American weapons and they lost those after you guys took out those bastards at the Embassy last night," Sommers answered. "For Christ's sake! Don't you want this mess to be over?"

"Of course we do," Encizo assured him, "but we want to make sure it really is before we head home and find out the terrorist attacks against U.S. personnel have started all over again."

"Well, I can interrogate some of the terrorists with scopolamine injections," Calvin James commented. "A few of them are too badly injured, though. Scopolamine is the most reliable truth serum, but it's also dangerous. Killing a man in combat is one thing, but I won't risk killing a person because his heart can't handle the effects of scopolamine during interrogation."

"I fail to see the difference," Ferrero remarked.

"Maybe I don't have malpractice insurance," James said with disgust. "If you don't see the difference, there's no way I can explain it so you'd understand, Major."

"Hector is still in good enough physical condition to survive a dose of scopolamine," McCarter stated. "I managed to just nail him in the arm with my trusty crossbow. Didn't use a cyanide bolt, of course."

"Mr. Goodman broke the bastard's wrist, too," James reminded the Briton, "but that's not what worries me. I'd have to run a physical on the dude. Check his heart, blood pressure and all that stuff. As long as he isn't doped up with painkillers, Hector ought to be a good subject if he doesn't have any unforeseen health problems. He'd sure be the most important ERP man to question about the terrorist activities in San Salvador."

"I'll contact Martillo and tell him you want to interrogate Hector and perhaps some of the other terrorists," Ferrero volunteered.

"Martillo has them?" Katz asked with a frown. "I had hoped your people were handling this, Major."

"Colonel Martillo does outrank me," Ferrero answered. "I couldn't demand that he allow military Intelligence to take the prisoners. Besides, his military connections include immediate access to bases with prison facilities."

"We'd better get 'em before Martillo and Ortiz set up their torture chambers," James warned.

"I'll contact him now," Ferrero promised, and headed for the door.

The major clearly wanted to avoid another violent confrontation between Phoenix Force and Martillo's staff. He left the conference room to radio Colonel Hammer. Sommers decided to open a bottle of champagne even though the mysterious five-man army was unconvinced the mission was complete.

"I don't know what the hell I'm supposed to tell the ambassador," the CIA man muttered as he peeled the foil from the mouth of the bottle. "My control officer has already been crying for a progress report. He hasn't been very happy about how you guys have handled this mission so far."

"What's his problem?" McCarter asked in a surly tone.

"He believes in keeping a low profile and trying to cooperate with the Salvadoran authorities to get results," Sommers replied. "Frankly I agree with him. That gunfight in the street by the Embassy received unwanted media attention, and you've managed to make some enemies among very influential Salvadoran military and civilians."

"In case you don't remember, you were with us in the bus when the terrorists attacked us in front of the Embassy," Manning commented. "Would you rather we hadn't stopped them from shooting the hell out of the vehicle and setting it on fire with a Molotov cocktail?''

"I didn't say that," Sommers insisted as he loosened the wire to the champagne cork. "It's just the incident was a bit public."

"You figure the terrorists would have agreed to not try to kill us until we could all move somewhere private to shoot it out?" James inquired. "Hey, if these guys are gonna be that considerate, maybe we can try to get them to agree to a nonviolent option. You ever try to have a nice polite debate with a fanatic who is frothing at the mouth and is armed to the teeth with automatic weapons and explosives? These are people who use violence not as a last resort, but as their *only* resort, man."

"In all fairness to your control officer," Katz began, making an attempt to keep tempers from flaring, "I understand his position. He's primarily concerned with maintaining security, gathering Intelligence and keeping reasonably good working relations with the Intel personnel in Central America. However, sometimes men who are sitting at desks in offices far from the battlefields can be very unrealistic about how operatives in the trenches should do their job."

"Damn right," McCarter agreed. "As for this bloke whining about the fact we haven't gotten along with some of the local high-mucky-mucks—who gives a shit? They can complain all they like. The President of the United States and the president of El Salvador will tell them to shut up. How much trouble will those bastards cause then?"

"And the reason we're not on good terms with them is because they were involved in the use of torture," Encizo added. "Now, I don't imagine they'll be stupid enough to admit that, but the men in high offices will know the truth. I doubt Veaga, Martillo or Ortiz will find much sympathy for using such methods."

Sommers worked the cork from the bottle. It shot out with a loud pop. The cork rocketed into the ceiling and punched a chunk of plaster from the surface. The CIA man gasped as he stared at the hole. Champagne gushed from the bottle in his fists and splashed on the floor by his feet. The cork ricocheted from the ceiling and bounced off a wall. Katz snatched it from the air with his hand.

"Perhaps you weren't aware that there is a lot of pressure there, and a champagne cork can travel more than thirty miles per hour," the Israeli remarked as he tossed the cork on the table. "That's a projectile capable of causing some damage. More than one person has lost an eye that way. In the future, cover the cork with a towel or napkin after you remove the wire and ease it from the bottle in a slightly tilted position. It should come out with a soft pop instead of a bang."

"Why didn't you tell me before I opened it?" Sommers asked as he looked down at the stains on his trousers.

"You didn't have the bottle pointed at any of us, so we weren't in any danger," Katz replied with a shrug. "We were involved in a serious discussion, and I thought you'd know better than to open the bottle incorrectly."

"Thanks," Sommers muttered with disgust. He reached for some plastic wine glasses on the table. "Anybody want a drink?"

"I still have work to do," James replied. "I'd better get my little bag of tricks and get ready to go interrogate the terrorists."

"You won't have to go anywhere tonight," Major Ferrero announced as he stepped back into the conference room. His grim expression warned that he wasn't the bearer of good news. "You won't be able to question Hector or the other survivors from your raid on the ERP base."

"Martillo doesn't want us to question them?" Manning asked and grunted sourly. "If that guy thinks he has jurisdiction over us in this operation, we'll show him he's wrong...."

"That's not the problem," Ferrero replied. "Martillo tells me the terrorists tried to escape on their way to the military prison. Hector and the others managed to seize some weapons from their guards, so Martillo's men were forced to shoot them. This time there were no survivors. Hector and his followers are all dead.''

James groaned. "Isn't that one hell of a coincidence? Did he happen to mention how Hector managed to grab a weapon? That's a pretty good trick, since his right arm and left wrist were broken and I gave him a shot of morphine to deaden the pain. Several of the other prisoners were in worse shape than Hector. I'd like to know how men in that kind of physical condition broke free of their riot cuffs and disarmed their guards to make a break for freedom.''

"I'm just repeating what the colonel told me," Ferrero stated. "I didn't say I believed it any more than you do."

"Unfortunately I think we can believe one thing," Katz remarked. "Hector and the others are certainly dead. Martillo may have destroyed any hope we had of learning whether or not the ERP cell was responsible for the attacks on the Embassy personnel.''

"Well, they probably were," Sommers said lamely.

"That's great," Manning replied. "If they weren't, it means the terrorists we've been looking for are still out there somewhere, and I wouldn't count on them deciding it's time to retire.''

17

At three o'clock in the morning, Rafael Encizo and David McCarter entered the hotel lobby. The other members of Phoenix Force were still involved in work connected with the raid on the terrorists. James was busy supervising autopsies while Manning was examining weapons and other gear used by the ERP group. Katz had the unenviable task of contacting Hal Brognola at Stony Man headquarters via a special satellite radio connection. The President of the United States was no doubt getting anxious about how the mission was progressing and probably wanted some information from Brognola.

Unfortunately Katz had little definite news for the Stony Man boss. Phoenix Force was faced with an unusual and frustrating situation. They weren't sure whether or not their mission was finished. The fact they had taken out more than two score of terrorists and rescued a U.S. citizen held hostage by the ERP wasn't proof of success. Brognola wouldn't be very happy when he learned that he'd have to inform the President that the success of the mission was only tentative.

There was no need for McCarter and Encizo to go without sleep, so they changed clothes at the safehouse and returned to the hotel, dressed in civilian garb and carrying innocent-looking attaché cases that contained Uzi machine pistols. Encizo also had to return to the hotel to attempt to contact Maria Santo before she left the building. Although McCarter didn't mention his concerns about Maria's roll of film, Encizo realized the Briton had accompanied him to the hotel instead of staying with the others, to make certain he didn't forget about this responsibility.

Katz had subtly reminded the Cuban to "talk to Miss Santo" before he and McCarter left the safehouse. The Israeli also remarked that he hoped she wouldn't try to leave San Salvador before Encizo had a chance to meet with her. Encizo understood what that meant. Katz had already made arrangements with Ferrero and Sommers to detain Maria if she tried to leave the city by any means. If she went to the airport or train station, she would be arrested. If she tried to hire a driver or rent a car, the Salvadoran Intelligence service and the CIA would find out. Even if she went to the Mexican embassy, she would probably be held in detention until the CIA could question her and no doubt confiscate her camera and film.

Encizo didn't like these tactics, but he understood why they were necessary. Maria's film presented a clear and serious danger for Phoenix Force. He was also offended that Katz had done this behind his back. However, he couldn't be angry with the Phoenix commander. Katz was doing the right thing, and he had lost some trust in his Cuban teammate. In all fairness, Encizo could not blame Katz for that. His defense of Maria and his willingness to protect her film even at the risk to himself and his team had caused Katz to doubt him. Encizo wasn't able to argue with that, although it upset him that his brothers in battle were losing faith in him. It was imperative that he got those damn photographs and negatives to regain the lost trust.

"Señor Cassias," the desk clerk called out to Encizo when he saw the Phoenix pair in the lobby. "I am glad you have returned. Señorita Santo has been calling my desk all night to ask if you have entered the hotel."

"Did she say what she wanted?" Encizo asked.

"No, *señor*," the clerk answered, "but it seemed quite urgent. Is there some important business you have with her perhaps? Not that this is any of my business...."

"No, it isn't," the Cuban replied as he took out his wallet and extracted fifty colones. He placed the money on the desk. "Will this help you forget about the messages she's left with you?"

"What messages, *señor*?" the desk clerk asked with mock innocence as he scooped up the cash.

"Gracias," Encizo said with a nod.

He and McCarter headed for the elevator. The Briton was less than fluent in Spanish, but he understood the language well enough to know what Encizo and the clerk had discussed.

"I hope this means your lady has those photos and she's going to keep her word," McCarter commented as they stepped into the elevator.

"Yeah," Encizo agreed. "Will you let me handle this alone, David? I know you're worried about this business, but I'd like to do this on my own."

McCarter thought for a moment. "If she doesn't hand over the photos and negatives this time," McCarter began, "we'll have to take them, anyway. Cal already talked to you about this."

"I remember," Encizo assured him. "And if she doesn't do it voluntarily, I'll get them from her myself. Even if I have to use force to do it. Fair enough?"

"There isn't much that's fair about any of this," McCarter said, shrugging. "I've known you for some time, mate. I figure you'll do what you can and, if that doesn't work, you'll do what you have to."

"That's about what it gets down to," the Cuban agreed.

ENCIZO KNOCKED on Maria's door. She immediately opened it and gestured for the Cuban to hurry into her room. Once inside, he closed the door and looked at her. Maria seemed to be gripped by conflicting emotions, excited and enthusiastic, yet somewhat nervous and a little afraid.

"I have been waiting for you all night," she complained as she paced around the throw rug in the center of the room.

"I was afraid you may have gotten killed. Especially if you were off somewhere with Colonel Martillo and his thugs."

"I'm here now," Encizo replied. "You have the photographs?"

"They're in the darkroom," Maria assured him with a smile. "That is to say, the bathroom. I developed the roll of film earlier tonight and left the pictures and negatives in there so you can see for yourself I haven't made any second copies of the photos. They should be dry now, and you can examine everything. There's one picture in particular you need to see, Rafael."

"Please show me," he urged.

Maria escorted the Cuban into the improvised darkroom. She made certain all the photographs were fully developed and dried before she switched on the light. Photos and negatives hung from wires strung across the shower stall to a peg near the door. Encizo looked at the closest photos. The terrorist gunmen at the Embassy were clearly displayed in the pictures, with the burning automobile and crippled bus in the background. Two Phoenix Force members stood with their backs to the camera. The shadows were too dense to even make out what color their hair was, but the orange flame of muzzle fire streaked from their weapons.

"These are good, Maria," Encizo told her with sincere admiration. "Very dramatic photos, and they don't put my people at any risk."

"I know," she said with delight. "Three other photos are a different matter, though. You'll want to take these."

She plucked three pictures from the collection and handed them to Encizo. He nodded with agreement when he saw his own face stare back from one photo. Another clearly showed Manning's features, and the third revealed Katz's prosthesis and the right side of his face. Encizo briefly checked the remaining photos. None of them showed any members of Phoenix Force clearly enough to offer any type of identification. "You can keep the rest, Maria," he informed her, "but I need the negatives."

"Take a look at them and you'll see which negatives match those photos," Maria said. "If you'll use a pair of scissors to cut out the ones that would endanger your group, then I can keep the rest. Agreed?"

"Absolutely," Encizo assured her. "I can't tell you how much I appreciate this cooperation, Maria. I'm also sorry this has caused you problems—"

"No." Maria cut him off. "I apologize to you for thinking only of my story and being difficult with you before. With your life and your friends' lives at stake, I should have been more understanding."

"What matters is we can agree on a compromise that protects my people and still allows you to have some excellent photos for your newspaper," he stated. "I'm glad we could work this out."

"Your friends were getting worried?" Maria guessed. "They put pressure on you to get the film, didn't they?"

"And they were right to feel that way," Encizo replied. "I just hoped that my own faith in you would prove to be valid. I'm glad to see you didn't disappoint me."

"Faith can be hard to keep," Maria said with a nod. She turned her attention to the other photographs while Encizo examined the negatives. "Now, I want you to take a close look at another picture here."

The Cuban snipped out the dangerous segments from the negatives and slipped them into a pocket. He would later show them to McCarter and destroy them in front of the Briton. After they told Katz the film was no longer a risk, the Israeli would have Ferrero and Sommers call off the watchdogs so Maria would be free to come and go as she pleased...or at least as much as anyone could in El Salvador.

"Get the magnifying glass, Rafael," Maria urged as she found the photo that seemed so important. "I can blow up this picture for more details, but for now you'll need the glass."

Encizo examined the photograph. Maria had snapped a shot of the terrorist gunmen at the corner of the U.S. Embassy. Light streaked from their MAC-10 Ingrams as they squatted low along the iron-framed fence. It was a good photo, but Encizo didn't see anything special about it until he passed the magnifying glass over the building behind the gunmen.

A man stood at a window overlooking the scene. He held a pair of binoculars in one hand and a walkie-talkie radio in the other. His face was grim and angry. Encizo had good reason to recognize that face.

It belonged to Colonel Martillo.

"That son of a bitch," Encizo rasped in English.

"What?" Maria inquired.

"I just made a rude remark about Colonel Martillo," Encizo explained. "He made a big show of arriving after the battle and after Ortiz and most of the other soldiers were already there. No wonder. He was probably talking to Ortiz on the radio to make certain none of the gunmen were taken alive. That explains why Ortiz killed one of the terrorists before Mr. Johnson could take the man prisoner. It explains a lot of things."

"Martillo is behind the terrorist attacks?" Maria asked.

"The FMLN and probably other groups to the political right as well as the Marxist left are responsible for their share of terrorism in El Salvador, too," Encizo replied. "But Martillo is the mastermind of the group we've been looking for. If it wasn't for this picture, he might have gotten away with it, too."

"I'll start working on a blowup of the photo," Maria volunteered. "I have a feeling this could be the biggest story to come out of Central America since Somoza fell from power."

"You'll have a very exclusive story, Maria," Encizo promised. "But I'll have to meet with my *compañeros* to arrange some exclusive business with Colonel Hammer, for a start."

18

The rain began at dawn. Dense dark clouds blotted out the sun as sheets of rain fell on San Salvador. The sky seemed to churn with angry gray swirls as if nature was displaying its fury for the people of the small Central American nation. Traffic slowed in the streets, and drivers had to switch on their headlights as the sudden change in the weather seemed to shut out the day and cast a gloomy, damp extension of the night over the capital of El Salvador.

Ron Sommers emerged from the U.S. embassy with an open umbrella over his head. Turning up the collar of his suit jacket, the CIA case officer hurried up the walkway to the gate. He splashed through puddles and cursed under his breath as his feet and pant cuffs were soaked in the process. Sommers reached the gate, opened it and quick-stepped to the minibus parked by the curb. A side door opened, and the Company man hopped inside the vehicle.

"This had better be good," Sommers remarked as he fumbled to close the umbrella. "I was in a meeting with the ambassador."

He was not pleased to see the five men of Phoenix Force and Ferrero seated in the bus. The Company man noticed the commandos were once again dressed in combat fatigues and armed to the teeth, as if ready to head for another battlefield. This made Sommers even less happy to meet with them again.

"You'll have to talk with him later," Yakov Katzenelenbogen stated. The Israeli leaned back in his seat and pointed the trident hooks of his prosthesis at Encizo. "Mr. Cassias has something to show you."

Rafael Encizo opened his attaché case and removed a blowup photograph, roughly twenty by twenty-five centimeters, and handed it to Sommers. Gary Manning held a penlight over the picture to cast ample light on it, ensuring the CIA man would clearly see the face at the window in the upper left-hand part of the photo.

"Martillo?" Sommers said, not sure he believed what he saw in the photo. "Martillo was watching when the terrorists attacked the Embassy?"

"Watching?" David McCarter snorted. "Hell, he was coordinating the bloody attack and the military patrols in the area. That explains why no patrol showed up until we'd already beaten the terrorists."

"They sure arrived fast after Ortiz blew away the dude I wounded and tried to take alive," Calvin James added.

"But an army patrol was killed when the terrorists assassinated McKeller," Sommers reminded them.

"No one is suggesting the entire Salvadoran army is involved in Martillo's conspiracy," Encizo answered. "The patrol that tried to rescue McKeller was sacrificed by Martillo's hitmen. It's obvious the colonel is ruthless enough to kill anyone who threatens his success. You know damn well he murdered Hector and the rest of the ERP prisoners."

"The colonel hates Communists," Major Ferrero stated. "That's well-known. It's regarded as one of his better traits."

"Murder is still murder," Katz replied. "Killing unarmed prisoners without benefit of trial, judgment and sentence is murder. There is no other term for it. Besides, Martillo didn't kill Hector and the others just because he's so dedicated to the fight against communism or the ERP and FMLN. He wanted us to believe the terrorists who kidnapped Convy were also responsible for the previous incidents. He knew we'd interrogate them and we wouldn't automatically assume Hector was lying when he denied having anything to do with the murders of McKeller and his bodyguards or the attack on the Embassy. Martillo may have even suspected we'd use truth serum. So he killed the prisoners. You can't interrogate dead men."

"Goddamn it," Sommers rasped. "I told the ambassador this mess was virtually over. Now I'll have to tell him Hector and the ERP weren't guilty? I'll have to explain that one of the highest ranking, most influential military officers in El Salvador is the prime suspect? A man who's regarded as a nemesis of communism in Central America?"

"That's about the size of it," James told him. "Sorry if you don't like the facts. Sometimes things don't work out the way you want them to. Your champion against the Red Menace is just another butcher fanatic with a slightly different creed to justify his actions."

"That sounds very nice, Johnson," Sommers said in a hard voice, "but in case you haven't noticed what's been going on in Central America, maybe I should tell you. Communist forces *are* trying to seize control in this part of the world. That's a fact, not just McCarthy-style paranoia. You think the FMLN aren't connected to the Cubans and the Sandinistas? They damn sure are. You think the people of El Salvador will be better off under Communists than they are under the present government?"

"And they won't stop with El Salvador any more than they stopped with Nicaragua," Ferrero added. "The Communist revolutionaries will continue on to Honduras and Guatemala. Then on to Costa Rica and eventually South America. Maybe they'll spread their political cancer north to Mexico. In the end they'll have enormous military might, and they'll roll across your borders into Texas and California."

"Well, judging from communism's past success in this region since Castro took over in Cuba," Gary Manning said dryly, "I figure the time between each takeover of another country is about twenty years. At that rate they ought to have control of Central and South America—and don't forget the West Indies and the Caribbean—in about three hundred years. That's when they'll be ready to invade North America, huh? Gee, I don't know that I'll be able to sleep nights now with that immediate threat dwelling on my mind."

"I don't believe you're really that smug," Sommers sputtered. "You're too intelligent to be that naive. It didn't take the Communists centuries to take control of Eastern Europe or Southeast Asia. It'll move even faster here if El Salvador falls to the Reds."

"If that happens," Encizo began, "half the reason will be because many of the non-Communist governments in Central America have been corrupt. Don't tell me how terrible the Communists are. I've seen it firsthand. Castro's regime cost me the lives of family members, several close friends and almost a year of my life spent in misery, pain and terror that I can't begin to describe to you. None of that changes the violations of human rights in Guatemala, Nicaragua under Somoza and right here in El Salvador."

"You're talking about the past," Ferrero insisted. "We have a new president, and things are changing despite this evidence of corruption by Colonel Martillo."

"Men like Martillo are exactly what I'm talking about," Encizo answered. "How can you expect the general population to be concerned about a Communist takeover when they already have to worry about being victimized by somebody like Martillo? He's killing people and getting away with it because of his status in the military. If you were a peasant, how much worse would communism seem to you compared to storm troopers who run you off your property, murder your family and might kill you, as well?"

"Well, what do we do about Martillo?" Sommers asked with a sigh. "Are you absolutely sure about him being a terrorist leader? He's supposed to be the top antiterrorist in El Salvador, you know."

"Martillo has been our lead suspect ever since we discovered two of the terrorists at the Embassy strike had formerly served under him in the army," Katz replied. "Of course, there was the possibility Martillo's right-wing extremist behavior could have steered them to the fanatical left. However, the fact that there were no military records, birth certificates or drivers' licenses on file proved someone with considerable contacts in the Salvadoran government had tried to erase any evidence those two men ever existed. I doubt the FMLN could have managed this, and there doesn't seem to be any advantage for them to carry out such a cover-up."

"But Martillo could have managed it, and he had good reason to want to keep the identity of those men secret as well as any connection to him when they were in the army," Ferrero added. "I'm afraid I have to agree with Mr. Goodman. Martillo is almost certainly the ringleader of the terrorists. Believe me, Mr. Sommers, I wish I could feel otherwise. My superiors aren't going to be very eager to grant a warrant for the colonel's arrest."

"We don't need a warrant," Katz announced. "We're authorized to handle this situation any way we see fit."

"Is that why you're carrying all that firepower?" Sommers asked with a frown. "You intend to kill Martillo instead of arresting him? What about that little lecture you made earlier about murder?"

"I haven't had a very high opinion of the CIA ever since the Bay of Pigs invasion," Encizo said dryly. "You sure aren't doing anything to change that opinion in a favorable manner."

"We don't want to kill Martillo unless it's necessary," Katz said. "A trial may be embarrassing for the Salvadoran government, but in the long run it would show that the new administration under Cristiani had the courage and sense of responsibility to see to it that even a man with Martillo's rank and status can't be allowed to commit such crimes."

"As for the firepower," McCarter added to answer the other part of Sommer's question, "you don't go after a terrorist leader with a salt shaker and a pair of handcuffs. If we have to go on a military base to get the bastard, there won't be any way of knowing who might be loyal to Martillo. We can safely assume Ortiz and Lopez are co-conspirators, but we can only guess how many more brainwashed soldiers are part of his private outfit."

"I don't understand why Martillo attacked U.S. citizens at the Embassy," Sommers admitted. "The United States is an ally of El Salvador. Over the last nine or ten years, Uncle Sam has given this country millions of dollars and military aid to resist the spread of communism. Martillo's interests are the same as our own. Why launch those attacks and kill some of the *yanquis* on his side?"

"Martillo gave me the answer without meaning to," Encizo replied. "He calculated that if Washington figures an El Salvadoran is vigorously fighting Communists and trying to hunt down the terrorists who committed the earlier incidents, the U.S. will increase aid to the country. He didn't have those people killed to drive away U.S. support. He thought it would do exactly the opposite. After we took down the ERP group, Martillo spoke to me about how Washington would renew support for El Salvador and even urged me to mention it in our report to the President. He was disappointed when I told him we don't report directly to the President and have nothing to do with policy-making in Washington."

"I bet when he got upset he started to get another headache, too," James commented.

"That's right," Encizo confirmed. "Do you think that means something?"

"I can't make an accurate diagnosis based on what little I know about the guy," James began, "but I'd say it's pretty obvious Martillo is losing all ability to deal with stress on just about any level and his judgment and decision-making ability is probably going down the tubes, as well."

"You mean he's going insane?" Ferrero inquired with a frown.

"That's a term I'm not sure I'm qualified to use in the evaluation of a person's mental condition," James answered. "I don't know if Martillo's migraines are mainly caused by psychological pressures, or, aside from the usual vascular symptoms leading to migraine, caused by a physical problem like a brain tumor. He's damn sure not fit to command other men, and the fact he is a high-ranking officer with a great deal of loyalty among his followers would make him a risk to Salvadoran national security even if he wasn't involved in terrorist activities."

"So, you guys are gonna go get him?" Sommers asked with a sigh. "Well, I'd rather let Major Ferrero and the Salvadoran government handle this than have you charge in like the Texas Rangers."

"Martillo has too many connections in the government," Katz replied. "If we let the authorities handle this, there's a very good chance an agent of Martillo's outfit might warn him in advance. The colonel could flee the country or go into hiding in the jungles or hills. No offense, Major, but there could be Martillo followers in military Intelligence, as well."

"I can't dismiss that possibility," Ferrero agreed. "If he could manage to get those personnel records on his former soldiers, we have to assume he's capable of just about anything."

"There's also the point that this mission is the reason we were sent to El Salvador," Manning added. "We want to see it through to the end."

"You're welcome to it," Sommers said. "Good luck. By the way, where'd you get the picture? That Mexican photojournalist?"

"It seems my men didn't get the right roll of film," Ferrero said dryly. "I never thought I'd be glad any of my agents were careless, but this time it proved to be to our advantage."

"Indeed," Katz commented, and glanced at Encizo. "And I have to acknowledge that Mr. Cassias proved to be a very good judge of character. When this is over, we need to give Maria Santo what details we can about the operation so she has the exclusive story before the rest of the press get any information. I'd say she's earned that."

"If that's the way you want it," the CIA man told them. "I'll let you guys handle that, too."

"Hopefully we'll be alive so we can," James said with a shrug.

CAPTAIN ORTIZ MARCHED into the office of Colonel Garcia. Water dripped from the captain's service hat, tucked under one arm, and his boots were squeaky damp from walking through the rain and puddles outside the headquarters building. Garcia was a full colonel and the commander of one of the largest bases in El Salvador. Ortiz had no idea why Garcia had ordered him to report to his office, but a junior officer does not ask questions when a field-grade officer requests his presence.

Ortiz snapped to attention and saluted. He failed to notice the two men seated on a couch along a wall near Garcia's desk. The colonel sat in his swivel chair and looked up at Ortiz with weary eyes that were set in a beefy, middle-aged face. He returned the salute and leaned back in his chair, and the sound of the rain pounding on the windowpane behind the colonel seemed to intensify. A bookcase stood near the window, and an El Salvador flag— blue and white with the national coat of arms in the center—was mounted on a pole in a corner.

"At ease, *capitán*," Garcia told Ortiz.

"*Gracias, jefe,*" Ortiz replied.

He glimpsed the figures on the couch out of the corner of his eye. Ortiz turned his head to get a better look. Rafael Encizo and Major Ferrero sat on the sofa. The captain's eyes widened with alarm and surprise.

Colonel Garcia pressed his palms together in front of his broad chest. "I believe you know these gentlemen," the colonel remarked. "They've told me a very disturbing story about Colonel Martillo and some of his men. He's involved in an ugly, disgraceful business, and you seem to be part of it."

"I don't know what this is about, Colonel," Ortiz declared, "but it sounds like someone is mistaken. Major Ferrero has obviously been listening to those *yanqui* Communist-lovers...."

"You will have an opportunity to defend yourself in court, Captain," Garcia told him. "Right now, you'd better answer the questions these men ask. The most important of which is, where is Colonel Martillo?"

"He's in the field," Ortiz replied. "Colonel Martillo is a field commander and often spends time with the patrols in the jungles and hills where the FMLN and other terrorists lurk. He's constantly searching for and fighting the true enemies of our country. Even the *yanqui* team is aware of this. They participated in a raid on an ERP base just last night with Colonel Martillo in command."

"Martillo is a busy man," Encizo commented. "Exactly where is he? You're his aide, Captain. You must have knowledge of your commander's whereabouts on a regular basis."

"Am I under arrest?" Ortiz inquired. "A Salvadoran officer accused by foreigners who don't give a damn about our country...
Why am I being subjected to this?"

Another figure appeared at the doorway. Ortiz turned and stared into the face of Calvin James. The tall black warrior smiled and smacked a fist into an open palm. The captain stiffened and glared at him.

"You remember me, Ortiz?" James inquired. "Want a rematch? I kind of enjoyed kicking your ass the last time. If I do it again, it'll be a lot harder on your backside."

"These men are going to interrogate you, Captain," Garcia announced. "I suggest you do not resist or do anything to draw attention to yourself while they escort you to a room that has been prepared for this use. I believe you are familiar with these men and know them well enough to realize it wouldn't be wise."

"What sort of interrogation?" Ortiz asked, his eyes wide and a tremor of fear in his voice.

"Afraid we might give you a dose of the sort of tactics you've used on people in the past?" James asked with a hard stare. "Maybe you deserve to be hooked up to an electrical generator and get a taste of the pain you gave that poor bastard I caught you torturing in the basement of Veaga's shop."

"Colonel," Ortiz said desperately as he spun about to face Garcia, "this is not military procedure. You can't allow them to do this...."

"Take it easy," Encizo said as he rose from the couch. "We don't believe in torture. You're going to answer a few questions under the influence of scopolamine. You'll tell us where to find Martillo, and then we'll hand you over to Colonel Garcia. I'm sure he'll be happy to put you in a military prison cell until you stand trial. Better get used to being behind bars, because you'll probably spend the rest of your life there."

"That may not be a long time," Ferrero remarked. "You and Martillo will probably face a firing squad for your crimes."

"Crimes?" Ortiz glared at the major. "Our crime was caring enough about our country to take action to protect it. Do you know what will happen to El Salvador when we're gone?"

"It ought to smell a little better," James replied. "Come on, Ortiz. Let's get the question-and-answer crap over with so we can go after the big fish next. You're damn sure gonna tell us where we can find Colonel Martillo."

19

The rain forest truly lived up to its name. Thunder echoed earsplittingly across the dark, gloomy sky as rain poured down on the dense foliage. Water flowed downhill to create meters of mud beneath the tall grass. The rain and heavy cloud cover caused a blanket of darkness. It was impossible to determine if twilight had fallen, because the jungle was already plunged into blackest night.

Phoenix Force, Major Ferrero, half a dozen Salvadoran paratroopers and three Nahuatl Indians made their way through the formidable terrain. They would have been completely blind in the darkness and the rain if they had not been equipped with special night-vision goggles. Rain pelted their ponchos, and water ran down the protective garments. Frequently each man had to wipe droplets from the lenses of his goggles in order to see.

The rain presented problems for the commandos and their allies, but it also provided certain advantages. The noise of the storm effectively concealed their progress through the bush, and the severe reduction of visibility would be an even greater problem for Colonel Martillo and his forces. They hoped that the colonel's fanatic followers didn't have sophisticated night-vision gear. When questioned about such details under the influence of scopolamine, Captain Ortiz said Martillo did not have such equipment . . . at least, not that Ortiz knew about.

By interrogating Ortiz with truth serum, Phoenix Force had learned Martillo had used his field commander status to cover a trip to a secret base of terrorists that included a number of Nicaraguan gunmen led by a former bandit chief known as *El Jinete*. Apparently Colonel Hammer wanted to meet with them to discuss future strategy after the raid on the ERP. Martillo was unaware his role in Salvadoran terrorism had been discovered, and he believed he had successfully convinced everyone that Hector and his gang were responsible for the attacks on U.S. Embassy personnel. He was probably eager to deliver the good news to Jinete.

Conditions seemed ideal for Phoenix Force to launch their raid on Martillo and his right-wing killers. The colonel had no reason to believe he was in jeopardy, and the weather would make the sentries at the covert base in the jungle less effective. Ferrero had personally selected the six Salvadoran paratroopers to assist in the mission and had vouched for their reliability. The Nahuatl guides had been hired from an Indian village in the area. The three Nahuatl were hunters and trackers, very much at home in the rain forest. Not surprisingly the Indians knew about the jungle camp, but they had assumed it was a legitimate military operation. The Nahuatl had learned long ago that it was safer to avoid contact with the army and not get involved in military and political matters. The Indians had in turn been victimized by the army, the government and the rebel FMLN.

The Indians had agreed to guide the assault team because the village needed the money offered for assistance by the mysterious *yanquis* and Major Ferrero. They also feared that failing to supply guides might suggest they were sympathetic toward the terrorists, which could mean problems with the Salvadoran government in the future. The Nahuatl had been assured that the guides would only be required to take them to the base. They would not have to risk their lives in battle against the terrorists.

They had already found Colonel Martillo's jeep parked off the road roughly half a kilometer from the heart of the rain forest. The Nahuatl guides had some difficulty adjusting to the night-vision goggles. The special fiber optics in the lenses, which magnified reflected light and transformed darkest night into dusk, also produced images in shades of yellow and green. The Indians were not used to finding their way in the jungle by viewing ghostly shapes in only two colors. One of the guides was frightened by this odd technology and only used the goggles when he absolutely had to see more than two meters in the extreme dark.

However, the Indians made their way through the jungle with greater ease than their companions. The heavy rainfall did not bother the guides as much as the others, because the Nahuatl were accustomed to the region's weather during the rainy season which ran from May to August. The Nahuatl tribesmen also traveled more lightly, not having to carry as much equipment as Phoenix Force and the soldiers. Although the Indians brought their hunting rifles and machetes, they didn't need to worry about getting pistols, radio units, ammo magazines or other gear clogged with rainwater. This made the trek a bit easier for them.

Phoenix Force tried to keep their equipment as dry as possible. The ponchos offered limited protection, and the tentlike garments also reduced their upper-body mobility. They reluctantly decided to carry fewer weapons than usual, due to the restrictions of the ponchos. Manning had chosen to bring his assault rifle and had left his Uzi machine pistol at the safehouse. The other four Phoenix commandos favored the more compact, close-quarters weapons, and carried their Uzis under the ponchos.

Major Ferrero and the paratroopers carried M-16 assault rifles. All the members of the team were armed with pistols, grenades, knives and other gear in addition to their rifles or subguns. However, the Phoenix commandos had the only silencers among the group, except for Major Ferrero's stainless steel .45 with a six-inch sound suppressor attached to the barrel.

"¿A qué distancia está el campamento?" Rafael Encizo whispered to a Nahuatl guide. He had to whisper fairly loudly to be heard above the storm. "How far is the camp?"

"Another kilometer northeast," the Indian replied. He pointed at the wall of living forest before them. "That way."

Encizo conferred with Katz and Ferrero. They agreed that the guides had done their job, and there was no need for the three Nahuatl Indians to go any farther. They told the guides to return to the village, then the assault team continued deeper into the rain forest.

Gary Manning took the point and scouted ahead for the unit. The Canadian muscled his way through the foliage, occasionally using his FAL rifle to hold aside low branches and tangled vines to force a path in the bush. Still, the demolitions expert took care to watch for booby traps and detection devices, and it was among a carpet of ferns that he discovered a trip wire at ankle level.

The Canadian gently extended the butt of his rifle past the wire and brushed the ferns to search for a secondary wire. He found a long, dark green cord instead. Manning suspected what the cord meant and carefully traced it to a clump of bushes. He avoided touching the trip wire and found that it followed the same pattern as the cord. The wire led to a tree trunk. It was attached to a small dark box at the roots of the tree. The speaker unit to the box revealed that it was a simple alarm-siren.

Manning searched in the bushes near the tree and grunted with satisfaction when he discovered a gray-green object of curved metal. The explosives master immediately recognized it. The American-made claymore mine was a device he had used on more than one occasion in Vietnam. The terrorists' booby trap was simple but extremely ruthless and deadly. The wire's function was to trigger an alarm to warn the enemy of invaders. Then they would press the plunger to an electrical squib connected to the claymore cord. The mine would explode and fire shrapnel in a massive radiating pattern of great destruction.

The Phoenix demolitions expert disconnected the cord from the firing mechanism of the claymore to render the mine harmless. He stayed alert for other alarms and traps as he continued to move closer to the enemy base. Every so often he used the Starlite night scope mounted on his FAL to peer through the gaps in the foliage, searching the area ahead. At last he spotted a group of camouflage-print tents in a clearing.

The terrorists appeared to be bogged down by the weather. Only two sentries stood guard, their oilskin ponchos drenched and their heads covered by rain hoods. Rifle barrels protruded from the hems of their protective garments, but the sentries seemed to pay little attention to watch duty. Their thoughts were probably centered on the miserable weather, and they considered the odds of anyone attacking the base in the middle of a rainstorm to be too small to present a serious threat. No watch commander supervised the sentries to keep them alert. Perhaps Martillo had already announced the good news to Jinete and the others, and the terrorists assumed the ERP had been blamed for their activities, thus dismissing the need to take camp security too seriously.

Manning scanned the camp in detail. There were six tents, each the size of an U.S. Army GP medium, which meant it could accommodate as many as ten men. Two deuce and a half trucks were located under a group of palms and were surrounded by large ferns. The survey gave no clue to Manning about how many opponents might be concealed at the base. Lights glowed under the canvas shelters of the tents, suggesting that the majority of the men in the camp were not asleep.

The Canadian crept back to the site of the trip wire and the claymore. He pressed the transmit key to a two-way radio twice, signaling Katz with a double beep on his radio. That told the Phoenix commander to lead the rest of the team forward. Manning waited for the others to make their way through the rain forest to join him, then showed them the trap.

"There are probably more of these," Manning warned. "A good demolitions man would set at least four mines to defend the camp on all sides."

"All right," Katz began as he wiped a finger across a fogged lens to his night goggles. "We'll divide the unit and surround the camp. The claymore must be located and deactivated before we can safely close in on the terrorists."

"Safely?" Calvin James said with a chuckle. "Who you think you're kiddin', man?"

"I have a suggestion," Manning volunteered. "Instead of disconnecting all the claymores, let's point a couple of them at the camp."

"Oh, I like that idea," David McCarter said with a sly smile. "If they try to blow us up, they'll nail themselves instead."

"Well, it is a pretty ruthless tactic," the Canadian admitted, a bit uncomfortable with the fact McCarter was delighted by one of his suggestions, "but it will sure take the fight out of a lot of the enemy."

"And there could be as many as sixty terrorists at the camp?" Major Ferrero asked, clearly alarmed by the odds. "May I remind you there are only twelve of us?"

"Sixty would be the maximum number that could fit in all the tents," Katz explained. "Most likely there aren't that many men crammed in those tents. The number could be less than half the maximum capacity. I doubt *El Jinete* would be willing to share his quarters with nine other men. More likely he has a tent of his own or shares it with one or two lieutenants who also act as personal bodyguards. The other tents probably have between six and eight men. Ten would be overcrowding and cause morale problems."

"They've probably also segregated the Salvadorans and the Nicaraguans at the camp," Encizo added. "Despite Jinete's claim he's with the Contras, the Horseman and his men are nothing more than hill bandits, according to Ortiz. Martillo's men resent having to work with Jinete's outfit. Of course, we have no way of knowing which tents are used by bandits and which have Colonel Hammer's men."

"What difference does it make?" McCarter said with a shrug. "They're all enemies and they'll all be trying to kill us when we hit the camp."

"Does that mean we aren't going to try to take any prisoners?" Ferrero inquired.

"That will be largely up to the terrorists," Katz replied. "Whatever you do, don't underestimate them. Martillo has already proved he can be very clever and dangerous. His men are well trained and well armed, and we must assume they've had some degree of combat experience. Jinete's men may be bandits, but that doesn't mean they'll be any easier to take on in a fight. They may in fact have more experience than the colonel's troops."

"That's a comforting thought," Ferrero muttered.

"If you wanted a comforting chore," Encizo replied. "you shouldn't have come with us, Major."

PHOENIX FORCE and their allies needed time to get into position and deal with the claymore mines before carrying out a raid. The rain gradually began to subside, making the working conditions easier, but it also meant the enemy would have greater visibility, too, and the sounds of the storm would no longer conceal any noise made by the assault team in the bush.

They were still preparing for the raid when a canvas flap moved at one of the tents. The familiar tall figure of Colonel Martillo and his burly NCO, Sergeant Lopez, emerged from the opening. They slipped the hoods of their ponchos over their heads and walked from the tent. A third man accompanied the pair as they headed for the rain forest.

Martillo may have stayed in the tent until the rain let up before starting the trek through the jungle to return to his jeep. The colonel was leaving the camp and would certainly discover the army trucks at the road when he reached the jeep. He would realize someone had found the secret terrorist base and would realize also that his role in the operations against the U.S. Embassy had been discovered.

However, the fourth—and hopefully last—claymore mine had not been located and deactivated. The Phoenix unit couldn't hit the camp yet, even though Martillo was leaving the area. The colonel, Lopez and a terrorist who knew the location of the booby traps and alarms marched into the jungle. Rafael Encizo, David McCarter and a Salvadoran paratrooper ducked behind cover as the enemy trio passed less than fifty meters from their position. The Phoenix pair and the soldier remained motionless and silent, weapons ready in case their opponents noticed them and forced them to take action.

The hoods of the ponchos reduced peripheral vision. Martillo and his companions walked past the hidden commandos without seeing them. Encizo started to reach for the Kraton rubber grips of his Cold Steel Tanto, but he didn't draw the knife. The chances of taking out Martillo, Lopez and the third opponent silently were too slim. At least one man would probably manage to cry out or fire his weapon before the Phoenix pair and the paratrooper could bring them down. That would alert the terrorists in the camp. With at least one claymore mine still active and ready to destroy the assault team, the risk was too great to allow the battle to begin.

Encizo watched Martillo and his companions shuffle out of view. They soon vanished among the dense foliage. The Cuban didn't want Martillo to get away. He turned to McCarter and pointed a finger at himself. Then Encizo pointed at the area where Martillo and the other terrorists had gone. McCarter frowned. He didn't like the idea of Encizo following the three terrorists alone. He pointed at their paratrooper companion, moved his finger toward Encizo and then indicated the jungle.

The Cuban nodded. He understood that McCarter wanted the soldier to accompany him. The paratrooper nodded to express his willingness to assist Encizo. They crept into the rain forest in pursuit of Martillo and his companions. McCarter was left to handle his position of the raid on his own. Encizo was somewhat reluctant to leave the British ace, but he realized McCarter could more than take care of himself in a firefight. Nobody was more at home on a battlefield than David McCarter.

GARY MANNING TRACED another green cord to a claymore mine hidden behind a pile of loose tree branches and high grass. The paratroopers with the Canadian warrior sighed with relief as Manning turned the claymore, aiming it at the enemy camp. He pushed back his poncho to unclip the radio unit from his belt. The transmit key operated on three modes. He could speak into the mouthpiece, key the beeper or send Morse code, or use the silent signal that triggered a flashing light on the receiver of another person's radio. He used the latter to signal Katz that he had found another claymore and taken care of it.

Yakov Katzenelenbogen glanced down at the flashing orange light on his radio unit. He had already received another signal from Calvin James indicating that he'd found a mine, and Katz himself had also located a claymore. Unless there were more mines set up for backup, all the heavy explosives at the rim of the terrorist camp had been taken care of. The Israeli considered the possibility the enemy might have some more destructive surprises Phoenix Force had failed to detect.

The final decision to start the raid was one Katz had to make. He realized there were always enormous risks involved in such an operation. Some things cannot be predicted, and good men could die when the enemy proved to be more resourceful or ruthless than appearances suggested. It seemed unlikely a terrorist outfit the size of Jinete's group would use more than four claymores to protect the camp, but Phoenix Force had not expected to find any mines at the site. If he had claymores, what else were the terrorists armed with? Mounted machine guns concealed inside the tents? Rocket launchers?

There was no time to waste dwelling on such matters, Katz realized. He had to make the decision based on what he knew and on what he could reasonably extrapolate from information he had acquired. He turned to face Major Ferrero and the paratrooper with their three-man section of the unit. The Phoenix Force commander nodded to inform them it was time to begin the assault.

Ferrero bobbed his head nervously. The soldier nodded in a firm, eager gesture. He was young and inexperienced in the ways of war. The paratrooper appeared enthusiastic about the battle and didn't seem to have a trace of fear. Youth tends to regard itself as indestructible, yet graveyards throughout the world have been filled with young corpses. The soldier was about to get his baptism by fire. He would learn the horror of the battlefield, the grief of causing death and seeing his comrades-at-arms slain, and discover that glory in war is a lie. That is, if he lived through the baptism.

Katz moved toward the camp. He braced the Uzi machine pistol across his prosthesis as he crept to the edge of the forest. A sentry shuffled along in the mud twenty meters from his position. Katz trained his Uzi on the guard's back and watched the man walk in the monotonous pattern he had established during watch duty. The sentry turned and started to circle around.

The Phoenix Force commander triggered his Uzi. Three rounds coughed from the silencer-equipped weapon. The guard's body twitched, and he staggered backward from the impact of the 9 mm slugs. The bullets tore into his chest, and burst his heart like a balloon. The man's rifle dropped from uncaring fingers as the sentry fell dead in the muddy slop.

The other guard heard a groan and turned to see his comrade fall. It was the last thing he ever saw. A 7.62 mm rifle round punched through the back of his skull. He fell facefirst to the ground, his rifle still clutched in his lifeless fists. Gary Manning had taken him out with a single well-placed rifle shot. The Canadian peered through his Starlite scope and examined the still figure. The bloodstained poncho hood revealed that his marksmanship had been precise. There was no doubt that his target was dead.

Manning felt a well-known twinge in his stomach. Although taking out the sentries was necessary, he still felt repulsion when he was forced to kill a man in a situation that was anything less than self-defense. He took some comfort in the knowledge that the kill had been swift and efficient. The guard hadn't suffered. The man was probably dead before he could feel the bullet crash through his skull into his brain.

"*¡Madre de Dios!*" a voice cried out from the camp. "*¡Carlos está muerto! ¡Maldito sea!*" A man stood at the open flap of a tent. He stared at the body of the sentry Manning had shot. The corpse was obviously Carlos, and the fellow at the tent had announced to the rest of the terrorists that their comrade was dead. Although the silencer attached to Manning's FAL had muffled the report of the rifle, the hole in Carlos's head made it quite clear he hadn't died from a sudden heart attack.

"Well," Manning said with a sigh, "here we go again."

20

"Rock 'n' roll," Calvin James rasped as he pointed his M-16 assault rifle at the enemy base.

An M-203 grenade launcher was attached to the underside of the barrel. James aimed with care and reached for the trigger to the M-203. He fired a 40 mm cartridge-style grenade and watched the projectile hurtle through the sky, a cometlike tail streaking behind it. The grenade crashed into one of the army trucks and exploded on impact. The blast tore the vehicle apart, and ignited the fuel in the tanks. Flaming gasoline splashed the second vehicle and set the canvas tarp ablaze.

Chunks of metal were propelled across the camp. A burning rubber tire rolled toward one of the tents as a number of terrorists tried to emerge. The giant doughnut startled the men and sent them running in all directions. The tire hit the tent, and more canvas began to burn.

Streams of automatic rifle fire tore into the ground in front of the panicked terrorists, convincing them not to bolt into the rain forest. They jumped back from the spewing clods of earth colliding with one another. Some tripped over their fellows and tumbled to the ground with deadly consequences.

"*¡Présten atención!*" Major Ferrero's voice bellowed from a bullhorn. "Attention! Throw down your weapons and surrender! We have you surrounded...."

Claymore explosions roared from the jungle. Two mines erupted simultaneously, and flying shrapnel rocketed from the east and west sides of the camp. The brilliant glare lit up the scene as terrorists were torn limb from limb by the blast. Tents were collapsed by the explosions, and those that remained standing were shredded by shrapnel. Wounded men screamed and thrashed about to the ground, and fire crackled among the torn lumps of canvas.

Maimed men crawled feebly in the mud. Some dragged along their smashed limbs or tried to stop the blood from pumping out of arteries severed by abrupt amputations of arms or legs. Others had been blinded by flying shrapnel. Crimson trickled from gouged sockets as the victims shrieked. One man endured his torment in silence. His jawbone had also been torn from his face by the explosion.

Katz heard one of his companions groan and cough violently. He glanced over his shoulder and saw the young paratrooper double up and vomit. So much for the glory of war, Katz thought. The ugly realities were less appealing to the green soldier. Major Ferrero's face was ashen as he viewed the scene with amazement and horror. The officer was a veteran soldier, but he had never witnessed the effects of two claymore mines at close quarters before. It was a setting which hell itself would find hard to equal.

Suddenly Ferrero was thrown against a tree trunk. Blood spurted from a trio of bullet holes in his chest. Enemy survivors within the camp had opened fire with their assault rifles. One gunman had spotted the major and had nailed him with a lethal burst to the upper torso. Ferrero slumped along the length of the tree and dropped to the ground. His eyes stared with the astonished expression of the dead.

Katz aimed his Uzi at the muzzle-flash of the gunmen's weapons and squeezed the trigger. A terrorist in a kneeling stance suddenly threw his M-16 into the air as his skull popped open from two parabellum slugs. Brains and blood spilled from his shattered head as the triggerman tumbled to the ground.

Another terrorist started to swing his rifle toward Katz's position, but the Israeli war-horse had already shifted his aim and sprayed the gunman with three 9 mm rounds. The bullets cut a diagonal line across the terrorist's chest. His heart and left lung were pierced by the Uzi fire. The terrorist toppled and triggered a harmless burst of M-16 fire into the stormy dark clouds above.

More terrorists adopted prone positions by their dead and wounded comrades. One mutilated victim pleaded with the healthier gunmen for help. A terrorist answered by smashing the injured man in the teeth with the barrel of his M-16. The maimed figure moaned and lay still, blood oozing from his crushed mouth, while his callous "comrade" placed the barrel of his rifle across the battered man's body. The gunman used the unfortunate terrorist for an improvised bench rest to brace his weapon as he fired at a Salvadoran soldier among the foliage.

The paratrooper groaned, a surprisingly subdued sound for a man who had been shot in the stomach and spleen by three 5.56 mm slugs. He fell backward and hung partly suspended by vines and low branches. Calvin James glanced at the wounded soldier. He wanted to help him and treat his injuries as fast as possible, but the battle was still in progress and any effort to assist the trooper would only put himself in the line of enemy fire.

"You assholes should have surrendered when you had the chance," James growled as he pulled the pin from an M-26 fragmentation grenade.

The spoon popped off the grenade, and James counted to two before he hurled the minibomb at the enemy position. The grenade landed between two terrorist gunmen. They cried out in alarm and reached for the grenade, desperate to throw it back at James. They bumped shoulders in their haste and got in each other's way in the panicked effort to grab the M-26 blaster.

Two other terrorists, who had been using the pile of dead and maimed victims for cover, bolted and ran for safety. James and the uninjured paratrooper under his command were ready for them. The Phoenix warrior and the Salvadoran soldier fired their M-16 rifles and chopped the enemy down before they could get three meters. The grenade exploded a split second later. The blast ripped the two clumsy gunmen apart and splattered them across the camp.

Other bodies were hurled in through the air or sent tumbling across the muddy earth. Among them were some who had already been dead and others who were formerly wounded—until the explosion terminated their suffering along with their lives. How many had been active combatants a moment ago was difficult to say. James regretted the necessity of taking out the wounded as well as the terrorists who presented a clear and present threat, but the enemy had forced his hand—men on James's side were suffering. Once again, the choice had been "us" or "them." In a philosophy class that attitude may be safely debated by those with differing points of view. On the battlefield, there is absolutely no doubt as to which choice one must make when survival is at stake.

FOUR TERRORISTS CHARGED for the rain forest at the position held by Gary Manning and two paratroopers. They had decided their odds were better if they took the offensive rather than remained boxed in at the base, where they would be blown to pieces by the mysterious invaders. They did not realize the most devastating explosions had been detonated by *El Jinete* himself when he set off the claymore mines intended to defend the camp instead of destroying it.

Manning saw the terrorists advance. Two fired assault rifles as they charged. Another carried an M-16, but the magazine well was empty and he used the unloaded weapon as a mount for a bayonet. The fourth man was armed only with a machete. The Canadian warrior concentrated on the opponents armed with loaded weapons, which presented the greatest threat. He trained his FAL on one gunman and drilled the guy through the heart with a trio of 7.62 mm slugs.

The terrorist stopped in his tracks and dropped his rifle. Blood spewed from his gaping mouth, and he wilted to the ground and died. However, the other enemy gunman sprayed one of the paratroopers with a burst of M-16 rounds. The soldier collapsed in a thick clump of ferns, his uniform splashed with his own blood. Manning and the other trooper fired on the second gunman simultaneously. Half a dozen rifle projectiles slammed into the terrorist. The force lifted the man off his feet and kicked his body two meters before it landed in a puddle.

Suddenly the machete-wielding opponent broke through the bush and attacked Manning. The terrorist was almost on top of the Canadian as he swung the big jungle knife in an overhead stroke. Manning gasped, surprised and frightened by the unexpected threat. He instinctively raised his rifle, forming a bar to block the big jungle knife. The heavy blade clanged against the steel frame of his weapon.

Manning swiftly delivered a circular butt-stroke with his FAL to strike his opponent's wrists and forearms before the terrorist could attempt another knife attack. The machete spun from the man's grasp, and Manning stamped the rifle buttstock into his chest. The blow knocked the terrorist backward and sent him staggering into the path of the fourth man, who was attempting to thrust his bayonet into the Canadian's abdomen.

Both terrorists stumbled awkwardly from the unexpected clash. Manning took advantage of the confusion and slammed his FAL across the barrel of the other man's M-16 to force the bayonet downward. The disarmed opponent snarled with rage and hurled himself at Manning. The weight of his entire body struck the Phoenix fighter in the chest and arms. The impact knocked the FAL from Manning's fingers as the frenzied terrorist clawed at the Canadian's throat.

Manning blocked the fingers at his throat with a brawny shoulder. Fingernails raked the leather strap of Manning's shoulder holster as the big Canadian drove a hard uppercut to his opponent's solar plexus.

The powerful punch drove the breath from the terrorist, and Manning's other hand thrust a heel-of-the-palm stroke under the guy's jaw. The blow sent the man hurtling into a tree trunk, but the terrorist with the fixed bayonet once again lunged for the Canadian's abdomen. Manning sidestepped the attack and avoided the deadly thrust. He grabbed his opponent's rifle at the center of the frame and yanked hard to increase the attacker's forward momentum.

Manning turned slightly to get the leverage to swing his opponent off balance. He released the other man's rifle and sent the terrorist reeling awkwardly into the vines and bushes. Manning glanced over his shoulder and saw that the first opponent had sufficiently recovered from the pounding he had received to reach for the Canadian's fallen FAL rifle.

The Phoenix pro whirled and drew his Walther P-88 from shoulder leather. He pushed back the poncho to point the pistol at the terrorist. Just as the man started to raise the rifle, Manning triggered the Walther twice and shot the fanatic in the face. One 9 mm slug crashed into the man's cheekbone and pulverized the left side of his face. The other bullet split the bridge of his nose and tore into his brain.

Automatic fire chattered near Manning's position. The glare of a muzzle-flash nearly blinded the Canadian, and bullets sliced air less than a meter from his left elbow. The warrior dropped to one knee and swung his pistol toward the gunman. Manning almost triggered the Walther, but saw the automatic rifle was in the hands of the surviving paratrooper.

Manning lowered his pistol and turned to see the soldier's intended target. The terrorist with the bayonet lay dead, his M-16 beside his still form and his torso riddled with bloodied bullet holes. Manning looked at the paratrooper and nodded with silent approval. He wasn't sure he needed to be rescued from the terrorist. The Walther in his fist more than evened the odds against the other man's bayonet. Nonetheless, he wasn't about to criticize the soldier's actions. The trooper had seen an opponent with a rifle in hand. He had done exactly what was required of him under the circumstances.

JINETE CRAWLED from under the canvas remains of his tent. The bandit had been stunned when the claymores swept through the camp. His legs were torn and bloodied by shrapnel, but he held a .38 revolver in each fist as he inched forward on his bloated belly. Jinete clenched his teeth to stifle a groan of pain as he rolled over and hauled himself to a seated position in the mud.

Rain splashed his face as he glanced about at the scene of incredible carnage. The camp was destroyed. Tents lay in tatters and some still burned despite the rainfall. One truck had been blasted into useless junk and the other was charred and blackened by smoke. His men littered the ground. Mangled corpses and grisly remains surrounded Jinete. The bandit had seen many battlefields in the past, but this was by far the most terrible because he was looking at his own defeat.

"Last chance to give it up!" a voice shouted from the rain forest in poor and halting Spanish. "If you want to live, throw down the guns and raise your hands. If you want to die...you know what to do next."

Jinete cursed and fired in the direction of the voice. He triggered both revolvers simultaneously, like a character in an old Western movie. The bandit's arms rose with the recoil as he blasted six rounds at the jungle, unable to see who he was shooting at. Jinete could only hope he had hit his invisible opponent.

David McCarter waited behind a tree trunk and listened to .38 slugs pound into it and chip bark from the surface. The Briton wondered if his Spanish had failed him and the son of a bitch hadn't understood what he'd said. McCarter hoped he could take the terrorist alive. If the idiot kept burning up ammunition, that would not be a problem. The problem with revolvers is they take longer to reload than an autoloader. Even if Jinete had speed-loaders, he would have to dump the spent shell casings from the cylinders before he could shove in fresh cartridges and close the cylinders.

Even if both revolvers were fully loaded with six rounds each, McCarter had more firepower with his 13-shot Browning Hi-Power, let alone the 30-round Uzi machine pistol. He purposely poked the barrel of the Uzi around the tree trunk and fired a short burst high above the heads of anyone in the area. The tactic was intended to draw Jinete's attention and lure him into wasting more ammo.

The terrorist responded with two more shots in McCarter's direction. The Briton ducked low as bullets tore at the trunk above his head. McCarter's pulse raced, yet he smiled thinly as the excitement blended with fear. He lowered himself to the base of the tree and drew the Browning. The British ace needed precision accuracy, and the Hi-Power was better suited for the task than the full-auto machine pistol.

The bandit leader held his fire, finally aware that he was being tricked by the elusive opponent. He pointed one revolver at the trees and started to crawl toward the only available cover near the wreckage of the motor pool. McCarter watched his quarry through the sights of his Browning autoloader. He chose his target with care and squeezed the trigger.

Jinete's scream accompanied the report of McCarter's pistol. A parabellum slug had struck Jinete in the left biceps. The 124-grain Federal Hydra Shok projectile struck the humerus bone and expanded on impact. Bone cracked and splintered. Tissue damage to skin and muscle increased, and the shock to nerves in Jinete's arm sent the revolver flying from his left hand.

The bandit rolled in the mud and howled. McCarter waited once more. Patience was not one of his greater virtues, but the Briton figured he could afford to give the man a moment or two to decide what he wanted to do. If Jinete tossed his other revolver and surrendered, that would be fine with the Phoenix commando. If not, another bullet through the terrorist's right arm would accomplish the same goal.

"You bastard!" McCarter growled when he saw *El Jinete* stick the barrel of the remaining revolver in his mouth.

The terrorist jammed the muzzle into the roof of his mouth as he screwed his eyes shut and squeezed the trigger. McCarter heard the muffled report of the .38 S&W and saw the spray of brains and blood when the bullet blew an exit hole at the back of Jinete's skull. The man's body slumped into the mud, quivered slightly and lay still.

"You bloody cheater," the Briton said with disgust as he returned his Browning to shoulder leather.

COLONEL MARTILLO HEARD the gunshots and explosions at the campsite. Sergeant Lopez whispered a prayer and crossed himself. The terrorist guide muttered an obscenity. The glare of explosions was visible despite the dense foliage. Columns of smoke rose above the treetops as if to challenge the rain clouds.

"What should we do, *jefe*?" Lopez inquired as he gripped his pump shotgun tightly in both fists beneath his poncho. "Do we go back to help the others?"

"I don't think that would do any good," Martillo said grimly. "You know as well as I do who must be responsible for the raid on Jinete's base."

"What are you talking about, Colonel?" the guide demanded. He flinched when the sound of men's screams of agony accompanied the explosions and automatic fire. "We can't just leave them...."

"You don't understand," Martillo told him. "The special team of *norteamericanos* must be behind this. Cassias, Goodman, Johnson...the names aren't important. They're all false identities, anyway. I know how they operate. I was part of the raid on the ERP base. The sergeant was there, too. These *yanquis* are very professional. They'll have Jinete's camp closed off and sewn up like a water bag."

"But the claymores..." the guide began hopefully.

"We didn't hear the alarms," Martillo stated. "If they found the trip wires to the warning system, they found the mines, as well. That's how these men work. Jinete has blown up our own people. Those U.S. bastards would turn the claymore toward the camp. I would in their place."

"Then we can get revenge," the youthful terrorist urged.

"We can go back and get killed," Martillo insisted. "You don't know these men. They'll have their troops divided up to cover every angle. They'll be ready for reinforcements to arrive and prepared to deal with them. They must have been setting up the raid when we left the camp. None of us saw or heard anything. We didn't suspect anyone was hiding in the rain forest. If we go back, we'll be lucky if we don't walk right into a trap."

"Why didn't they try to stop us?" Lopez wondered aloud. "Perhaps they didn't recognize us dressed in these ponchos."

"They knew," Martillo stated. "They probably think they can catch up with us at any time. I'm far too visible and well-known in El Salvador...."

He clutched the hood of his poncho and yanked it from his head. Rain poured down on the colonel's throbbing skull. The migraine seemed determined to burn up his brain. Martillo massaged his head as he tried to decide what they should do, since all his plans had obviously been ruined in one fell swoop.

"Colonel?" Lopez asked, worried about his commander.

"The only chance we have is to try to get out of the country," Martillo declared. "We'll continue north to the border and cross into Guatemala. Eventually we'll move on to Mexico. It is a large country, and we can hide there far better than in Guatemala or Honduras."

"I know members of the Contras in Honduras," the guide stated. "They'll help us—"

"You damn fool!" Martillo cursed. "They'll expect us to flee to Honduras because Contras are there. Getting into Guatemala will be difficult enough. Of course, if your men don't want to accompany me, I'll understand. You may indeed be safer on your own."

"I'm still with you, Colonel," Lopez assured him.

"I don't have anywhere else to go," the guide commented. "I'll stay with you, too, Colonel."

Martillo carefully looked at the man as if he had never taken note of him before. In truth, he hadn't really paid much attention to the guide Jinete had given him to get through the forest. The young terrorist was a small man, wiry and thin, with a small weak jaw and a few whiskers on his upper lip. Martillo couldn't make out much more of the man's face, because the hood covered most of his features.

"What is your name?" Martillo asked.

"Roberto," the youth answered. "Roberto Garfalo."

"You are welcome to join us, Roberto," the colonel assured him. "Although I can't promise we are heading toward any destination except our graves."

Garfalo took little comfort in Martillo's remark, and they didn't speak as they continued to trek downhill to the jeep. The mud was thicker, due to the rainwater that ran down the path and mixed with the rich soil. The storm had subsided by the time they approached the vehicle. Hopefully the roads would not be flooded and blockades had not already been set up near the borders. Of course, they would not be able to drive across the border to Guatemala. Perhaps the best way would be to go to the coast and take a boat north....

"¡*Alto*, Martillo!" a voice ordered from the tree line behind the trio. "If you run for the jeep, we'll blow up the vehicle and the three of you with it!"

The colonel turned and stared at the jungle. He recognized the voice. It belonged to the Cuban who called himself Cassias. Martillo didn't see the commando, but he was certain the commando could see him from wherever he was concealed in the rain forest. He was equally certain the threat to blow up the jeep was genuine.

"If we start shooting and run for cover," Garfalo whispered to his companions, "we might be able to flush them out."

"We don't know where they are or how many we're dealing with," Sergeant Lopez warned. "We're more or less in the open. They can cut us down before we can get three meters."

Martillo continued to gaze at the trees. He barely seemed to pay any attention to anything Lopez and Garfalo said. The colonel's entire life, dreams and ambitions were all falling in ruin right before his eyes.

"Show yourself, Cassias!" Martillo demanded. "Come out and face me like a man. Even if you are a Cuban, you have Spanish blood in your veins. Does machismo mean anything to you or did Castro cut off your *huevos* before he ran you out of your own country?"

"You don't like me, Colonel?" Encizo's voice called back in a mocking tone. "I'm really upset about that. Now, drop your weapons and remove those ponchos so we can see you're unarmed. That means *all* three of you. If we have the slightest reason to suspect one of you is planning to escape or reaching for a weapon, we'll kill all of you. *¿Comprende?*"

Martillo lowered his rifle to the ground and slipped off his poncho. The colonel reluctantly took his .45 from leather and dropped it next to the rifle. Sergeant Lopez frowned and followed the officer's example. He placed his shotgun and pistol on the ground and stripped off his poncho. Garfalo still held his M-16 in both fists.

"Do it, Roberto," Martillo ordered.

Garfalo's face flushed with anger, but he bent his knees and laid the rifle near his feet. Colonel Martillo raised his hands to shoulder level, and his companions once again followed his example. The rain and wind tore at the trio with a damp, clammy grip as they stood quietly and waited for the Cuban to make the next move.

Rafael Encizo and the paratrooper who had joined him in the pursuit of Colonel Martillo emerged from the trees. The Cuban pointed his Uzi machine pistol at the terrorists. The soldier carried an M-16 and smiled in victory at the captives. He quick-stepped toward the trio, eager to gather up their arms and bind their hands and wrists.

"*Un momento,*" Encizo urged. "Just a moment. Don't get too close...."

The Phoenix warrior wanted to make the captives move away from their weapons and the jeep before securing them and getting their firearms. However, the young paratrooper had already hurried forward and stepped between Encizo and Garfalo. The anxious terrorist took his opportunity to make his move, hoping Encizo would hold his fire for fear of hitting the trooper. Garfalo also noticed the soldier was paying more attention to Martillo than his companions. A better chance was not likely to happen, Garfalo decided.

He dove to the ground and grabbed his rifle, but he had overestimated his chances. The paratrooper swung his M-16 toward the sudden movement and opened fire. Garfalo's body was knocked sideways by a burst of 5.56 mm slugs through the rib cage. The terrorist youth rolled over on his back, rifle still in his grasp. The paratrooper triggered his weapon again and chopped Garfalo's chest open with another salvo of M-16 rounds.

Sergeant Lopez reacted instinctively. One of his men had been killed, and the NCO immediately responded. He also took Encizo's warning seriously and assumed they would all be shot, anyway, so there was nothing to lose. Lopez scooped up his shotgun. The soldier swung his M-16 at the new threat as the sergeant raised his 12-gauge blaster.

The assault rifle blazed another salvo of full-auto rounds. Bullet holes tore Lopez's massive chest. Blood streamed down his shirt, but the big NCO triggered his riot gun. The mighty boom of the shotgun joined a clap of thunder above to create a single, long angry roar. The paratrooper was pitched two meters by the blast of buckshot at extremely close range. His torso was chewed into a strawberry smear of pulp and smashed bone. The soldier slammed to the ground. The crater in his chest left no doubt whether he was alive or dead.

Although Lopez also been shot in the upper torso, he worked the slide action of his shotgun to jack the spent shotgun shell casing from the chamber and pump a fresh round under the hammer. The sergeant began to swing his weapon at Encizo. The Cuban fired his Uzi, and a trio of 9 mm parabellums ripped a column of destruction across Lopez's forehead. The top of his skull was literally blasted away, and half of the NCO's brains spewed from his smashed head in a hideous halo of scarlet and gray.

"Lopez!" Martillo cried out as he saw his sergeant fall.

Rain showered down on Lopez's lifeless face, his blood seeping into a mud puddle. Colonel Martillo hissed with rage and reached for the hammer in his belt. Encizo pointed his Uzi at the officer.

"Don't try it," the Cuban warned. "It's over, Martillo. You and your band of paramilitary trash are finished."

"You filthy traitor!" Martillo snarled. "We would have destroyed communism in Central America! After we crushed the FMLN in El Salvador, we planned to move on to our neighbors and form a strong, united force against the Communists in Nicaragua. Eventually we would have conquered Cuba and liberated your homeland of Castro's oppression...."

"And replaced it with your own brand of oppression?" Encizo asked. "You used murder, torture, deceit and terror. You murdered innocent people to try to trick the United States into supporting your plan. You might hate the Communists but you're blind to the fact that you've become as bad as what you're opposed to."

"You can only fight a ruthless enemy by ruthless tactics," Martillo replied. "What we did was justified for the greater good in the future."

"I'm sure Hitler, Stalin, Mao and Castro made similar claims," Encizo snorted. "Fanatics can always see the evil in others, but never recognize it in themselves."

"What about honor, Cassias?" Martillo inquired with a smile. "What about repaying your debts to a man who saved your life? Do you believe in that or do you have cowardly excuses to avoid that responsibility as well?"

"I'm not letting you go because you bailed me out in the firefight against the ERP, Colonel," Encizo told him. "The fact I haven't already killed you is as close to repaying that debt as I can come."

"There is something else you can do," the terrorist leader insisted as he lowered a hand to the steel hammer in his belt. "You carry a knife and I carry this hammer. Put down the guns, and we'll see which one of us is truly the better man. No politics, no excuses, no laws and no philosophy. Your skill against mine in hand-to-hand combat to the death.''

"I don't have to agree to that when I've got the gun," the Cuban informed him, and raised the Uzi to point the barrel at his opponent's face.

"You owe me, Cassias," Martillo insisted. "I don't want to stand trial and have the humiliation of prison and courtrooms before I finally face a firing squad. If you don't have the courage to face me in a fair duel, just shoot me now and get it over with."

Encizo's angry gaze drilled into Martillo, sizing the man up. The Colonel's hair was plastered to his head by the rain, and his clothes were soaked and clung tightly to his athletic physique. The storm still reduced visibility, but Encizo did not need the night goggles to see the raw fury—perhaps even madness—in Martillo's expression.

"This is an idiotic demand, Colonel," Encizo began as he reached inside his poncho with one hand and kept the Uzi in his other fist. "It would be foolish for me to agree to it...."

Suddenly his poncho split open as six inches of Cold Steel sliced through the garment. Encizo had drawn the knife from the belt sheath under the poncho. He cut the cloth from chin level to the middle of his torso, then shrugged out of the poncho as if shedding an old skin like a serpent.

"But sometimes I agree to foolish things," he confessed, and tossed the Uzi to the ground.

The Cuban warrior still carried a Walther P-88 in shoulder leather under his arm, but he wasn't about to disarm himself of all firearms just to please Martillo. The Tanto was in his fist. At close quarters the blade was as lethal as a gun, and it was in his hand and ready. Even if he reached for the pistol, Martillo could stop him with a blow from the hammer if the colonel was close enough to his opponent.

"*Bueno,*" Martillo declared as he drew his hammer.

THEY SQUARED OFF. Encizo adopted a low stance, back arched, knife held low, free arm in front to guard and strike, as well. The mud made his footing slippery and at times bogged down his feet. A knife fighter needs to be able to move nimbly on his feet, and the conditions were not favorable. Martillo stood in a fighting posture similar to that of a prizefighter. The steel head of his hammer weaved slightly like a cobra unsure whether to bluff or strike.

Encizo let Martillo make the first move. The colonel obliged. He attacked and swung his hammer in a figure-8 pattern. Encizo weaved away from the slashing tool. He was almost too slow in the soft muck under his boots. The hammer whirled at his knife hand in an attempt to strike the Tanto from the Cuban's grasp. Encizo pulled his arm away before the hammer could land a punishing, if not crippling, blow.

Martillo kept on the offense and altered the attack to a diagonal swing. This time Encizo closed in and slashed the Tanto in a high arc to meet the attack. The ultrasharp steel cut Martillo's shirtsleeve and sliced a deep wound in his forearm. The colonel groaned as blood flowed from the gash.

The terrorist shuffled back two steps and tossed the hammer from his right hand to his left. Encizo followed up the slash with a quick thrust for his opponent's torso. He realized as he made the stroke that Martillo had suddenly swapped hands with the hammer. The tool swept down, and Encizo tried to move clear of the attack. He almost succeeded. The shaft of the hammer struck him across the forearm and chopped the Tanto out of his hand.

Martillo glimpsed the knife fall and slashed a backhand sweep with the hammer. Encizo snapped his head back to dodge the steel claw of the hammerhead as it whirled only centimeters away from the tip of his chin. His right hand quickly shot out and grabbed Martillo's left wrist. He pushed upward to keep the hammer at bay and grabbed the colonel's wounded right forearm with his other hand.

Encizo whipped a knee upward for Martillo's groin while the terrorist struggled to break free of Encizo's grip. The colonel grunted when the Phoenix pro's knee kick hit him in the inner thigh. Martillo snapped his head forward and butted his skull into Encizo's forehead. The Cuban's skull filled with pain, and his vision became filled with a swirl of bright lights that seemed to appear on the insides of his eyelids.

Luckily the lights popped brilliantly in Encizo's head and vanished to leave his vision restored. The Cuban managed to hold on to Martillo's wrist and forearm. The colonel stamped a boot along Encizo's shin and drove the heel into his instep. The Phoenix fighter's leg felt as if he had banged it on the world's hardest coffee table and the table had hit back, as well.

Encizo squeezed Martillo's right arm and dug his thumb into the knife cut above the colonel's wrist. Martillo gasped in pain, and his body convulsed from the sharp agony in his arm. Encizo still held on to Martillo's left wrist to keep the hammer in check and released the wounded arm to swing an *empi* blow to the side of Martillo's jaw. The front of Encizo's bent elbow struck hard, and the colonel's head recoiled from the *empi* stroke.

The Cuban quickly grabbed Martillo's left wrist in both hands and twisted hard in an effort to force him to drop the hammer. Martillo drove his right fist under Encizo's ribs. The commando grunted from the sharp pain under his lungs and immediately slashed a backfist to his opponent's face. A knuckle struck Martillo at the bridge of the nose hard, and blood seeped from his nostrils.

Encizo grabbed his left arm with both hands and shoved it down hard to slam the limb across a bent knee. Martillo groaned from the pain that coursed along his ulnar nerve, and the hammer popped from open fingers. Martillo hooked his right fist to the side of Encizo's skull. Both men groaned in pain. Encizo's head stung from the punch, and he lost his grip on Martillo's arm. The colonel broke a knuckle on the Cuban's hard skull, and the impact on his wounded right arm caused the cut to bleed more freely.

Lightning flashed above, and the Cuban saw Martillo's face clearly illuminated by the harsh, brief glare. The colonel's mouth and nose bled. Bruises marred his features, yet the furious gleam remained in his eyes. Encizo hoped he had enough fight left to take on the demented terrorist. His head still ached, one leg was numb and his ribs felt as it someone had stuck thumbtacks in them. Martillo's punch must have bruised the floating rib at the bottom of the rib cage.

If someone had to score a lucky punch, Encizo thought bitterly, why couldn't it be me? He needed to take down Martillo in a hurry before the colonel got the upper hand. The man advanced, his hands poised like twin claws. Encizo raised a fist high to distract Martillo and draw his attention upward as he swung a front-kick to the colonel's abdomen. His boot slammed into Martillo's stomach with enough force to make him double up from the kick.

Encizo's other foot had slid in the slippery mud when he executed the kick. He lost his balance and fell to the soft damp ground. The Cuban rolled on his left side and pushed himself to a kneeling position. He glanced up and saw that Martillo had retrieved his hammer. The colonel charged forward, both fists wrapped around the shaft of the hammer. He raised the tool overhead, prepared to finish Encizo off with a final powerful blow to the skull.

Rafael Encizo grabbed the hilt of the Gerber Mark I dagger in his boot sheath as he scrambled to his feet. He drew the knife as he rose and held it low by his right thigh to conceal it from Martillo, who was virtually on top of him. There wouldn't have been time to draw the Walther from shoulder leather, but Enci014 had instinctively reached for the dagger instead. He was committed to his counterattack and he had to follow it through to the end whether it worked or not.

One way or the other, one of them was about to die.

Martillo swung his arms overhead, but Enci014 stepped forward and thrust his left arm high to jam the heel of his palm under the colonel's fists. Enci014's arm was straight, his right leg braced behind him to form a strong wedge with his body. Martillo's attack was blocked, his fists and hammer unable to complete the killer stroke. Enci014's right hand carried out the final move swiftly.

The Phoenix warrior's arm shot out, and he drove the tip of the Gerber dagger into the hollow of Martillo's throat. Double-edged steel plunged deep into soft tissue. Martillo's mouth fell open, and blood gurgled from his lips. Enci014 twisted his wrist and slashed the knife across Martillo's carotid artery. Blood arced onto Enci014's shirtfront as a crimson fountain flowed from the wounds.

As Martillo's hammer fell from twitching fingers, Enci014 shoved him to the ground. He watched Martillo twitch in the mud, then lie still as the final remnants of life vanished. The Cuban stepped back and allowed the rain to wash down over his head and face. He turned away from the corpse of Colonel Martillo and breathed deeply, relieved that he was still alive.

The rain forest around Enci014 came alive as the other four members of Phoenix Force and the surviving paratroopers emerged from the trees. Katz stepped forward and glanced at Martillo's body. He turned to Enci014.

"Are you all right?" he asked.

"We've completed our mission?" the Cuban inquired.

"Absolutely," Katz answered with a nod.

"Then I'm just fine," Enci014 assured him with a sigh. "I'll feel even better when we get out of El Salvador."

"We can leave in the morning," the Phoenix Force commander assured him. "That should give you time to say a proper farewell to Maria."

"Yeah," Encizo replied soberly, then a slow smile lit his face and eyes. "I'll do my best, since luck was with me and not the colonel."

AVAILABLE NOW

A Shiite-Mafia drug cartel leads The Executioner to Lebanon's deadly Bekaa Valley ... where uninvited visitors don't get out alive.

DON PENDLETON's

MACK BOLAN.

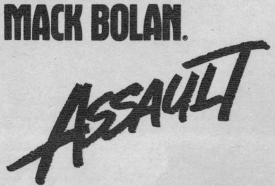

A powerful Shiite-Mafia drug cartel prepares to supply bargain-basement drugs, bringing Iran's holy war right to America's doorstep.

Enlisting the aid of rebel factions, Bolan stages an explosive raid that ends in Lebanon's Bekaa Valley and demonstrates to those who profit in war and human suffering the high cost of living ... and dying.

**A treacherous tale of time travel
in a desperate new world.**

JAMES AXLER

Time Nomads

Trekking through the blasted heart of the new America, Ryan Cawdor and his band search the redoubts for hidden caches of food, weapons and technology — the legacy of a preholocaust society.

Near death after ingesting bacteria-ridden food, Ryan Cawdor lies motionless, his body paralyzed by the poison coursing through his system. Yet his mind races back to the early days in the Deathlands...where the past is a dream and the future is a nightmare.

TAKE 'EM NOW

FOLDING SUNGLASSES
FROM GOLD EAGLE

Mean up your act with these tough, street-smart shades. Practical, too, because they fold 3 times into a handy, zip-up polyurethane pouch that fits neatly into your pocket. Rugged metal frame. Scratch-resistant acrylic lenses. Best of all, they can be yours for only $6.99.

MAIL YOUR ORDER TODAY.

Send your name, address, and zip code, along with a check or money order for just $6.99 + .75¢ for postage and handling (for a total of $7.74) payable to Gold Eagle Reader Service. (New York and Iowa residents please add applicable sales tax.)

Remove from pouch.   unfold once

unfold twice   and they're ready to wear

 Gold Eagle Reader Service
901 Fuhrmann Blvd.
P.O. Box 1396
Buffalo, N.Y. 14240-1396

GES-1A

Offer not available in Canada.

Do you know a real hero?

At Gold Eagle Books we know that heroes are not just fictional. Everyday someone somewhere is performing a selfless task, risking his or her own life without expectation of reward.

Gold Eagle would like to recognize America's local heroes by publishing their stories. If you know a true to life hero (that person might even be you) we'd like to hear about him or her. In 150-200 words tell us about a heroic deed you witnessed or experienced. Once a month, we'll select a local hero and award him or her with national recognition by printing his or her story on the inside back cover of THE EXECUTIONER series, and the ABLE TEAM, PHOENIX FORCE and/or VIETNAM: GROUND ZERO series.

Send your name, address, zip or postal code, along with your story of 150-200 words (and a photograph of the hero if possible), and mail to:

LOCAL HEROES AWARD
Gold Eagle Books
225 Duncan Mill Road
Don Mills, Ontario
M3B 3K9
Canada